the Beach

Debbie Macomber is a number one *New York Times* bestselling author and one of today's most popular writers with more than 170 million copies of her books in print worldwide. In addition to fiction, Debbie has published two bestselling cookbooks; numerous inspirational and nonfiction works; and two acclaimed children's books.

The beloved and bestselling *Cedar Cove* series became Hallmark Channel's first dramatic scripted television series, *Debbie Macomber's Cedar Cove*, which was ranked as the top programme on US cable TV when it debuted in summer 2013. Hallmark has also produced many successful films based on Debbie's bestselling Christmas novels.

Debbie Macomber owns her own tea room, and a yarn store, *A Good Yarn,* named after the shop featured in her popular *Blossom Street* novels. She and her husband, Wayne, serve on the Guideposts National Advisory Cabinet, and she is World Vision's international spokesperson for their *Knit for Kids* charity initiative. A devoted grandmother, Debbie lives with her husband in Port Orchard, Washington (the town on which her *Cedar Cove* novels are based) and they winter in Florida.

Also by Debbie Macomber available in Arrow

Debbie Macomber

A Walk along the Beach

arrow books

1 3 5 7 9 10 8 6 4 2

Arrow Books
20 Vauxhall Bridge Road
London SW1V 2SA

Arrow Books is part of the Penguin Random House group of companies
whose addresses can be found at global.penguinrandomhouse.com.

Penguin
Random House
UK

First published in Great Britain by Arrow Books in 2020

www.penguin.co.uk

A CIP catalogue record for this book is available from the British Library.

ISBN 9781784758776

Typeset in 11.25/15.5 pt Adobe Garamond Pro by
Jouve (UK), Milton Keynes
Printed and bound in Great Britain by Clays Ltd, Elcograf S.p.A.

MIX
Paper from
responsible sources
FSC
www.fsc.org   FSC® C018179

Penguin Random House is committed to a
sustainable future for our business, our readers
and our planet. This book is made from Forest
Stewardship Council® certified paper.

In memory of Roberta Stalberg,
my beloved friend

Summer 2020

Dear Friends,

If you read the dedication, you might not recognize the name. My friend Roberta Stalberg, who wrote under the pseudonym of Christina Skye, died of cancer in May 2018. She was my best friend and I miss her every single day. I've come to hate the word *cancer*. It's robbed us of too many of those we love.

After Roberta died, I decided I needed a break from writing. I told my agent and editor I was taking a year off. Her loss devastated me. As the weeks progressed, I thought perhaps the best way I could remember my friend wasn't to stop writing but instead to do the opposite. I decided to write this book in her memory.

A huge note of appreciation belongs to Michael Hanson, who willingly guided me with his own experiences and adventures as a freelance photographer. Another debt goes to Ron and Katie Robertson, who shared the journey of their daughter Karina and her battle against cancer. Katie's book, *Anchored*, written after Karina's death, deeply touched my heart.

I hope you enjoy this story with the familiar characters from *Cottage by the Sea* in the small town of Oceanside. It is exactly the kind of place Roberta and I would have gone to plot and knit and laugh ourselves silly. My hope for each of you is that, in your own life, you will find a friend as wonderful as the one I had in her.

Warmly,

Debbie Macomber

P.S. You can always reach me via my web page, Debbiemacomber.com, or by writing me at P.O. Box 1458, Port Orchard, WA 98366.

A Walk along the Beach

Chapter 1

Willa

"He's cute." My sister Harper stage-whispered when I joined her at the table in Bean There, my small coffee shop in Oceanside along the Washington coast. I knew exactly who she was talking about and refused to look. I really shouldn't pay him any mind. I shouldn't look. Shouldn't look.

I looked.

"Who?" I asked, doing my best to hide my interest. I'd noticed the tall, lean man with sandy-colored hair who stood at the counter with regularity. My sister was right. He was cute. Not the drop-dead gorgeous of a cover model, though. His appeal was subtle, understated. His hair fell haphazardly across his forehead and his blue eyes were warm. Some days they were a deeper shade than others, depending on what he wore. He had a small cleft in his chin with a single dimple on the right side of his cheek. I knew his first name was Sean for the simple reason I'd written his name across the cup.

He'd corrected me the first time he ordered when I spelled it *S-h-a-w-n* and explained it was spelled with an *e*.

"Don't be coy, Willa. You know exactly who I mean. That man is gorgeous. Admit it."

Shrugging, I acted disinterested. "If you say so."

"Does he stop by often?" Harper leaned forward, as if to get a better look.

My sister was an outrageous flirt. She always had been, although her relationships never seemed to last more than a few weeks. She was the outgoing one in the family, while I was the introvert, the shy, retiring one. Harper taught yoga and fitness classes at the Oceanside Fitness Center two blocks over from my coffee shop. She was their most popular instructor, and with good reason. Everything was fun with Harper, even exercise, and that was saying something.

"What's his name?" she pressed, unwilling to drop the subject.

Normally I would suggest she introduce herself, and she would make sure she did. For my own selfish reasons, I didn't. I knew that within minutes they would likely be involved in a friendly conversation. That was Harper. She was blond, beautiful, physically fit, and the kind of friend everyone hopes to find. It rarely took more than the fluttering of her stunning blue eyes for a man to be captivated and fall under her spell.

"Sean," I answered, and immediately felt guilty. It wasn't like I had a claim on him or that he'd be interested in me. We'd shared only a few brief exchanges. His smile was warm and engaging. I hesitated for more reason than my own interest. I knew if Harper went for him the relationship wouldn't last. None ever did with her, and I didn't want to see him hurt. He seemed the sensitive type. Oh heavens, what did I know? I was being ridiculous.

"Sean." Harper slowly repeated his name. "Like Sean Connery?"

"You should introduce yourself," I suggested, swallowing back my reluctance. I was being self-seeking and judgmental.

Harper's lovely face broke into a huge smile and she shook her head. "Not happening."

"Why not?"

"This one is for you, Willa," she said with a playful wink.

I opened my mouth to protest and the words stumbled over the end of my tongue, twisting around in my head before I could admit or deny my interest.

"Excuse me," Sean said, speaking to Alice, the high school girl I had recently hired. "I believe this is a macchiato instead of an Americano."

Alice glanced nervously toward me. As a new hire, she worried about making mistakes. "I thought . . . I heard you say you wanted a macchiato."

"Go," Harper urged, nudging me with her elbow. "You don't want a dissatisfied customer."

Scooting back my chair, I walked to the front of the shop. "It's all right, Alice," I told the teenager. I probably shouldn't have left her alone at the counter, as this was only her third day on the job.

Looking to Sean, I avoided eye contact for fear he'd overheard my conversation with my sister. "I apologize for the mistake. Do you want your usual Americano with room for cream?"

"Please."

"I made fresh cinnamon rolls this morning. Would you like one? It's on the house." I worked hard to keep my customers happy.

He glanced at the display case, considered the offer for a few seconds, and then reluctantly shook his head. "Not today. Perhaps another time."

"Sure thing," I said as I went about preparing his drink. As soon as I finished, I handed him the cup.

Sean added the cream, adjusted the lid, and then started for the door when Harper stopped him. "Hi," she said, beaming him a smile that was guaranteed to charm Scrooge. "Do you have time to join my sister and me?"

Walking three paces behind Sean, I frantically waved my hands at Harper, silently demanding that she stop. I knew what she was doing, and I wanted no part of her playing matchmaker between Sean and me.

"I'm sure Sean has better things to do," I said quickly. "Besides, I should get back to work."

Sean hesitated and looked over his shoulder at me. "I'd be happy to join you, if you don't mind."

"Willa doesn't mind. And, there's no one in line," Harper said, and gestured for Sean to take a seat.

I hesitated and scowled at my sister, a look that she ignored.

"Sit down, Willa," Harper insisted.

As if unsure what to do, Sean remained standing with a

look akin to a deer caught in headlights. I hated that Harper had put him on the spot.

Carefully watching me, Sean pulled out a chair and joined us at the table.

Harper shot me a look that said I should make my move.

Yeah, right. My little sister had yet to realize I had no moves. Our mother died of a brain aneurysm when I was thirteen and in junior high, so I'd completely missed out on those carefree teen years. As best I could, I'd taken over the duties at home, cooking and cleaning for our older brother, Lucas, Harper, and my dad. As soon as Lucas had graduated from high school, he'd joined the Army. In the years that followed losing Mom, our dad had slowly fallen apart, sinking his woes in the bottom of a whiskey bottle. After Harper's bout with cancer, he'd gone to AA and was mostly sober these days, although he had occasional slips. He lived in a trailer park and worked as a dealer at a tribal casino just outside of town.

After Sean joined us, silence circled the table. Harper glared at me, waiting for me to lead the conversation.

I couldn't. My mouth went dry and I stared down at my cooling coffee as if it held the answer to world peace. Rarely had I felt more awkward. Harper was a natural when it came to drawing people out. She, more than anyone else, should recognize how uncomfortable this situation made me. I couldn't begin to imagine what she hoped this would accomplish. Already I could feel the heat warming my cheeks.

"So, Sean," Harper said, dragging out the sentence. "You must be new in town? I don't remember seeing you around."

He stretched his arms out in front of him and held his

coffee with both hands. He, too, seemed keenly interested in its contents. "I've been living in Oceanside about a year now."

"That long?" I asked, surprised. He'd come in for coffee a time or two a few months back, but then I hadn't seen him again until just recently. For the last week, not that I was counting or anything, he'd been in every morning. He always ordered an Americano, and every so often took a bakery item to go. Generally, he stopped by around ten, after the morning rush.

"I bought a place about a mile outside of town, off Harvest Road."

"The Andrews house," Harper said knowingly.

The Andrews were good people and their home was beautiful. I'd gone to school with their youngest daughter, Lenni, although we were never good friends. Because I was involved in caring for our family, I was unable to participate in a lot of school activities. Lenni was a class officer and a cheerleader. We didn't exactly run with the same crowd.

"Funny I haven't seen you around before and now you're here," Harper continued with enthusiasm, as if meeting him was predestined. She continued to send me encouraging looks, apparently in hopes I would pick up her line of questioning, learn all I could about him.

Sean's gaze bounced back to me. "I travel quite a bit for work."

"How does your wife feel about that?"

I kicked my sister under the table at her blatant attempt to find out his marital status. She couldn't be any more obvious had she tried.

"Unfortunately, I'm not married."

"Really? Neither is Willa."

I nearly groaned aloud from embarrassment. "Sean," I said, taking up the conversation, "I apologize for my sister, I . . ."

His knowing smile stopped me. "It's fine, Willa."

"You say you travel," Harper continued, ignoring my censure. "What do you do?"

"Photography."

"Really?" That spiked Harper's interest, and she straightened in her chair.

"I've always liked the name Willa," he said, in an abrupt change of subject, cutting Harper off before she had a chance to drill him about his career. It was clear to me, if not my sister, that Sean preferred not to talk about his work.

"My mother had an aunt named Willa," he continued. "You rarely hear that name these days."

Again, it was Harper who answered. "Willa was named after Willa Cather, who was one of our mother's favorite authors."

"And Harper then for Harper Lee?" Sean asked, making brief eye contact with her.

Harper grinned. "Yup, and our older brother is Lucas. He isn't named after anyone. From what we understand, Mom and Dad made an agreement before they married. Dad got to name the boys and Mom got to name us girls."

"How long have you had Bean There?" he asked, looking to me.

"Almost six years now." I had a small inheritance from

our grandparents that had originally been set aside for college. I'd attended the community college in Aberdeen, daily driving the twenty-three miles each way. I'd taken every business class available and used the rest of the money to buy equipment and set up shop. It hadn't been easy those first couple of years, but now Bean There had a faithful clientele. I did a brisk business, especially in the mornings. I took my coffee seriously and baked nearly everything myself. That meant a lot of early mornings, not that I minded. I loved what I did, and it provided enough income for Harper and me to share an apartment without worrying about how we would pay the rent.

Seth Keaton walked in and glanced my way before he stepped to the counter. Alice was in the back, cutting cookies from the dough I'd made earlier that morning. I welcomed the opportunity to escape this uncomfortable situation.

"If you'll excuse me," I said, grabbing hold of my coffee mug as I stood.

"Back to the grind," Harper teased, "pun intended."

Sean grinned. "I need to get back to work myself. Thanks for the conversation," he said, looking at me.

"Ah . . . sure."

Relieved, I headed to the counter and Keaton. His first name was Seth, but no one called him that. His size was something to behold. He must have been close to seven feet tall, and his shoulders were massive. He worked as a house painter, but he was far more talented than most folks gave him credit for. It was a surprise to learn Keaton was the one who'd painted the murals in town. He was married to the local doctor, Annie Keaton, who headed up the health clinic in Oceanside.

"What can I do for you?" I asked.

"Give me a vanilla latte. Sixteen ounces. Make it extra hot."

"For Dr. Annie?"

He nodded. "She didn't have time for breakfast this morning and I'm guessing her blood sugar is low right about now."

"You got it." I recognized the order. Keaton wasn't a latte kind of man. He liked a double shot of espresso and baked goods. Especially my Danish, but he was equally fond of my cinnamon rolls.

Business slowed until lunchtime. My sandwiches made with homemade bread were a popular item. With only a few tables available, most of my business was takeout. I'd recently expanded our luncheon menu, and sales were picking up.

When business slowed again in mid-afternoon, I took a break and went for a short walk along the beach. I tried to do that as often as time afforded. With a hectic work schedule, I needed to breathe in the fresh air and center myself. The seagulls squawked as they soared overhead, carried by the wind. Although it was only mid-June, the sunshine shone down on me, relaxing the tense muscles of my shoulders, easing my worries.

The ocean had always been my solace. The sound of the waves as they crashed against the shore reverberated in my head, offering me a peaceful contentment. I once heard it explained that being near the ocean, with the surf and the swirling waters, was like being tucked inside a mother's womb. I wasn't sure if that was scientific or not, but in some ways, it made sense. The rhythm of the tides, the predictability of it all, offers reassurance and a certain sense of security.

I'd badly needed that, especially when Harper had been deathly ill. The long months of fighting cancer had taken a toll on my sister. On all of us. I thanked God every day that she'd survived. Still, the threat that the leukemia might return hung over our heads like a dark, threatening storm cloud.

I closed my eyes and let the wind buffet my face. Even though Harper had been cancer-free for three years, I worried. I couldn't help it. My sister was everything to me and I couldn't bear the thought of losing her. Lately, I had this feeling, this sense that things weren't as they should be with her.

Chapter 2

Willa

Once I was back at the apartment, the feeling about Harper refused to leave me. Reaching for my phone, I sent my brother a text, asking him to call when it was convenient. I brewed myself a cup of tea and waited.

Thankfully, he responded almost immediately.

"Hey," Lucas said, "I got your message. What's up?"

Now that I had my brother on the phone, I wasn't sure where to start. Getting right to the point, I blurted out, "I'm worried about Harper."

My brother snorted. "When are you not worried about Harper?"

I knew he'd react this way. Lucas became the rock of our family when our father crumbled. I would much rather have had this talk with Dad, but I knew he would freak out. Dad was incapable of handling negative news without reaching for a bottle. His sobriety was shaky at best, and I didn't want to give him an excuse to drink.

"Did you know Harper's planning to climb Mount Rainier this summer?"

Lucas took the news calmly. "Cool. If anyone can make it to the summit, it's Harper."

He was right—however, that wasn't the issue. "I agree, but this follows the bungee jump she did two weeks ago."

"And your point is?"

"I don't know what my point is," I confessed, "except this adventurous behavior has all come about in the last few weeks. It seems out of the blue, you know?" Lucas was probably right, and I was making more of this than necessary. Still, it was concerning. He was also right about me fretting over Harper. I couldn't help myself.

"Listen, Willa, I get it. When someone comes that close to death, I think they have a certain fire within them to make the most of a second chance. To her way of thinking, these are bonus years and she's squeezing as much out of life as possible while she can. I don't blame her; I'd probably do the same thing."

"She ate fried bugs." I cringed as I said it.

"Harper? She won't eat green beans."

Despite my concern about our little sister, I laughed out loud. "I know, I couldn't believe it either. She went to this Indonesian restaurant in Seattle with one of her friends and fried bugs were on the menu, and she went for it."

"She survived."

Lucas was right. "I know what you're saying, and I agree,

but mountain climbing and bungee jumping? You and I both know how afraid of heights she is, and yet she made herself do it. Leesa told me Harper was so afraid she threw up before she jumped." My sister seemed to be facing her greatest fears and I didn't understand what was driving her, especially now. What if she knew something I didn't? That possibility had thrown me into a tailspin. When I mentioned this to Lucas, the phone went silent. "Did you ask her?"

"Of course. I've tried to talk her out of climbing Mount Rainier, but she won't hear of it. It's like she's flirting with death. Something's going on with her, but she tells me I'm imagining things. She said if she had a death wish she wouldn't have fought so hard to win the battle against leukemia."

"She has a point."

"I know, but Lucas, my gut is telling me something is up. Like the fact that she doesn't stay in any relationship for more than a few weeks. That girl has left a string of broken hearts from here to Canada and back."

Again, Lucas paused, as if taking it all in. "Maybe I should talk to her. Where is she now?"

"Training to climb Mount Rainier. She's going with a group of other amateur climbers and they have a rigorous training schedule. She's out every evening strength- and endurance-building, and that's after teaching several classes during the week." Little wonder she had the figure of a model.

"Okay, I get it. I'll make a point of coming to visit this weekend. I haven't seen Dad in a while. Have you?"

"Yeah. I had him over for dinner last Sunday."

"How is he?"

"About the same, I guess." I wasn't sure what to tell my brother. It was difficult to know with our father. He hid his drinking well. For a long time, I didn't realize how much he'd come to rely on alcohol.

"I'll bring Chantelle with me."

My spirits lifted. I loved Chantelle. She was good for my brother, who worked as a longshoreman on the Seattle docks. Chantelle and Lucas had been dating for two years. I didn't know why Lucas hadn't proposed. I'd asked him about it once and got the message this was his business and I was to butt out.

"Would you like me to cook dinner?"

"No, that's too much work."

I appreciated my brother's thoughtfulness. He knew I set my alarm clock for three-thirty and was at Bean There by four each morning. It'd only been in the last three months that I was grossing enough to hire another baker. Having Shirley take over some of the early-morning responsibilities gave me leeway, and I was grateful. I opened at five and had a steady stream of customers from the moment I unlocked the front door.

"I'll stop off and check on Dad, too."

"He'll be glad to see you." None of us ever doubted our father's love. He'd been a lost soul since Mom died. She'd been the love of his life. We all missed her dreadfully. Our mom was the best mother in the world. Sort of a modern-day June Cleaver from the 1950s sitcom *Leave It to Beaver*.

"I appreciate being able to talk to you about this, Lucas."

"I'm grateful you reached out. Don't ever worry that you're bothering me or that I can't handle it."

"I don't. You're my rock."

It was Lucas I'd turned to when Harper's health had started to go south. At the time he'd been in the military, serving in the Army as an Airborne Ranger. He'd planned to make the military his career. Everything changed when we learned Harper had leukemia. It'd all started so innocently with a bad case of hives.

Hives.

Who would have even suspected those hives were an indication of something far, far worse? Dr. Bainbridge was the local physician at the time. We all assumed Harper had some food allergy. I was allergic to strawberries and it made sense that Harper must be, too, even if it didn't show until she was a high school senior. But the hives persisted, and my sister was irritable and uncomfortable. When I took Harper back for a second visit, Dr. Bainbridge seemed to think she might have mononucleosis. We teased her and asked who she'd been kissing. Miserable as she was, Harper didn't take kindly to the joke. Next, Dr. Bainbridge ordered a full set of blood work, and that was when everything changed.

Even now, nearly three years later, I would always remember the day when the call came. Harper had recently graduated from high school and planned to spend her summer working at a local church camp. Our pastor, Heath McDonald, had written her a glowing recommendation the year before, and Harper was great with the junior-high kids. They'd loved her.

The camp was thrilled to have her back and she was just as eager to return.

Dr. Bainbridge gave the news to me instead of our father, knowing I would handle it better than Dad. He said the test results showed Harper had leukemia and that we needed to get her to the University of Washington Medical Center in Seattle as soon as possible so she could be assessed.

Harper was as shocked as we were. We clung to each other the same way we had the day our mother died, weeping, afraid, uncertain of the future. Harper pulled it together before me, asked what she needed to do, and immediately packed a bag and asked that I go with her to Seattle. I don't think I've ever admired my sister more than I did that day.

Our entire world was turned upside down that summer. Lucas was due to reenlist and instead gave up what he'd hoped would be a promising career in the Army. He got an apartment in Seattle and the two of us lived together while I finished up my business classes online. Harper was in bad shape and she needed our support.

Dad came by to visit every now and again. Seeing his youngest daughter deathly ill was more than he could endure. His visits usually resulted in tears and pleading with Harper not to die, as if she had any real control over the outcome. She was desperately ill. Worse than we could have imagined.

"Willa? Are you there?" Lucas asked, cutting into my thoughts.

"Yes, sorry. My mind drifted there for a minute. I was remembering when we first got word of how sick Harper was." Our sister had come face-to-face with death and walked away a winner. Lucas was right. I was overreacting. If Harper wanted to live an adventurous life, then who was I to question her? Even knowing I had no control over the future, I couldn't help being concerned.

"I'm afraid for her," I admitted, lowering my voice. I couldn't help it. I felt responsible for keeping a close eye on her and her health. Last winter when she'd gotten the flu, I'd watched her like a hawk. Harper had gotten angry with me and insisted I leave her to her misery.

"You're such a worrywart," Lucas joked, lightening my mood. "Harper is fine. She's not showing any signs of a recurrence, is she?"

"I . . . I don't think so." I knew what to look for—at least I thought I did.

"When was her last blood test?"

"A few months ago. Her next one isn't until July." Only a month away. I dreaded each one, barely slept the night before, and then breathed easier when everything showed Harper remained in remission. My stomach tightened. I wished this feeling, this sense of foreboding about my sister, would go away so I could let go of my worries, but they persisted.

"Then it's coming right up," Lucas said. "That should put your mind to rest."

Then and only then would I be able to let go of my concerns.

"I'll look forward to seeing you and Chantelle."

We spoke for a few minutes longer, deciding on the time and what restaurant. When we ended the call, I felt better.

Bouncing my fears against Lucas had a calming effect on me. He always knew the right thing to say.

Although it was still light out, following my talk with Lucas, I headed for bed. I was still sitting up and reading when Harper returned from her training session. My bedroom door was open. With sweat beading her forehead and a hand towel around her neck, she leaned against the doorjamb, breathing heavily.

"That was a killer workout," she said, loudly exhaling.

I ignored her choice of words. "When's the climb scheduled?"

"August twenty-second. We'll do a practice climb to Camp Muir. If I can't make it to Camp Muir, I won't be allowed to go the following weekend. That's why I'm training this hard."

"You'll be ready."

"I'm ready now." Her face, already red from exertion, reddened more with excitement. "Imagine climbing Mount Rainier. It's something I've always wanted to do." She wiped her face with the towel. "I'm heading for the shower and then bed. See you in the morning."

"Sure thing."

Because I left the apartment early, Harper stopped by for coffee on her way into work at Oceanside Fitness. Her first class was at eight. She taught yoga at nine and another exercise class at ten three days a week. She had a break then until the afternoon. The woman was a machine. No one drove themselves harder than my sister.

"Are you turning the light out soon?" she asked.

"Another fifteen minutes." It was far too easy to fall into

the trap of staying up late. I had to set a rigid bedtime—otherwise I was worthless come morning.

"Dream of Sean."

"Very funny." I rolled my eyes. "What you did today wasn't cool."

"Yes, it was. He's into you."

"Hardly." I didn't know why my sister would ever say that.

"Willa, don't be dense. Of course he is." She gave me a look that suggested I was a complete idiot. "He couldn't keep his eyes off you. Surely you noticed?"

I didn't believe her for a minute. It seemed Sean had concentrated on his coffee with the same intensity that I had my own. He'd been as uncomfortable as I'd been, and too polite to say anything.

"I hope you realize you embarrassed us both."

My sister shook her head as if giving up on me and headed for our shared bathroom to shower.

Fifteen minutes later I heard her enter her own bedroom. I set my book aside and turned out the light. It was barely dark out. During the summer months in the Pacific Northwest, it was close to ten o'clock before it went completely dark. I would be sound asleep by then.

Closing my eyes, I tucked the sheet up close around my shoulders, and instantly Sean's face came into my mind. I liked him. I wanted Harper to be right, but I didn't dare allow myself to get caught up in the fantasy.

Chapter 3

Sean

I didn't even like Americanos, and here I was driving into town every day for a cup I tossed after the first few sips. Not that it mattered, I would gladly pay ten times the price of that Americano for an opportunity to see Willa.

What got me was how beautiful she was without knowing it. She was tall, nearly five-eight, I'd guess, and curvy in all the right places. She wore her straight brown hair in a short bob, parted in the middle, and often looped the ends around her ears. Her dark brown eyes reminded me of a teddy bear. She was warm and friendly and completely unlike other women I'd dated.

The first time I stopped by Bean There wasn't for coffee, nor was it the reason I returned. I happened upon it one early morning and I smelled those freshly baked cinnamon rolls. It was the same aroma I remembered from visits to my grandmother's. I wasn't thinking of Grams, however, when

I first met Willa. One look and I was mesmerized. I'd watched her deal with an unpleasant customer with patience and grace, not allowing the belligerent man to ruffle her. She listened to his complaint, soothed his anger, and treated him with kindness and respect, none of which he deserved. I knew then this woman was special, and I wanted the opportunity to know her better.

Her sister was lovely, too, but in an entirely different way. Harper was bubbly and outgoing, strikingly beautiful and vivacious. From those handful of times I'd interacted with Willa I recognized her to be an introvert, quiet and intense, yet also sincere and approachable.

So here I was back again, ordering coffee I wouldn't drink on the chance of spending a few minutes chatting with Willa. It wasn't a caffeine fix I needed; it was a Willa fix.

Today was the day.

I was determined that this was the morning I would ask her out. Dinner? A movie? Videogames? Basically, I was willing to do or go anywhere that interested her.

It shouldn't be difficult. It was what guys did, right? When it came to women, I didn't usually get tongue-tied and awkward. I'd been in relationships before—several, if the truth be known, especially when I'd played professional baseball. In retrospect, I recognized they had mostly been shallow and empty, based on my fame and the size of my bank account.

Then I blew out my knee and that was the end of that. Not only did I lose my career in sports, but the woman who I'd assumed was the love of my life went with it.

That was a harsh lesson and I'd been gun-shy ever since. Nikki was out of my life and had been for three years. I'd pretty much been living like a monk ever since.

It was time to break out of that mold. Willa gave me hope. She had no idea I'd played professional baseball and wouldn't have recognized the name Sean O'Malley even if she had. I'd played for the Atlanta Braves for two years, and the biggest splash I'd made, other than a few vital home runs, was when I injured my knee. Even now I walked with a slight limp.

Parking my car, I walked over to the coffee shop and nearly changed my mind when I saw there was a long line ahead of me. This wasn't encouraging. Lines meant Willa had to shuffle everyone along. I did take heart when she saw me. She paused and offered me a shy smile. Playing it cool, I lifted my chin, acknowledging her. It seemed her face was flushed, and while I'd like to think it was due to me, I had to assume it had more to do with the heat from the drinks she served. The woman was a marvel when it came to coffee and baking.

When my turn came up, I stepped forward until I stood in front of the cash register.

"Your usual?" Willa asked, offering me one of her signature smiles.

"Sure thing, and I'll take one of your cinnamon rolls today."

"You got it." She immediately set to work filling my order.

It was now or never. "So," I said as nonchalantly as I could manage. "What are you doing . . . you know . . . Are you interested in later?"

Willa paused and her gaze shot to mine. She looked

confused, which was no wonder. I couldn't have been less clear. I had no hope I'd do better a second time around, so I stood like an idiot and prayed she'd forget I'd said anything.

"Doing? I'm working . . . later. We don't close until three."

"Right . . . good to know."

Kill. Me. Now.

Grabbing my Americano and cinnamon roll, I headed out the door before I made an even bigger fool of myself. I had no clue where the smooth, confident man I'd once been had disappeared to. Willa did that to me. I couldn't leave the shop fast enough.

With my heart pounding like a locomotive struggling up a steep incline, I speed-walked across the street to a small park and slumped down on the bench. I felt like a loser. How was it that I could face a raging bull elephant in the Maasai Mara in Africa with no more protection than a camera lens without a qualm? Yet facing a pretty girl and asking her to dinner left me shaken to the core. How had that happened? I had to wonder if Nikki had played a role in that and decided she hadn't. This was all me and my own insecurities.

The array of brightly colored flowers surrounding the base of a tree captured my attention, and, seeking a distraction, I took a shot with my phone. I took another picture of the front of Bean There, too. I was far more comfortable behind the lens of a camera than I ever was standing before a pitcher in a major league game.

I considered coming back later with something more professional than my phone and taking additional photos of Willa's shop. I could enlarge one and frame it for her.

While I was staring at the shop, I noticed a stray dog. I'd caught sight of him several times over the last few weeks. He was excessively thin, to the point that his ribs were showing. He lingered near the entrance to Willa's place of business. I imagined the mutt smelled the baked goods she used to lure in customers and suspected she might have fed him a time or two.

Sure enough, the minute the door opened the stray was ready. A middle-aged woman I didn't recognize walked out with coffee in one hand and a white sack in the other. As if this was exactly what he'd been waiting for, the dog sprang forward. He grabbed hold of the sack and raced off.

The woman screeched, but it didn't help. Her goodies had been ripped from her hand and the dog had made it look easy.

The stray was a blur as he raced toward the beach. Usually I saw him hanging around the local pizza parlor. How he'd managed to avoid getting taken to the Humane Society before now was proof of his craftiness. This dog was street-savvy. I had to admire his ingenuity.

Dogs were my weakness—well, other than baristas, and Willa Lakey in particular. If my career didn't involve as much travel as it did, I would gladly have taken a dog as a pet. My life was solitary. If I wasn't taking photos, I was spending time in front of my computer, editing my work. I would have enjoyed a canine companion.

After watching the dog's quick moves, I felt the least I could do was see about making sure this fella found a good home. One thing was for sure, I'd need to be as cagey as he was, and that required a bit of help. Thankfully, I knew the best place to find it.

I dumped my nearly untouched Americano into the garbage and jogged over to the beach. I found evidence of what was left of the stolen breakfast. The white sack was tattered and torn, and there wasn't a crumb left of its contents. I picked up the bag and tossed it. Glancing up and down the beach, I thought I caught a movement and saw him take off in the direction of the pizza parlor.

Getting back into my car, I drove past the back entrance of the pizza place and saw nothing. From there I went to the animal shelter. I knew Preston Young and his wife, Mellie, were big animal lovers. Mellie helped nurse sick and injured cats and dogs back to health, and Preston made sure they went to good homes.

I walked inside the shelter to a cacophony of barks and other noise. Preston was great about getting volunteers to come in and care for the animals. He had an entire crew that walked the dogs and saw that they all received an ample amount of tender loving care. He glanced up when I entered the building and greeted me with a mildly curious look. From the moment we'd met, Preston had been after me to adopt a pet.

"Hey, Sean, good to see you."

I nodded. "You, too. I got a stray for you."

"With you?"

"Nope. This dog is smart. I've seen him around town a few times. Watched him snatch a woman's breakfast right out of her hand this morning."

"Brown, long hair, medium size, and on the thin side?"

Apparently, I wasn't the only one who'd noticed the stray. "You talking about the dog or the woman?" I joked.

"Funny." Preston had a quirky sense of humor. "The dog.

"I've been hearing about him," Preston continued, grinning. "Keaton had a run-in with him last week." His smile grew bigger. "The stray got one of his sandwiches right out of his lunch box. Clever, too. He managed to figure out how to open his container. He left the peanut-butter-and-jelly sandwich for Keaton and took the homemade meatloaf sandwich that Annie made him. Keaton was madder than a hornet."

I couldn't keep from smiling myself. This was one smart dog. "I saw him around the back of the pizza parlor and think that might be where he's holed up. There's a spot behind the dumpster that would be a perfect hiding place."

"I'll check it out."

"You want company?"

"Wouldn't hurt. I'll give you a call later when I'm ready to head over."

"Do that."

Preston held his look. "A dog that smart could use a good home, you know. Seeing that you've taken an interest in him, you might consider keeping him for yourself. It's clear he doesn't belong to anyone. Mellie can check him out for you and make sure he's healthy."

I was sorely tempted and sadly shook my head. "I'm waiting on an assignment. Wouldn't be fair to give him a home and then abandon him for a few weeks."

"Last I heard you were waiting for an assignment and that was over a month ago. How much longer do you have to wait?"

"Don't know. I've taken a few smaller jobs that require a bit of travel, but I can drive to those."

"Take him with you."

I rubbed the side of my face, considering it. "On second thought, maybe I could take him in." The dog reminded me a bit of myself, not that I'd ever been homeless. When my baseball career ended, I'd been at a loss about what to do with the rest of my life. I floundered for a bit, paralyzed about facing a future that didn't include baseball. I'd lived and breathed the sport from the time I was five years old and started playing T-ball with my dad as my coach. Briefly, I considered taking a position as a high school coach, but that meant returning to college. The appeal wasn't there.

"First let's see if we can catch him," I said, forcefully turning my thoughts away from what I'd lost. If and when we managed to capture the dog, I would make that decision.

"Sounds good. I'll give you a call later this afternoon."

"I'll wait to hear from you."

I left shortly thereafter and returned to the house. The more I thought about bringing home the stray, the stronger the appeal grew. When I did travel, and there were times when I was away three to four weeks at a stretch, I'd need to figure out what to do with him. Before I could leave, I'd need to make sure the dog understood that this was his home and he belonged to me. That might not be an easy task, especially since it was clear he'd been on his own for a good long while.

Once home I was curious to see if *National Geographic* had sent word about two possible assignments, one in Bolivia and another in the Philippines. I went to my computer to check my email. Quickly scanning my inbox, I saw there was nothing of interest. I would be a good choice for the Bolivia assignment because I spoke fluent Spanish. When my mother returned to work as an attorney, she'd hired a housekeeper from Mexico, and I'd picked up the language at an early age. Later, I'd majored in Spanish in college, although my real interest was baseball. It'd always been any- and everything having to do with baseball.

The only assignment I had on the books was from *Seattle Magazine,* asking me to photograph the murals of Washington State. I'd already gone to several towns in close proximity and had literally thousands of shots. There was a town in eastern Washington called Toppenish I wanted to hit that was known for its murals. Once I made the decision about the dog, I'd make the trip across the Cascade Mountains to the other side of the state.

After reading through my emails, I made myself lunch and was about to look through the photos I'd taken earlier when my phone buzzed. Checking the number, I saw that it was Preston.

"You ready to head out?" I hadn't expected to hear from him this soon.

"No need."

"What do you mean?" For some reason an irrational fear came over me and I was afraid Preston was about to tell me the stray had been hit by a car. I'd witnessed a near accident with him the first time I'd seen him, and it'd sent my heart racing.

"Keaton got him."

"You mean you have him?"

"Yup. He's at the shelter. Mellie is checking him over as we speak."

"How'd Keaton catch him?" This had to be good. Keaton was a big guy, and while he was agile, I didn't think he was able to move as quickly as this dog could.

Preston chuckled. "I told him what you'd said about the dog hiding behind the dumpster, so he went over there, set out his lunch, and turned his back. Sure enough, the dog couldn't resist. He might not be as smart as we think, because he assumed Keaton was foolish enough to be tricked a second time."

I laughed. Leave it to Keaton. The guy was the size of a giant, and smart besides.

"So, the question is," Preston continued, "do you want him or not?"

It didn't take me long to decide. "I'll take him."

It looked like I was going to get a dog after all.

Chapter 4

Willa

Lucas sent a text letting me know he and Chantelle planned to arrive early Friday evening. Once I was home from work, I took a nap so I wouldn't fall asleep over dinner. Having our brother visit was a treat.

Harper was as excited as I was at the chance to see Lucas. Having Chantelle join him was a bonus. The minute his car pulled in front of our apartment we both flew out the door like the place was in danger of exploding.

Lucas caught Harper in his arms, the impact causing him to take a step in retreat. Wrapping his arms around her waist, he whirled her around and around. Being a bit more subdued, I hugged Chantelle.

"Are you staying the whole weekend?" Harper asked. "You must, you really must! It's been forever since we last saw you."

Harper and I were in Seattle every six months for her routine blood work. The doctors had insisted on keeping a close eye on her. Thus far, the test results showed that the cancer hadn't returned. We held on to the hope future tests would continue to show she was in remission. When we were in Seattle, Lucas loved to treat us. Last January he'd taken us to the 5th Avenue Theatre for the off-Broadway production of *Come from Away* and then dinner afterward. On Harper's last birthday, he'd splurged on an amazing lunch at the Space Needle.

With his arms around both of us, he answered, "Chantelle and I leave tomorrow afternoon."

"So soon?" Harper pouted, jutting out her lower lip. When Lucas did visit, he never stayed long. I suspected it had a lot to do with the memories of the home we'd all once shared that was forever lost to us.

"I'll be back later in the summer," our brother promised, and kissed the side of Harper's head.

"With Chantelle?" I urged, casting a glance toward the woman I hoped would be my future sister-in-law.

Lucas looked toward his girlfriend as if to gauge her response before he nodded. "With Chantelle."

Harper hugged them both again. Then I did, too. Everything felt right when Lucas visited. It was as if the responsibility I carried shifted from my shoulders when my big brother was around.

With our arms around them both, we walked back to the apartment. I had homemade snickerdoodles and lemonade waiting, knowing that after the long drive they'd both be thirsty and hungry. Sitting around the kitchen table, we caught up with one another as if it'd been years since we'd last talked. It was like this with the three of us. We chatted nonstop, pausing now and again to laugh. Chantelle joined in the fun and updated us on her summer plans.

"Did you know Willa's got an admirer?" Harper said, jiggling her eyebrows like this was highly valuable information.

"I don't," I insisted, blushing. "She's making this up."

"Am not," she returned, waving a cookie at me. "Sean comes into Bean There every day. You should see the way he looks at her. He's cute, too. I'd go for him myself if I thought I had a chance."

"Harper," I snapped, hating the way she went on about Sean and me. Nothing was there, although I secretly hoped that might change.

Lucas grabbed another cookie off the plate. "You two sound like you're in junior high."

"His name is Sean, spelled like Sean Connery," Harper continued, all too willing to fluster me. "Come on, Willa, admit it. He's delicious-looking."

"Delicious?" I repeated and rolled my eyes. "You make him sound like one of my cinnamon rolls."

"He frequently orders those, too."

"Will you please stop?" I all but begged. This was highly embarrassing.

Kindly, Lucas took pity on me. He checked his wrist and announced, "Chantelle made us dinner reservations at the casino. I thought it would be good for Dad to join us."

"Great idea." Lucas was thoughtful like that. He wanted to make the most of his visit, and I was happy he'd wanted to include our father. My one worry was that Dad might be drinking. If that was the case, it would put a pall over the evening.

"He's working tonight but was able to schedule his dinner break at the same time as our reservation."

Chantelle was a natural organizer, and it made sense that Lucas would ask her to make the arrangements. We had discussed restaurants earlier, but this worked out much better.

"I thought tomorrow we could all visit Mom's grave."

"I'd like that," Harper said, setting the cookie back on the plate. As the baby of the family, Harper lost Mom before she'd even had a chance to really know her the way Lucas and I did.

We made a point of taking flowers to Mom's grave site whenever Lucas was in town. Our mother might be gone, but she remained a large part of our lives. We missed her. I hoped that our father might join us this time. For whatever reason, he rarely did, always coming up with a convenient excuse.

"Now, what's this I hear?" Lucas said, looking pointedly across the table at Harper. "A little birdie told me you plan on climbing Mount Rainier this summer."

My sister's eyes rounded, and she glanced at me. "You told him?"

"I might have mentioned it." I shrugged, hiding how concerned I was over our sister's plan. Climbing 14,411 feet was no small endeavor. Only those in top physical and mental condition would have what it took to complete such a challenge.

For the next ten minutes Harper spoke nonstop about all

she was doing to prepare for the adventure. She mentioned the equipment she would be using, the team she was working with, and the friends she'd made in the process, including a young physician, John Neal, who currently worked at the University of Washington Medical Center, the very place she'd spent so much time while dealing with leukemia. Just the way she said his name told me he had caught Harper's eye. Whenever she mentioned him, Harper became animated. It appeared the two had become training partners. My hope was that her interest in this physician would last longer than it had with other men. This climb was important to Harper, but I had to wonder if the challenge was as key as her budding romance with this young man.

"Sounds great," Lucas encouraged her.

Hearing her determination and seeing her enthusiasm, I felt guilty that I'd made a fuss. Lucas was right, I tended to worry about Harper more than I should. She was doing great. Seeing the way her face lit up when she spoke about this new goal of hers was all the convincing I needed.

Lucas's gaze connected with mine.

"Did you hear I went bungee jumping?" Harper continued. She took back the cookie she'd recently set down and bit into it, chewing appreciatively.

"What prompted that?" Chantelle grimaced, her entire upper body shaking as if to say bungee jumping was the last thing she'd ever consider.

Harper leaned back in the chair and paused before responding. "I did it on a bet."

"Someone dared you?"

She shrugged. "Sort of."

"But you're afraid of heights," Lucas reminded her.

"I know. I was scared out of my mind, but I did it!" She beamed with pride. "When I stood on that bridge and looked down, I nearly lost my nerve. I don't think I've ever been more frightened in my life."

"You jumped off a bridge?" Lucas asked, as if he could hardly take it in. This from the man who leaped out of airplanes!

"Yup! Crazy, huh?"

"You won't get an argument out of me." Chantelle placed her hand over her heart. "You're a lot braver than me."

"No worries, I don't plan on doing it again. This was a once-in-a-lifetime thing. I survived to tell about it."

"Thank goodness," I chimed in. "If I'd known what you planned that day, I wouldn't have let you leave the house."

"You're such a mother," Harper teased.

What she said was true. It was the role I'd been cast into after Mom died. My teen years were lost to me. All three of us had to grow up quickly; we'd had no choice. I'd filled in for our mother, Lucas had enlisted in the Army, and Harper, although the most protected of us three, had faced leukemia. The only one to stumble had been our father.

Chantelle checked the time. "We should leave now, or we'll be late for dinner."

We stood, eager to be on our way. Lucas grabbed the last two cookies and shoved them into his jacket pocket. Snickerdoodles were his favorite.

"Lucas," Chantelle warned, "you're going to ruin your dinner."

Harper looked at me. "She already sounds like a wife, doesn't she?"

Lucas sent a warning look our way, but it didn't faze Harper. Looping her arm through Chantelle's, she added, "I thought our brother was smart enough to know a good thing when he saw it. Apparently, I was wrong."

"Stop," he ordered. "That's between Chantelle and me."

Harper slowly shook her head. "Just saying."

Frowning, Lucas said, "Kindly keep your thoughts to yourself, little sister."

I knew better than to harass him. I'd basically said the same thing when we spoke earlier and had been shut down. I didn't know what held him back, but as he'd pointed out, his and Chantelle's relationship was none of my business.

Lucas drove the four of us to the casino, which was less than five miles from Oceanside on the tribal reservation. On a Friday night, the parking lot was nearly full. I was grateful Chantelle had thought far enough ahead to make reservations at the restaurant.

When we arrived at the restaurant, our father sat waiting just outside. He brightened and stood up as we approached.

"Lucas. Chantelle." He shook hands with his son and then hugged all three of us girls. "This is great."

"You'd think it was Thanksgiving," Harper joked. "That was the last time all of us had dinner together."

"It couldn't have been," I said, and then realized Harper was right. It had been more than seven months since we'd all been together for a meal.

Chantelle approached the hostess and we were escorted to our table. Friday nights offered a seafood buffet with crab, shrimp, salmon, and all the fixings. We decided to go for that, since Dad was on his dinner break and had only an hour. Seeing how busy the restaurant was, we couldn't guarantee we'd be finished within sixty minutes if we ordered off the menu.

When the server came to take our drink order, we collectively held our breath, fearing Dad would opt for wine with his meal.

"Water's good for me," he said, smiling up at the server.

The four of us released a simultaneous sigh of relief. Once Dad started drinking, he couldn't seem to stop. The casino had a no-drinking policy for employees while working. If Dad lost this job, I don't know what he'd do with himself.

Once we placed our drink order, we went through the buffet and returned to the table with our plates loaded down with an abundance of seafood.

"How long are you in town for, son?" Dad asked, looking to Lucas.

"Chantelle and I will head out tomorrow afternoon."

Dad looked a bit surprised, but then slowly nodded as if he understood.

"We're planning on going to the cemetery to visit Mom in the morning," I said, wanting to encourage Dad. "Won't you come with us?"

Seeing his face fall, I wished I hadn't asked. Even mentioning that we were going to visit Mom's grave site was an unwelcome reminder of all he had lost. All that we'd lost as a family. It was beyond our father's comprehension how the three of us had bonded after losing our mother. All he saw and felt was loss. I understood and didn't judge.

"Another time," he said, and dug into his food as if he hadn't eaten a decent meal in weeks. And he probably hadn't. I invited him to dinner on Sundays, my one day off from my small café, and he came about once a month, if that, because of his shifts at work.

"No problem," I assured him. Reaching for his hand, I gave it a gentle squeeze. He smiled back at me, silently thanking me.

Our time together passed far too quickly. Following dinner, Dad returned to dealing at the blackjack table. Seeing that we were in the casino, we lingered and played the slots, allotting ourselves twenty dollars each. None of us left as winners, but we had an enjoyable evening and that was what counted.

It was close to ten by the time we returned to the apartment. Lucas and Chantelle had booked a hotel room, and they left after dropping Harper and me off.

The next morning, Harper and I cooked breakfast and Lucas and Chantelle joined us. I made French toast and Harper fried the bacon. When we finished, I stopped in briefly to check in with Shirley and Alice to make sure everything was running smoothly at Bean There. From what I could tell, all was fine without me, and Leesa was a backup if Alice needed help. It felt good to take an extra day away from the business, although it was never far from my mind.

"Did Sean stop by?" Harper asked, making a point to mention his name in front of Lucas and Chantelle.

"Not today," Alice said.

"Oh." My disappointment showed before I could keep it in check.

"See," Harper said, cocking her head toward Lucas. "She doesn't want us to know she likes him, but she does."

I could feel the color fill my face.

"I'm sure he'll be back on Monday," Alice assured me.

Embarrassed, I tried to pretend it was no concern of mine.

We stopped off at the local market to purchase a large bouquet of colorful spring flowers for Mom, along with a bottle of water so they would remain fresh. The mood was somber as we headed to the cemetery. Because of our frequent visits, we had no problem finding Mom's grave site.

Lucas poured the water into the small vase and I set the bouquet inside. Then we bowed our heads and each said our own special greeting to the mother we so deeply loved and would always miss.

Harper looked up and her gaze drifted from me to Lucas. "I have something to tell you . . . I probably should have before now." She paused and tears clouded her eyes.

I reached for her hand and she gripped hold of it so hard I nearly cried out.

"When I was the sickest, when I was sure I was going to die, Mom came to me."

Chapter 5

Willa

"Mom came to you?" Lucas repeated.

Harper nodded and smeared the tears across her cheeks. "For a long time, I thought I must have been hallucinating, but the more I think back to that day, the more I realize she was there. Mom was with me."

"You actually saw her?" Lucas asked, looking as stunned as I felt.

Harper hesitated before answering. "I . . . I don't think I saw her as much as felt her presence. I knew she was there, although I don't know how I knew . . . I just did."

"You said she spoke to you?"

"I didn't hear an audible voice, if that's what you mean. It's hard to explain. I was so sick and weak; everything hurt. Nothing seemed to make it better. Willa had been with me all day and refused to leave my side until you came," she said, looking to Lucas. "You convinced her to take a break and go with you down to the hospital cafeteria, so for the first time I was alone."

"What happened?" I asked, struggling to hold back my own tears. The fact Harper had managed to keep this to herself for this long shocked me. Not once since she'd gone into remission had she mentioned anything about this incident.

Harper nodded. "It was at a point where I didn't care any longer if I lived or died. Sick as I was, I would have welcomed death just to make the pain go away."

If memory served me right, it must have been soon after the initial treatments began. Harper was in the hospital twelve days for the first round of chemotherapy. She lost all her beautiful blond hair, but that was the least of her problems. The treatments left her violently ill, and to complicate everything, she developed an intestinal infection. We were told this was a common side effect of chemotherapy. In Harper's case, it had almost been a deadly combination. Fearing we were going to lose her, I was at her side almost twenty-four/seven.

"The thing is, I kept drifting in and out of sleep. After Lucas took Willa away, I felt this strange comfort. I still hurt and would have done anything to make the pain stop. That was when I felt a presence in the room. Not a physical presence, like a nurse checking on me. A spiritual one. Right away I knew it was Mom. I didn't hear her voice, but I felt it in my heart just as if she had spoken. Mom told me I needed to hold on. That I would survive, and I did."

"Yes, you did," I said, blinking back my own tears. "And look at you now. You're climbing one more mountain."

Harper smiled at me through her own tears. "Yes, I am. Mount Rainier, here I come."

Monday, I found myself waiting for Sean to stop by and was disappointed when the morning passed without my seeing him. Harper almost had me convinced that he was interested, and I'd been foolish enough to believe her.

Harper dropped in between classes, as cheerful as ever. "Has Sean been here today?" she asked, as I made her the drink she had created with kale, wheatgrass juice, and protein powder, then dished up her favorite whole-grain spelt brownie.

Doing my best to hide my disappointment, I shook my head. "Not today."

"Oh," she murmured, pouting a bit. "That's disappointing."

"I told you he wasn't interested." I was intent on making busywork at the counter. Alice had phoned in sick, but I had a feeling it had more to do with fun over the weekend than any virus. As a result, I was left manning the counter single-handedly. Shirley had made it clear when I hired her that she was no barista and preferred to bake and stay in the kitchen.

Harper finished her brownie and returned to work and I went about my day. Near closing time, Sean arrived. My heart did a little jig when I saw him. Thankfully, the business had died down and it was only the two of us in the café.

"Your usual?" I asked when he stepped up to the counter.

He nodded. I noticed he looked tired. "Busy day?" I asked.

"Busy weekend," he answered, holding my look. "I was

on a last-minute assignment. The timing couldn't have been worse."

I was curious and wanted to question him but wasn't sure if it would be appropriate. I knew next to nothing about his work and wished I did. If I was more like Harper, who naturally engaged people, I would have encouraged a conversation.

He lingered for a moment and it seemed neither one of us knew what to say. "I suppose I should be going," he said. "Before I do, I have something for you."

"For me?" For the first time I noticed he had a yellow manila envelope with him. He handed it to me. When I opened it, I found a beautiful black-and-white photo of the front of Bean There. Staring at it for several moments, I didn't know what to say. Even though the photo lacked color, the shadows and the lighting offered a warm, welcoming sensation. "Sean," I whispered as I pressed my hand over my heart. "This is . . . perfect."

"I wanted to be sure you liked it before I framed it."

"I . . . love it. Thank you . . . I hardly know what to say."

"No thanks necessary. It was something I wanted to do." He turned away, prepared to leave.

More than anything, I wanted him to stay. "Ah, it's pretty quiet, if you'd like to sit for a bit?" I asked, stopping him.

He hesitated. "Will you join me?"

"Um, sure, but if someone comes in, I'll need to get up." This would be the first time ever that I'd prayed for a lack of business.

"Understood."

I made myself a latte and joined him, my hands trembling, nervous and feeling awkward. Sean didn't seem any more at ease than I was.

He smiled when I sat down and I released a small sigh, wondering how best to start the conversation. I knew most everyone enjoys talking about themselves. When I heard that Sean was a photographer, I was intrigued, even more so now that I'd seen his work. I would treasure the photo he'd given me. With a single picture, he'd managed to capture everything I'd hoped my small coffee shop would be.

"How did you get into photography?" I asked. "Is it something you've done all your life? I hope you don't mind me asking." I glanced down at the photo once more, impressed with his talent.

"I don't mind in the least." He stretched out his arms and held on to his cup with both hands the way he had earlier. "I started out with another career that unfortunately didn't pan out. It was a major disappointment, and afterward I floundered, unsure what I wanted to do. For years I had a single focus. For a time, I was angry and lost."

"That must have been unsettling."

"It was. I'd always enjoyed photography and had played around with it for years. I was bored and killing time, taking photos. It was my dad who suggested that I go into photography for a career, since I was so interested in it. His encouragement was all I needed."

"Sometimes all we need is a nudge."

"Dad was right. Soon I lived and breathed photography. It filled the void and gave me the opportunity to pour my passion and energy into something I genuinely loved. And the beauty of it was that I didn't need a degree or a certificate."

"Did it take long for you to make a living?"

His responding smile said more than words.

"It wasn't easy in the beginning, but I managed. I'm grateful I'd made enough money in my earlier career so that I was able to make an investment into the equipment I needed and had the time to develop a portfolio."

I noticed that he seemed evasive about his previous job, and while I wondered what he'd done, I didn't ask. If he didn't want to tell me, then I wasn't about to put him on the spot.

"I took a few classes and got a job working for a fine art photographer."

So he'd learned on the job, the same as me. I'd worked as a barista while in college. I'd enjoyed the work and made a lot of friends. I'd been terribly shy as a teenager, still was, but not nearly as bad as before. Having to greet people and make light conversation had helped me tremendously with my shyness.

"What was your first sale?" I asked.

He grinned, his look almost boyish. He pushed a lock of sandy-colored hair from his forehead. "A garbage dump."

"You're teasing me, aren't you?"

"Okay, that's a bit of an exaggeration. It was the glass recycling center. I happened by one day to drop off my recyclables. The sun broke out from behind a cloud and shone down on the glass in a large storage bin. Light bounced around the multicolored glass stored there. I was never without my camera. I grabbed it and took a zillion pictures until I got the right one. I submitted it to a local magazine and was paid a whopping fifty dollars."

"Enough for a bottle of champagne," I said.

"I worked hard to build my portfolio and eventually was able to make enough to support myself."

"It's clear you enjoy your work."

"I do. Very much."

"You were on assignment this weekend, you said?"

"Yeah, in Seattle. I finished editing the shots this afternoon and decided to take a break."

His gaze briefly met mine. I could be wrong, but his look seemed to say he wanted to see me more than he needed the break. While I longed to believe that, I doubted it was true.

"I'm glad you did."

He was about to say something more when a customer entered the café. Although reluctant to leave, I had no choice. Taking one last sip of my latte, I stood. "Thank you again, Sean. This photo means more than I can say."

"I'm glad." He stood with me and said, "Let me frame it for you."

"No, please, let me do that. Thank you again."

I was sad to see him go. In those brief moments I felt that I'd gotten to know him a bit more. How I wished we could have talked longer.

By the time I closed for the day and got the dough mixed for the following morning, I was exhausted and at the same time exhilarated. Although hesitant to admit it, I knew the smile I wore was due to Sean's visit and the photo he'd given me.

When I arrived back at the apartment, Harper was lounging on the sofa. As soon as I walked in the door, she catapulted off and stood before me. Guilt was written all over her. My sister was incredibly easy to read.

"What did you do?" I asked, not giving her a chance to speak.

"Don't be mad."

I froze, afraid to discover what scrape she'd gotten herself into this time. "Why would I be mad?" I asked tentatively, waiting while I held my breath.

Rubbing her palms together, she paced in front of the sofa, avoiding eye contact. "I'm sorry, Willa, but I couldn't help myself. I couldn't say no."

"No to what?" I asked, lowering my voice.

"Wait here." She held out her arm to keep me from following her. Hurrying into her bedroom, she returned with a small white kitten cuddled up against her midsection. She held it as though it was the most precious object in the world.

"You got a cat?" I cried, aghast.

"A kitten," she corrected.

"Who will grow into a cat." Did I seriously need to remind my sister that this kitten wouldn't stay small?

"Yes, I know, but isn't she adorable?" She stared down lovingly at the white puffball.

"She?" I could already see the vet bills mounting.

"Well, I think she's a she. It's hard to tell. She could be a he, which is why I chose a generic name."

As hard as it was, I felt I needed to remind her of what we already knew. "Harper, our lease states that we aren't allowed to have pets in this apartment."

"Who will know?" she asked. "Think about it, Willa. When was the last time we saw our landlord?"

She had a point. If we paid the rent on time, there was no reason for the landlord to make a visit.

Tucking the kitten below her chin, Harper rubbed its tiny head. "I named her Snowball."

"Snowball," I repeated, which I had to admit was the perfect name.

"You aren't upset, are you?"

"Honestly, Harper, we can't keep her. We could get kicked out of the apartment if anyone finds out."

My sister had apparently thought this through, because she shrugged as if that would be a small inconvenience. "If that happens, we'll move, or maybe I'll move myself. You could keep the apartment. We aren't attached at the hip, you know. The time will come when you'll want your own space and I won't be here."

"What?" I started to argue, but she cut me off.

"You don't need to worry, I'll take care of her. I'll keep Snowball in my room with a litter box."

"You can't keep that sweet kitten a prisoner in your room," I insisted. "That would be unfair to Snowball."

"Don't make me take her back," Harper pleaded.

"Where did you get her?"

Petting the tiny kitten, Harper explained. "Candi Olsen from my yoga class. You remember Candi, don't you?"

I did. She was a frequent customer.

"Anyway, Candi found the mother and this litter under her back deck. She brought the kittens into class with her, looking for homes. Snowball was the only one left. The funny part is, Snowball was the one I wanted. It was fate, I tell you. She was meant to be with me."

Looking at the tiny kitten, I was torn. It was hard to refuse Harper, especially when she was this adamant. And I certainly didn't want her to move. Her eyes continued to plead with mine. Heaving a sigh, I reluctantly nodded.

"I knew you'd agree," she said, dancing about our small living area. "You have a home, Snowball."

"As long as you remember she's your cat, and you're footing the bill for all the costs of the vet."

"Gotcha." Harper beamed at me.

Although I was hesitant to admit it, Snowball was irresistible.

Chapter 6

Sean

I decided to name the dog Bandit, seeing that it seemed that he had a habit of stealing. He seemed to adjust quickly enough to a more domesticated lifestyle, although in the beginning it'd been hard on both of us. Regular feedings seemed to have persuaded him that it was worth keeping me around.

Mellie, Preston's wife, had examined him and found him to be a mixed breed. Her guess on the specifics was as good as mine. She suspected he was part shepherd and several parts something else. Whatever it was, it appeared he'd gotten the best of all sides, smart as he was. We both guessed he'd had a home before and had been either lost or abandoned. There'd been no identification on him and no chip. After all these weeks, if he'd been lost there would have been some effort to find him. As far as we could see from an internet search, no one was looking.

According to Preston, abandoning pets in Oceanside was

a common practice, though who knew what people were thinking, bringing their pets to a resort town and leaving them behind. Myself, I couldn't understand anyone being that heartless and cruel. How long Bandit had been on his own was hard to tell. Two or three weeks, possibly longer.

Now that he'd accepted me, I found him to be an amiable companion. I bought a bed for him and kept it in one of the four spare bedrooms that I used as an office. He seemed content to sleep at my side as I sorted through the various photographs that I'd taken on the assignment I'd gotten that weekend from Starbucks. I'd been honored to do repeat business with them, even if it was last-minute. A couple of years earlier, I'd documented coffee origins for the Seattle-based company, traveling to Colombia, Panama, and Ethiopia.

When I was certain that I had several photos that would satisfy my client, I emailed them and awaited word back. Caught up in the project, time had passed quickly, and I realized if I didn't leave soon, Bean There would be closed.

Watching the way Willa's face had lit up when she'd first seen the photo was more than enough thanks. I would do almost anything to see her smile. She'd been full of questions and I enjoyed telling her about my photography, although I'd avoided talking about my baseball career. From experience, I knew the minute I mentioned I'd played in the majors, that was all anyone wanted to talk about. Baseball was my past and I was no longer a part of that world. Nor did I wish to be.

As hard as it'd been to accept at the time, I was grateful to have gotten away from professional sports. Photography was my all-encompassing passion. Not a day passed when I didn't have a camera in my hand. All those years I'd been the star. How odd it was now to feel the comfort of being behind the camera instead of in front of one.

Bandit woke and stretched. He looked up at me as if to remind me it was dinnertime. It seemed like this dog's appetite would soon eat me out of house and home.

"Don't worry," I told him, "I'm going to feed you; I haven't failed you yet, have I?"

Although I'd had Bandit less than a week, he was already filling out, and with good reason. I'd fill his dish, which he'd promptly scarf down. As if to say he'd been cheated, he'd look up, asking for more. Seeing how thin he was, I willingly obliged. Already his ribs didn't stick out quite as much as they had when I'd first brought him home.

Leaning back in my chair, I raised my arms over my head and stretched. I needed to check my email and almost dreaded what I would find. I was waiting on word from *National Geographic* about a Research and Exploration Grant that would send me to a series of islands off the coast of the Philippines. It would take some time for the team to be assembled. My hope was that I'd receive word any day now. Already I hated the thought of having to leave Bandit behind. Mellie and Preston had assured me they would find a good foster home for Bandit when the time came, if that was what I chose to do. That had been the deciding factor when I agreed to adopt him.

"I was going to do it, you know," I told Bandit, who cocked his head at me. The poor dog didn't have a clue what I was talking about. I was talking about Willa. She was almost constantly on my mind. "I had every intention of asking her out and would have if a customer hadn't arrived when they did." I was a victim of poor timing. It'd taken all my self-control not to tell her customer she was closed for the day.

Bandit continued to stare at me. "I agree, asking a woman out shouldn't be this hard. Guess I'm rusty when it comes to this dating business." That was an understatement if ever there was one. From the time I'd left baseball and started freelancing, every spare moment had been tied up with building my portfolio. Although I'd saved a nice nest egg from my time in the majors, it wasn't enough to support me for more than a few years, especially considering my traveling expenses for freelance opportunities. I'd worked night and day, hustling for jobs, investing in top-of-the-line digital cameras, a laptop, lights, and a website. That didn't leave time for much of anything else.

Traveling as often as I had in the last few years had made it difficult to maintain a relationship, even with my own family. I'd lost count of the number of holidays I'd missed. The truth was I hadn't found a woman that had caught my interest nearly as much as Willa had. She was almost entirely the exact opposite of Nikki, who'd flaunted her beauty.

Looking back, I realized I'd had a lucky escape. It baffled me that I had been so foolish, unable to accept what was right in front of me. Nikki was greedy and self-absorbed. Everything was about her and what she could get. The last I'd heard, she'd hooked up with another player, my replacement, in more ways than one.

"Next time I see her, I'll ask her out," I told Bandit. I could have sworn I heard him snort as if he didn't believe me. "Just you wait."

The opportunity came sooner than I expected. After filling his bowl twice for dinner, I realized Bandit had gone through an entire bag of dog food. I didn't want him to go hungry come morning, and decided to make a run into town that evening, heading to the local grocery store.

My mistake had been in purchasing a small bag. I didn't want to waste money on a brand Bandit didn't like. I should have known that after living off scraps and whatever he could steal, he wouldn't be picky.

I loaded a twenty-five-pound bag into my cart and headed to the cashier. As I rounded the corner, I nearly bumped into another cart.

"Willa." I gasped, shocked to see her.

She looked as surprised as I did. "Hello, again," she said after her initial reaction. "Funny running into you here."

"Yeah. Funny." My wit had failed me, which it seemed to do whenever I was around her.

Staring at the huge bag of dog food in my cart, she raised her gaze to meet mine. "I didn't know you had a dog."

"Bandit is a recent addition."

"Harper and I have a new addition ourselves. She brought home a kitten this afternoon." Lowering her voice, she added, "Our lease doesn't allow pets, so I don't know how this is going to pan out."

"Bandit was a stray in need of a good home."

Willa smiled knowingly. "That tells me Preston and Mellie Young got ahold of you."

Barking a laugh, I nodded. "That they did, although to be fair, I wasn't all that averse to adopting him. He's proved to be a good companion."

"I'll let you know how it works out with Snowball," she said.

It seemed neither one of us knew what else to say after that. "I guess I better get back home," I said, "Bandit is waiting."

"Me too, although I just started."

I noticed she had only a few items in her cart. She went in one direction and I headed in another. Once I paid and hauled the heavy bag out to my car, I returned the cart to the store.

A light rain had started to fall, and I hurriedly got into the car and was ready to pull out of the parking lot when I stepped on the brake and slammed my hand against the steering wheel. I heaved a sigh big enough to lift my shoulders. I'd let yet another opportunity to ask Willa out slip through my fingers.

Not happening. Not again. Hadn't I told Bandit less than two hours ago that I would ask the next time I saw Willa?

Turning off the engine, I opened the door to pelting rain and raced back into the store. It took me three aisles to find her.

"Willa," I called out loudly, capturing her attention. I was a man on a mission, and this time I wasn't backing down.

She looked up and blinked. I must have been a sight. Rain had plastered my shirt against my front and back. Water dripped from my hair onto my shoulders and into my eyes.

"It's raining?"

"It's a monsoon," I said.

"I didn't hear anything about rain in the forecast," she said, as though I'd returned to the store to warn her.

"Listen," I said, "I don't mean to be rude, but I'm asking you not to say anything for the next few minutes."

She looked concerned and confused. Not that I blamed her. That wasn't how I should have started, but I wasn't stopping now.

"Okay," she agreed. "What's this about?"

I'd already started down this path and was unable to make a course correction now. It was my do-or-die moment. "Every time I try, I flub this up, so please be patient." I paused as if awaiting her response before I realized I asked her not to give me one.

Sucking in a breath, I charged forward. "I like you, Willa, and I'd enjoy getting to know you better." I brushed my wet hair off my forehead. "You should know I don't drink coffee. I don't like the taste. The only reason I stop by Bean There is for the chance to see you."

Her dark eyes widened as if my words had offended her. I probably shouldn't have admitted that.

"Don't get me wrong. You make good coffee; it just so happens that I'm not a coffee drinker. I felt I had to justify coming in every day. I add cream to make it tolerable." Seeing

that Starbucks was one of my major accounts, I felt the need
to add, "If you ever have the opportunity, promise me you
won't let the folks at Starbucks know that."

"Ah . . ."

"That's beside the point." Already I was screwing this up.
"What I'm doing a piss-poor job of saying is that if you're
agreeable I'd like to date you. We can go out to eat, take
in a show, take a walk along the beach. I'm willing to do
anything you want."

She continued to stare at me with her mouth half open
as if she didn't know what to say.

Finally I couldn't stand it any longer. "Say something," I
urged.

It appeared she had no words.

"If you're not interested, tell me." She should know her
silence was deflating my ego. And physically I was already
all wet.

"Okay," she said.

A single word, and it was as if someone had resuscitated
me back to life. "Okay you'll say something, or okay you're
willing to go out with me?"

"Both, I guess."

"You will?" I had to be sure I understood correctly.

She nodded.

"Good." Nervous as I was, I left her and walked all the
way to the end of the aisle before I realized that I'd abandoned
her. Doing an abrupt about-face, I hurried back to her. "When
would you like to start?"

"I . . . anytime," she said. She seemed to have gone pale.

"I wouldn't be able to stay out late, though. Three-thirty comes early."

"You get up at three-thirty?" That seemed unbelievable. "What time do you go to bed?"

Lowering her gaze, Willa gave the impression that if she said too early, I'd have a change of heart. I needed to correct that impression.

"It doesn't matter—nothing does, as long as you're willing to go on a date with me." I was convinced the pleading in my voice destroyed my man card.

"Lights are off around nine." She sounded unsure, as if her hours remained a deal-breaker.

I did the math in my head. "Is that enough sleep?"

"I can stay out later if you want."

"No need," I rushed to assure her. "I'm willing to take whatever time you give me. I'll get up at three-thirty, too, if that helps."

Willa smiled. The only thing I could equate her smile to was watching the sun rise, spilling light over the Olympic Mountains. I'd managed to capture that shot in one of the several magazine covers I'd had over the years. The photo, which I considered my best to date, took my breath away once the film was developed. I swear I stared at it for a good fifteen minutes, unable to tear my eyes off the image I'd captured.

The same feeling flowed over me with Willa's smile. "Is tomorrow too soon?" I asked, calmer now, my heart returning to an acceptable beat. From the way it had pounded earlier, I should have been light-headed.

"Tomorrow would be perfect."

"What would you like to do?" I was game for anything, as long as it was with Willa.

She met my gaze. "Would you mind a walk along the beach?" she asked.

A walk along the beach. "That sounds perfect."

I would have gladly taken her to the priciest restaurant in the state, had she asked. This was Willa, though. Nothing fancy. Nothing out of the ordinary. A simple walk along the beach. If I wasn't half in love with her already, this simple request would have done it.

Chapter 7

Willa

I arrived home, bubbling with excitement, eager to tell Harper about running into Sean. I flew in and nearly tripped over the rug in my eagerness. My shoulders deflated when I found her in her room, fast asleep. Snowball was nowhere in sight. Careful to keep the screen door closed as I traipsed back and forth hauling grocery bags into the apartment, I kept an eye out for my sister's kitten.

Snowball didn't make a showing and I could only imagine where she was hiding.

I made dinner and went to wake Harper. "Dinner's ready," I told her, gently placing my hand on her shoulder.

Stretching her arms over her head, she yawned and briefly looked up at me. "I'm tired. I want to skip dinner tonight."

"You sure?" Normally Harper had a good appetite.

"I did a hard workout this afternoon and was up late on the phone with John last night. Let me sleep."

John, if I remembered correctly, was a fellow climber. From the beginning I'd had my doubts about this mountain adventure of Harper's. She was exhausted and she had yet to set foot anywhere close to Mount Rainier. "Sleep," I whispered. She'd wake later and change into her pajamas and probably raid the refrigerator.

In the meantime, Snowball was AWOL. Hoping to lure her out from her hiding spot, I set a bowl of food on the kitchen floor. She was a no-show. Surely the kitten would be hungry by now. So much for Harper's promise to take care of her.

Mumbling under my breath as I headed into my room, I found Snowball curled up and asleep on my pillow. How she'd managed to get all the way up to the bed was a mystery.

"So here you are," I said, lifting her and gently petting her. "I have food out for you." I carted her into the kitchen and placed her on the floor. Snowball found the bowl and quickly ate. When she'd finished her dinner, I carried her back to Harper.

"Harper," I said softly, not wanting to startle her. "I have *your* cat." I set Snowball down on the pillow next to my sister's head. While half asleep, Harper smiled and gently tucked Snowball against her stomach. The kitten immediately curled up and took a nap.

Shaking my head, I left the two of them.

I didn't talk to Harper until the following morning, when she stopped off at Bean There on her break between her fitness classes.

"Hello, Sleeping Beauty," I said, and handed her a protein drink along with a vegan blueberry scone. There'd been evidence that morning of her kitchen raid sometime during the night.

"I know. Can you believe I slept nearly twelve hours?"

"Yes. I think these workouts are stretching you to the limit." I didn't want to claim they were too much for her, for fear of sounding like the mother she'd accused me of being.

"Hogwash," Harper insisted. "I didn't get enough sleep the night before and needed to catch up is all."

"Whatever you say." I wasn't sure I believed her, and resisted rolling my eyes.

Seeing that Alice was dealing well with the customers, I grabbed a coffee and joined my sister. Lowering my voice, I said, "I happened to run into Sean last night."

"And?" Harper arched her neatly trimmed eyebrows.

Hiding my smile would have been impossible. "He asked me out."

A knowing smile quivered at her lips. "Told you."

No use arguing. Besides, I didn't want to. "You did."

"Where's he taking you?"

"He asked me what I wanted to do." That had impressed me. "I suggested a walk along the beach."

"What!" Harper cried, shaking her head as if I'd committed some terrible faux pas. "No way. After he kept you waiting all this time. The least you can do is ask him to take you to dinner."

"Next time," I said, amused at her outrage. "At the end

of the day, I'm tired. I'd rather get to know him without all the fuss of us sitting in a crowded, noisy restaurant, trying to have a conversation."

Harper considered my words before slowly shaking her head. "You and I are different people."

I laughed. "You mean to say it's taken you this long to realize that?"

My sister smiled. "Not really. If it was me, I'd have Sean wine and dine me and make sure he understood how fortunate he was that I was willing to spend time with him."

That was Harper, all right. "But then you get ten men all wanting to date you to my one."

She bit off the end of her scone. "You're exaggerating."

"Hardly." We both knew I was right, and we both knew it wasn't worth arguing over. Time to change the subject. "Where did you put you know who?" I asked, my voice a whisper. I figured she'd understand I was referring to Snowball.

Harper nearly spit out a bite of her scone. "You mean Snowball?" she asked, as if this was all one big joke.

I glared back at her. We couldn't very well blurt out that we were keeping a cat in an apartment complex that didn't allow pets. "Yes," I admitted.

"It isn't like we're hiding an escaped felon."

"Whatever. Where is she?"

"My room, like I promised. I got a box with kitty litter and have a bowl of food and water out for her. She'll be fine until I'm back this afternoon."

"Did you close your bedroom door?"

Harper blinked and shook her head. "Of course not. You're the one who insisted that would be cruel."

I could see it all now: Within a few weeks Snowball would grow big enough to curl herself up in the front window, lazing in the sun for all the world to see as they passed by. There would be a tenant revolt because others in the complex would demand to know why we had a pet and they weren't allowed one. Then the landlord would be notified, and we would be asked to move. It came to me as clear as a termination notice.

"You've got that look again," Harper murmured, frowning at me. "You're thinking too much."

One of us needed to. "We're going to lose our apartment because of that cat. Mark my words, Harper Lakey. Mark my words."

Following the lunch hour, Teresa Hoffert stopped by. She wasn't a regular customer and I enjoyed seeing her. Teresa cleaned houses and was the hardest-working woman I knew. Her daughter, Britt, had worked for me during her senior year in high school and was one of the best employees I'd ever hired. Like mother, like daughter.

"Teresa," I said, happy to see her. "What can I get you?"

"How about a turkey sandwich and a cup of coffee."

"Sounds good." I removed the sandwich from the refrigerated glass case and poured her a cup of coffee.

She paid me and took a seat at a table close to the counter. We chatted for a bit, and it was good to catch up with her and get the latest news about Britt and her younger brother,

Logan. After Teresa finished her lunch, she left. I knew that her buying herself lunch was a rare treat and that she did it because she wanted to support me and the café.

As the afternoon progressed, I found myself watching the clock. Sean knew I closed the shop at three, but I often stayed longer to get everything ready for the following morning. When Shirley arrived that morning, I'd asked her if she would cover for me and she'd readily agreed.

When Scan came by for our date, I was as ready as I was likely to be. I'd changed into white jeans and a sleeveless red blouse with ruffles on both sides of the long row of buttons. It was one of my favorites.

"Hey," he said.

"Hey." I nervously wiped my hands down the front of my pants.

"You ready?"

I nodded, letting him know that I was. He looked wonderful. Better than ever, in a checkered shirt and khaki pants.

"I brought Bandit with me. He's in the car. You don't mind, do you? I hated leaving him alone at the house."

"Sure, no problem." Even though I'd made a fuss over Harper's cat, I was an animal lover and was especially fond of dogs.

Shirley locked the door behind me and winked, letting me know she approved. Earlier, when I'd asked her to stay late, she'd said she felt it was high time I made a life for myself. And she was right. I'd invested so much of myself in my tiny café at the cost of everything except family. I couldn't remember the last time I'd gone out with someone I was excited to see. I'd dated some in the last few years, thanks to Harper. My sister often took pity on me and asked me to double-date with her. Most were blind dates and had petered out quickly. With my irregular hours and dedication to making my café a success, there wasn't a lot of room in my life for romance. Sad to say, I was a sorry disappointment to Harper.

Sean was the exception. Almost from the time he'd started showing up, I'd felt drawn to him. When my sister suggested that he was interested in me, I'd wanted to believe it but dared not hope. I didn't want to set myself up for disappointment. Even now, I wasn't sure what it was about him that I found so compelling. Yes, he was attractive in a boyish sense. I liked that he wasn't overconfident and had downplayed his success.

Okay, I'll admit it. I'd gone online soon after meeting him and checked out his website. I soon discovered that he'd worked all around the world and taken photographs for major corporations, done catalog shoots, and had several magazine cover photos—including more than one for *National Geographic*. Sean was successful, and yet he'd never once bragged about his work or made it apparent he was as well known as he was. I couldn't help but admire that about him.

Sean opened the rear door of his car and a midsize dog leaped from the backseat. I recognized him as the stray I'd fed a couple of times. Sean had him by a leash. Once out of the vehicle, Bandit paused and looked around. Sitting on his haunches, he turned his head and looked back at Sean.

Bending down on one knee, Sean spoke to him softly, rubbed his ears, and then righted himself. "Bandit is nervous and needed a bit of reassurance."

"Why is he nervous?" I asked, joining him as we sauntered toward the beach, Bandit leading the way.

"Preston and I suspect his previous owner brought him into town and abandoned him. Bringing him back here, I think he's afraid I'm going to do the same thing."

"Poor Bandit." I bent forward and gently stroked his fur. He looked at me with deep brown worried eyes. "You have nothing to be afraid of, fella," I told him.

Once we reached the beach, we found it crowded with the normal summer population. Kids raced, kicking up sand as they flew kites up and down the beach. Several cars were parked up from the surf and there was a line of multicolored umbrellas offering shade. The remains of sandcastles littered the area as we walked side by side, Bandit taking the lead.

After a bit, Sean reached for my hand.

"I missed seeing you this morning," I said, "which is silly, because I knew you'd be by later."

"I nearly came in."

"Why didn't you?"

He chuckled. "The truth? I thought I might look a bit overeager, which I confess I was."

I smiled to myself, not wanting him to know how much I'd been looking for him to show even though I now knew he wasn't a coffee drinker.

"I'm going out of town on Thursday. I'll be gone all day and probably won't return until late."

"Where are you headed?"

"A small town in eastern Washington called Toppenish. Have you ever heard of it?"

I didn't know that I had. "Maybe," I ventured.

"I have an assignment to shoot town murals, and apparently Toppenish is known for them."

"That sounds interesting." Another day, possibly two, without my Sean fix.

"I'll need to bring Bandit with me. It's going to be a long day, so if I don't show up for a couple of days, you'll know why."

So I was right. "You travel a lot, don't you?"

"On occasion. I'm waiting on a big assignment but got word this morning of another assignment I'd be foolish to refuse. The big one is in the Philippines, but it doesn't look like it's going to come through for another couple of months. I have another planned on spec in Bolivia."

He wasn't kidding. He got around. "How long will you be in South America?"

"A couple of weeks."

"That long?" I asked, before I could hold it back.

His hand squeezed mine. "Will you miss me?"

"I think I will."

Bandit tugged on his leash, disliking our slower pace. The wind whipped around us and the scent of the ocean wafted along the beach. Seagulls flew with the wind current. I saw a pretty shell and bent down to retrieve it.

"What about Bandit?" I asked. "Who's going to watch him while you're away for an extended time period?" I'd volunteer if I could, but that was impossible. Not with the no-pet policy and my hours at the café.

"Preston's got someone lined up for me. A boy by the name of Logan Hoffert. It seems he trained a puppy Keaton gave him a few years back and is quite good with dogs."

"I know Logan. In fact, his mother was in today for lunch. Logan will do a great job."

"Preston said the same thing."

Winding my arm around his elbow, I asked him the same question he'd posed to me. "Will you miss me while you're away?"

He grinned down at me, holding my gaze. "Like crazy. I'm already dreading the one day when I'll be in Toppenish."

If we were going to be in a relationship, and that was a big if, then I would need to adjust to his traveling schedule. The same applied to him. Sean would need to accept my irregular hours.

"Hey, I've got an idea," Sean said, stopping abruptly, his eyes brightening. "Come with me."

"With you? Where?"

"To Toppenish. It's just one day. I'll be leaving soon afterward for Bolivia, and this might be the only time we have together for the next few weeks. Do you think you could take time away from work?"

My head was spinning. Shirley and Alice had filled in for me last Saturday when Lucas was in town. Everything had gone smoothly at the café. Shirley was great, and if Alice wasn't available, then maybe Harper could fill in. She'd done it before and was great with the customers. The thing was, I wanted this day with Sean. I wanted it badly.

"I'll make it work," I said.

Sean beamed me a huge smile. "Great. We leave early Thursday morning."

"I'll be ready whenever you say." Harper might want to be wined and dined. I was completely happy spending time with Sean, driving to the other side of the state for a photo shoot.

Chapter 8

Willa

When I arrived home, I found Harper sitting with Snowball on her lap and her phone to her ear. She glanced up when I entered the apartment and excitedly waved her hand at me, indicating I should sit down next to her.

"Hold on, Lucas, Willa's here."

"It's Lucas?" This was a surprise.

Harper nodded. "He wants me to put the phone on speaker."

Having recently spent time with our brother, I hadn't expected to hear from him this soon. "What's up?" I asked, sitting down next to my sister.

"I don't know," Harper said, as she set the phone down on the coffee table. "He said he had something to tell us but would wait until you could be here, too."

"Is it about Dad?" I fretted that he might have gotten

drunk on the job and been fired. Or, worse, that he'd been arrested for driving while intoxicated.

"Nothing like that," Lucas's voice came through the phone. "Both of you better sit down."

I drew in a deep breath, wondering from the seriousness of his tone what this could be about. "Okay, I'm ready. What is it?" I couldn't help being nervous. "What's going on?"

"I wanted to mention it last weekend but promised I wouldn't," he started.

"Mention what?" Both Harper and I said at the same time. We shared a worried look, fearing the worst.

"Chantelle and me."

I leaped to my feet and braced my fists against my hips. "Lucas Lakey, if you tell me you've broken up with Chantelle, I don't know that I'll ever forgive you."

"Hold on, sis, we didn't break up. We're getting married."

Harper and I both gasped with delight.

"You're getting married!" Harper nearly tossed Snowball from her lap.

"When?" I asked.

"December fifth."

"You've already set the date?" Harper cried.

It was clear that the wedding plans had been in the works for some time and that we'd been kept in the dark.

"You'd already proposed when you were here last Friday, hadn't you?" I said, voicing my suspicions.

"Yes, he had." It was Chantelle who spoke. "And my ring is everything I hoped it would be."

"Why keep it a secret?" Harper asked before I had a chance.

"The ring was being sized and wasn't on her finger yet," Lucas explained. "Besides, we hadn't told Chantelle's family."

"That's no excuse," Harper complained. It wasn't like either of us were in contact with Chantelle's family or would spoil their announcement.

Once more Harper said the same thing that was on my mind. It happened often, I suppose because we were that close, we shared each other's thoughts.

"No wonder you were upset when we started bugging you about marrying Chantelle," I said. His frown had been fierce enough to melt concrete.

"It's my fault," Chantelle was quick to chime in. "I wanted a ring on my finger before we told my parents. Lucas said he wouldn't tell his family then, either, and so we didn't. I'll admit it was hard to keep it to myself, especially when we were with you and your dad."

"So tell us about the ring!" Harper relaxed against the back of the sofa, looking smug. "A diamond, I presume. How many carats did he spring for?"

"Harper!" The fact that our brother was marrying the love of his life was far more important than the size of the diamond.

"Two carats, and it's stunning."

I could envision Chantelle holding out her hand and examining her engagement ring.

"Congratulations, you two," I said, genuinely pleased for Lucas, although it had taken him long enough to make the leap. Chantelle was exactly the right person for my brother. I couldn't help wondering why he didn't recognize it when I did.

"I want both of you to be bridesmaids," Chantelle said. "My sister will be the maid of honor."

"Bill and Ted will serve as ushers," Lucas added.

I recognized the names of two friends Lucas had while serving in the Army. Both had remained in the military and had stayed in touch with our brother.

"Charlie has agreed to be my best man."

Charlie was our cousin, the son of our mother's sister.

"That's wonderful." The two were close in age and had been good friends nearly their entire lives.

"We've thought about this a lot and we've decided we want to be married in Oceanside."

"Here?" This came as a huge surprise.

"We're being practical," Lucas explained. "It isn't like this is the most romantic spot in the world. It's cheaper. Do you have any clue what a wedding costs in Seattle? I'm not talking about a fancy venue, either."

Both Harper and I shook our heads. Wedding costs weren't exactly on our radar.

"We want to put our money into a down payment on a house instead of blowing it on a huge wedding."

My brother had always been practical.

"I'm sewing my own dress," Chantelle said. "The design is simple and elegant. I can't wait to show you the pattern. I'll sew your bridesmaid dresses as well. We don't want you to put a lot of money into an outfit you're only likely to wear once."

I knew Chantelle was an accomplished seamstress and worked with a fashion designer. I couldn't imagine her buying off the rack when anything she created herself would be stunning. "I couldn't hope for any better bridesmaid dress." It went without saying that our dresses would be beautiful as well.

Giving their wedding some thought, I realized I could help, too. "I'll bake the wedding cake," I offered

The line went quiet.

"What's the problem?" I asked.

"How many wedding cakes have you baked?" Lucas asked suspiciously.

"None . . . yet. I'll practice and I promise I won't let you down."

"Thank you," Chantelle said, and sounded sincerely pleased.

I knew her family had money and could afford a lavish cake. Seeing how much time I spent in the kitchen, baking for Bean There, I felt I could do a worthy job of it, given the opportunity.

"That's so thoughtful of you, Willa." Chantelle was gracious, even if my brother wasn't.

"Have you talked to Chantelle's father yet?" I asked, knowing my brother well enough to expect him to want his future in-laws' approval.

Immediately, Chantelle burst into giggles.

"Stop laughing, it wasn't funny," Lucas warned.

"What happened?" I was smiling now, too, and eager to hear the story.

Chantelle answered for Lucas. "I don't think I've ever loved Lucas more than I did the night he spoke to my father," she said, her voice wavering with emotion. "My darling love was a nervous wreck."

"I was a little on edge," Lucas reluctantly admitted.

"A little? I thought you were going to vomit."

Lucas snorted. "It wasn't that bad."

"Close."

"Maybe," Lucas concurred.

Glancing over at Harper, I saw that she'd covered her mouth to hold back her laughter. I had trouble containing my own. I could well imagine how nerve-racking this conversation must have been for my brother.

"So, what happened?" Harper plied.

Again, it was Chantelle who answered. "We stopped by the house and Lucas said he wanted to speak to my dad privately. Then the two of them disappeared into my dad's home office. When he closed the door, Lucas gave me a look like he was walking toward the electric chair."

"Very funny," Lucas muttered in the background. "You and I both know your father has never been fond of me."

"You're imagining things," Chantelle muttered.

"No, I'm not," Lucas argued. "They had someone other than a longshoreman in mind for their beautiful daughter."

"You're exaggerating, Lucas."

"Don't think so, babe."

"Well, anyway, it was very sweet," Chantelle said, her voice soft and full of love. "Here was a man who'd faced the

Taliban, IEDs, and fought for his country, who was shaking in his boots facing my father."

"A divorce attorney, I'd like to remind you."

"Daddy takes other clients, too," Chantelle said.

"It must have gone well," I said, seeing that they were now officially engaged.

"It did," Chantelle hurried to tell us. "Thirty minutes later they came out of the room and my father said he had a few questions for me."

"Right," Lucas muttered. "He wanted to be sure Chantelle was convinced I would make a good husband, as if he was in doubt."

"And I told my parents I was the fortunate one to have fallen in love with a man who is kind and honorable and who loved me with all his heart."

"So romantic," Harper said and sighed.

"It wasn't as problem-free as you make it sound," Lucas added. "Chantelle's parents wanted to throw us the wedding of the century."

"Like they did with my sister," Chantelle explained. "I don't want that, and neither does Lucas. Knowing my mother, she'd take over and everything would be to her liking and not mine. What's important to us is that those we love most are there to share our wedding day."

"For my part, Chantelle and I are both adults, and frankly, I didn't like the idea of Chantelle's father paying for the wedding. I feel like I need to prove myself to him."

"Lucas, you don't have anything to prove to my family."

I silently agreed with her.

"Mom was horrified when I told her I would be sewing my own wedding dress," Chantelle continued.

"Well, yes, considering they paid the price of a small car for the one your sister wore."

"It took some convincing that we wanted to do this our way," Chantelle said. "In the end, they agreed. I don't need or want a large wedding. I've got everything I could ever want with Lucas as my husband and the man who will father our children."

I had to admire Chantelle for sticking up for what she wanted and not expecting her family to foot the bill for their wedding.

"I couldn't be happier," Chantelle said. "I meant every word I told my parents. I'm the fortunate one."

"My brother knew a good thing when he found it," I said.

"And in the bargain, I get two new sisters."

"Two sisters who welcome you into the family with open arms." We were the fortunate ones. I'd known Chantelle was the one for Lucas the first time I'd met her. Lucas had dated several women since leaving the Army. Harper and I had met a couple of his love interests, neither one of which I'd felt a connection to. Chantelle seemed to be the perfect match for him.

I was happy for them both. December couldn't get here soon enough to suit me.

Chapter 9

Willa

"I've got you covered," Harper told me.

Her gleeful smile didn't evoke confidence. It was hard for me to stay away from Bean There, even if it meant I would be able to spend the day with Sean.

"Leesa and I will take over for you. No problem. We have everything under control."

Leesa was Harper's best friend. They both taught yoga and fitness classes at Oceanside Fitness and had been friends since their grade-school days. I'd come to appreciate what a good friend Leesa was when Harper was first diagnosed with leukemia. She'd been a constant encouragement to my sister. Although it was inconvenient to travel into Seattle from Oceanside, Leesa had made the trip at least once a week during the worst of Harper's treatments and long recovery.

Traveling with Sean, especially when he was on an assignment, was highly tempting. Even though I'd already agreed, second thoughts hounded me. I wasn't sure I could say this was such a good idea after all. It was like leaving my baby unattended.

To be fair, Harper knew how to steam a mean cappuccino; she was good with the customers, too. Still, I hesitated. I was the responsible one. The one who made sure that everything ran smoothly, and I kept my customers happy. Leaving it in the hands of Harper and Leesa gave me pause.

"Are you looking for excuses to get out of this trip?" Harper asked, hands on her hips. Her narrowed eyes challenged me. My sister didn't back down often, and I knew she was determined to see me out the door at the crack of dawn and in the car with Sean on our way to eastern Washington.

"No . . . I want to go." And I did, in the worst way.

"We got this, Willa. It's one day. One. Day. How much damage could we possibly do?"

The answer wasn't something I wanted to contemplate.

"Don't even think about it," Harper warned, wagging her finger at me. "You're going."

"Okay, okay."

My sister knew all the buttons to push to convince me. And maybe, just maybe, that is what I needed, what I wanted from her. This thing, whatever it was with Sean, unnerved me. I wasn't accustomed to men being interested in me, especially after they met Harper. I'd never minded, and didn't now—I was just surprised and a little intimidated.

Thursday morning, Sean picked me up bright and early. Bandit was stretched out, taking up the entire backseat. I joined Sean in the front with a small basket of freshly baked cinnamon rolls and two coffee drinks, which I set in the cupholder. The basket went down by my feet, next to my purse.

"You ready?" he asked, after I adjusted my seatbelt.

"Yup," I said, smiling over at him.

For one awkward moment, Sean sat there and stared at me, his dark eyes intense.

"Is something wrong?" Harper had helped me dress and fussed with my hair, giving me advice, which she seemed to think I needed. And to be frank, I probably did.

Embarrassed, I looked away.

"Sorry," he said, and abruptly returned his attention to the road before shifting gears and starting out. "You're beautiful."

"Oh." I was sure I blushed. Unsure how best to respond, I placed my hands in my lap and looked straight ahead.

After a couple of minutes, Sean reached for his coffee and took his first sip. "Hey, what's this? It's not coffee and it tastes . . . different."

"It's a dark chocolate mocha. You said you didn't enjoy coffee, so I decided to mix it up a little. How do you like it?"

"It's fantastic!" He continued to sip the drink, keeping it in one hand and steering with the other.

"A lot of men order cold-brew coffee, but I didn't think you'd want to start the day off with a cold drink." I bent forward and retrieved the basket. "I wasn't sure if you took time for breakfast. I have a couple of cinnamon rolls if you're interested."

"Does a bear . . ." He hesitated. "I'm always interested in your cinnamon rolls. We'll take a break and eat when we get to Snoqualmie Pass, if I can wait that long."

Before we left, I'd Googled the route and saw that the drive between Oceanside and Toppenish would take nearly five hours. That meant we'd be spending ten or more hours on the road. Sean had warned me it would be a long day. That hadn't been a deterrent; I considered it a plus. The time in the car would give me the opportunity to get to know him better.

"Harper and her friend Leesa are minding the café," I mentioned, looking to start a conversation.

"Are you worried?"

"Not overly. Harper's helped me out before, and Alice is there if she runs into trouble. She can make most of the drinks without a problem. It'll be fine."

"You sound worried."

"I kind of obsess over things." I couldn't help it. Ever since Mom died, I'd been a worrier and a caretaker. Even now, when we were all adults, I hadn't been able to stop, as evidenced by my constant concerns about Harper's health. "Not just Bean There. Although this is the second time in a week that I've left the café in someone else's hands. That's not like me."

"I'm happy you agreed to come with me."

"I am, too." I didn't want Sean to think otherwise. Since our conversation in the grocery store, I'd been on a natural high, giddy. Of course, Harper had picked up on my mood. To hear her speak, his interest in me was akin to a wedding proposal. She might have been inspired by Lucas and Chantelle's wedding announcement. My mistake was telling her. From that point on, Harper had been full of relationship advice, guiding me on how best to reel Sean in. I listened with half an ear, amused and at the same time interested. I found it laughable that the girl who hadn't stayed in a relationship longer than a few weeks insisted on giving me advice.

I hadn't seen Sean since I'd spoken to my brother and his fiancé, so I told him Lucas was engaged.

"You like Chantelle?" he asked.

"Love her. She's a good match for Lucas. I wondered why it took him as long as it did to make it official. In looking back, I believe it has something to do with her family."

"Oh?"

"They have money, and, well, we don't. My guess is Chantelle shut down that argument, which is probably why Lucas insists on paying for the wedding on their own."

"I can understand his point of view. A man has his pride, you know. We all do."

I paid close attention to that piece of knowledge. It helped me understand my brother better and would help me with Sean, too, if we continued seeing each other.

After the first hour on the road, Bandit stirred and stuck

his head between the two seats. "Well, hello there," I said, patting his head.

"I bet he smells those cinnamon rolls," Sean said. "You know how he got his name, don't you?"

I laughed, remembering the story. "I should have brought a treat for him, too."

"He's not getting my cinnamon roll, so don't even think of offering it to him."

"No worries. You're good."

Once we reached the top of Snoqualmie Pass, we took a short break. Sean walked Bandit and then returned to the car. I had everything ready for him when he joined me. We ate our breakfast and I shared part of my roll with Bandit, who licked my hand in appreciation. Or it might have been on the off chance a bit of the icing remained on my fingertips.

Once we were back on the road, Sean gave me the lowdown on this assignment. "*Seattle Magazine* asked me to shoot several murals around the state. I was up in Anacortes a week ago, and Seattle has a number of murals as well."

I remembered seeing one or two over the years, mostly near Seattle Cancer Center and the University of Washington Medical Center, where Harper had spent much of her hospital stay.

"Have you shot any in Tacoma?" I asked, thinking there were sure to be several there.

"Tacoma's interesting," he said, glancing toward me before returning his attention to the road. "They have what's known as Graffiti Garage, and that's literally what it is. The city banned graffiti, but they allow artists into this garage every

Sunday to paint the walls. I stopped by one week and the artwork was fantastic. Some of the best I've been able to shoot."

"Did you get a look at the two that are in Oceanside?" He couldn't very well have missed them. Not many people were aware Keaton had painted those.

"It was those murals that inspired the idea. I took pictures of them and a few in Seattle and approached the magazine with the idea and they went for it."

"So you drum up your own work?"

"Yes. I am often approached to do a shoot, but others are on spec. My trip to Bolivia is on spec, which means I'm footing the cost in the hopes of finding a publication that will find it newsworthy."

More and more, I was learning what it meant when Sean said he was a freelance photographer.

"Thus far, my assignments pay the bills, but there's a lot of hustle that goes along with this career. The thing I've learned is that when I do what I enjoy, then the money will follow. It didn't come easy. It involved a lot of sweat equity, but there's nothing else I'd rather do."

"I know what you mean," I said. "In the early days, I'd stand on the sidewalk in front of Bean There and hand out samples of my drinks and home-baked goods to any poor unsuspecting soul who happened to walk by."

"It takes effort and ingenuity to build a business. Good for you."

It was certainly stepping outside my comfort zone, but I didn't mention that. "Success came slowly and involved a lot of sleepless nights, but looking back, I wouldn't change a thing."

Briefly taking his eyes off the road, Sean smiled. "Me, neither."

The five hours it took for us to arrive in Toppenish flew by. Normally I'm an introvert, quiet and reserved. Sean had a way of drawing me into conversation. We talked in spurts. The silence was relaxed and comfortable. I learned more about his family and shared stories of my own. I told him about losing our mother and how our father had struggled in the aftermath of her death. His sympathetic look told me he had read between the lines and understood Dad's struggle with alcoholism.

When we arrived in Toppenish, we ate lunch in an authentic Mexican place that seemed to be doing a robust business. The building looked like it was weeks from being condemned, but the parking lot was full. The food was a different story. We ate like kings and queens. Bandit was tethered to the table where we ate al fresco. Bandit lapped down an entire bowl of water and the dry dog food Sean brought along.

It was at the restaurant that I learned Sean spoke fluent Spanish. The man was full of surprises. On the server's recommendation, I ordered a tamale with asparagus and it was oh, so good. Sean had chicken enchiladas. The salsa was spicy and delicious.

As we sat in the sunshine, I couldn't help but notice the painted murals that covered the sides of every building in town for as far as I could see.

"There are seventy-five here," Sean explained between bites of his enchiladas. He gave me a brief history of how they had come into being. What I found fascinating was that the town had decided to paint murals in a day, involving a dozen or more artists until they had completed all seventy-five with historical themes, a reminder of the history of the community.

As soon as we were done with our food, Sean retrieved his cameras from the car. I held on to Bandit's leash while Sean and I walked around town. He took one photo after another, paying attention to the light and shadowing. Several times I noticed that he slyly added pictures of me and Bandit.

"Sean," I complained, uncomfortable to be the object of his pictures.

"What?" he asked, and barked with laughter. "Why shouldn't I take photos of my dog?"

"Very funny."

"And a beautiful woman." His eyes held the same dark intensity they had earlier.

Two hours later, when Sean had taken no less than three to five hundred photos, we headed out of town and back to Oceanside.

The afternoon grew warm and we stopped in Ellensburg for a break. We each got ice-cream cones with two scoops and a small bowl of vanilla ice cream for Bandit. Sitting in the shade of a park close to the Central Washington University campus, we licked away at the melting goodness. I paused long enough to mention how delicious it was and gestured with my arm, stretching it out. Seeing an opportunity, Bandit immediately snatched the cone out of my hand and gobbled it down, looking pleased with himself.

"Bandit," Sean chastised. "Bad dog."

Sean might not think it was funny, but I did and burst into giggles. "I should have known better, especially when I know how he got his name."

At Sean's gruff voice, Bandit lowered his head and placed his chin atop my thigh, as if to apologize.

"It's all right; I forgive you," I assured him, and petted him until it was time for us to go.

With his head down, Bandit returned to where Sean had parked the vehicle. "You need to reassure him he's forgiven," I urged Sean. Seeing how distressed the poor dog was tore at my heart.

"You're forgiven," Sean repeated, and patted his head.

Bandit looked up with deep, dark eyes and crawled into his spot in the backseat.

"He has abandonment issues," Sean said. "Leaving him behind for this trip to Bolivia concerns me. I wanted to wait to adopt him until after I returned, but Preston talked me out of it."

"Preston is all about finding good homes for all the animals he rescues. Harper has a heart for animals, too, hence Snowball." While Harper had given me every assurance that she intended to take care of the kitten, it seemed Snowball had glommed on to me. The tiny cat insisted on sleeping on my bed and seemed to follow me around, despite Harper's efforts to prove ownership. While I hated to admit it, I rather enjoyed having a kitten. I wasn't sure how I'd feel when she was full grown. Time would tell.

Just outside of Seattle, I must have fallen asleep. I hadn't meant for that to happen. Dusk had come and gone. I found it harder and harder to hold back my yawns. At what point I'd closed my eyes and leaned my head against the passenger window, I couldn't remember.

"Willa." Sean gently shook my shoulder.

I jerked upright, shocked to find we were parked outside my apartment complex.

"We're home," he whispered.

I raised my hands over my head and stretched. "I'm sorry, I didn't mean to drift off. How long have I been asleep?"

"Awhile."

"I fell down on the job of keeping you awake," I said, and pressed my hand over my mouth to squelch a yawn.

"Don't worry. I enjoyed listening to you snore."

"I didn't?" I asked, horrified.

"No, you didn't, but you did drool a bit."

I was speechless until he laughed.

Bandit poked his head between the seats again and looked from Sean to me, as if waiting for me to leave.

I could take a hint. "I had a wonderful day. Thank you, Sean."

"I had a good time, too." He placed his hand around the back of my neck. "Would you mind terribly if I kissed you?"

"Ah . . . sure." I closed my eyes and leaned toward him. He didn't keep me waiting long. His mouth covered mine, and wow. This guy knew how to kiss. I placed my hands on his shoulders and leaned into him. My heart and my head soared as the kiss became fully involved. I loved the taste and feel of him, and found myself wanting more of him, wanting to give him more of me.

When we broke apart, Sean's eyes held mine. "Wow," he said, and cleared his throat. He didn't sound anything like himself.

"Wow," I echoed, and I realized I didn't sound like myself, either.

Chapter 10

Sean

Although I'd been planning this trip to Bolivia, I was reluctant to leave Willa. Time with her was a gift. After our all-day trip to Toppenish, we were together every day for the next week. I made it a habit to stop by the coffee shop for another of her specialty drinks. I'd tried several now and found I rather enjoyed drinking coffee when it was disguised. She'd quickly wrapped herself around my heart. This was different from any other relationship I'd had. Willa was unlike any other woman I'd dated. She helped me view the world in ways I never had before; she showed me the importance and appreciation of family. Since I'd started spending time with her and saw the closeness she shared with her siblings, it made me want to grow closer to my own family. Both my parents noticed and had commented. Once it was clear my career in baseball was over, I rented an apartment close to my parents. I used the next couple of years to build my portfolio as a professional photographer. Being raised in Colorado Springs had its downfalls. Despite my efforts to start over, everyone knew me from my baseball career. I needed to move someplace where the entire city hadn't watched me grow up in the sport. I happened upon Oceanside, as fate would have it, doing a shoot of the Olympic rain forest. The town and the community immediately appealed to me. I could remain anonymous in this tiny burg. While in town I walked past a real estate office and a photo of a home captured my attention. On impulse, I went to see it and saw the potential. I made an offer that day, and learned I got the house the next. And as they say, the rest is history.

My flight out of Seattle was scheduled for July 5, and after all the effort I'd taken to get what I needed lined up, I stared at the date on my calendar with regret. This wasn't a good time to leave. Still, my head was looking forward to learning what I could about the Bolivian people in the backcountry. My heart, however, would remain in Oceanside with Willa.

Willa told me Harper planned a barbecue for the Fourth of July holiday on the beach and invited me to join her, along with Harper and her friends, later in the afternoon after she closed the shop. I was concerned that she might be exhausted after doing a hard day's work, but when I saw her, she immediately brightened. Happiness radiated from her as she waved and hurried to meet me.

Unable to leave Bandit behind, I brought him along. The moment he viewed Willa, he strained against the leash, anxious to get to her. She'd changed into a sleeveless yellow summer dress with white polka dots and was barefoot. I'd never seen her look more beautiful. Her natural beauty was unlike the other women I'd dated. Willa didn't need a full array of makeup or expensive clothes or jewelry.

The beach was crowded with those celebrating the holiday. Harper had apparently staked out her territory early that morning. She set up a barbecue and table, along with blankets and a huge multicolored umbrella. I noticed several folding umbrella-style chairs. The firework display was not to be missed, or so Willa had told me. I'd lived in the area the last Fourth of July but had avoided the crowds and the tourists, preferring to stay at home instead of joining my family.

Harper raced across the sand to greet Willa, me, and Bandit. She introduced me to her friend John Neal and a couple of others. I remember Willa had mentioned that John and Harper were part of a group that would be climbing Mount Rainier later in the summer.

"I hope you're hungry," Harper said, motioning toward the table, covered with a variety of salads and chips and dips, along with the accouterments for the barbecue hamburgers and hot dogs.

"Starving." I'd finished the mural project and sent the photos and the article I'd written on to *Seattle Magazine*. I was pleased with how it had turned out. By far my favorite photos, however, were the ones I'd taken of Willa and Bandit that day. Half the time she was unaware I had my camera focused on her. I'd printed out my favorite five of those and pinned them on my office wall. After seeing her every day for the last week, I wasn't sure how I would fare for the next twenty-three without her.

Communication would be difficult. There likely weren't many cell phone towers anywhere close to where I planned to stay. From the research I'd done, I accepted that the remote area would likely have primitive conditions and no Wi-Fi. I'd have to go into town to find an internet café, and I knew I wouldn't be able to make that trek often.

The day was perfect. Then again, it could have been overcast and raining and I wouldn't have cared, as long as I was with Willa. Although it might not be entirely true, I'd never been in a relationship where a woman was interested in getting to know me. The real me and not the sports hero. Again I might be exaggerating, but it always felt as if the relationship was based on what I could do for them, their social standing, their ego, or what I could give them.

I used the excuse of building my career as a photographer to avoid dating. I left the big city behind, sequestered myself. Seeking out a woman, wooing her, was an entirely new experience for me. Deep down, I recognized Willa was worth the effort, and I had no intention of letting her slip through my fingers.

Sitting in the sand with her at my side, we ate fresh-off-the-grill hamburgers that Harper and her friends made along with all the fixings. Although Willa protested, Harper insisted on bringing us plates piled high with a variety of picnic food.

It seemed the entire town of Oceanside was on the beach. Sitting just down from us were Annie and Keaton, along with Mellie and Preston. I remembered hearing that at one time Mellie had been an agoraphobic, afraid to leave her home. Looking at her now, I found that hard to believe. It appeared the two couples were close friends. Keaton was a gentle giant. It was clear from the way he looked at his wife, and the exchanges between them, how deeply in love they were. For a short while I found it hard to look away. That kind of love was what I wanted, what I'd hoped to find in my own life.

"You leave tomorrow?" Willa asked, breaking into my musings.

A group of teens played volleyball down the beach as children raced back and forth, kicking up sand. Kites flew overhead and the surf eased against the shore, leaving a haphazard trail of bubbles edging the sand in a lacelike pattern.

"I'll be off first thing tomorrow, changing planes in Atlanta and flying into La Paz." Willa knew all that; I'd gone over it two or three times since I told her I'd be leaving right after the holiday. Placing my arm around her, I brought her closer to my side. Sighing, Willa leaned her head against my shoulder.

"I'm going to miss you."

"I'll miss you too, babe." I heard the same reluctance in her that I'd been experiencing myself. The attraction I felt for Willa was unexpected. My life was comfortable. When I'd moved to Oceanside, I'd done it for a fresh start, a new beginning. What I hadn't expected when I made this move was meeting Willa.

Her hand drifted to Bandit and she scratched his ears, giving my dog comfort and perhaps seeking it for herself.

"I'm dropping Bandit off with Logan later tonight." I'd be taking a couple of days in La Paz, Bolivia, to acclimate to the change in altitude. I intended to head for the Bolivian Apolobamba region. My idea was to document how climate change had affected the alpaca herders. I knew I would need to take a couple of days to connect with my guide and to sort through and secure my equipment.

"I should be able to be in touch with you while I'm in La Paz, but probably not much after that." I knew this wasn't what Willa wanted to hear. What I doubted she understood was that not being able to talk to her would be equally hard on me. I'd grown accustomed to sharing my day with her and hearing about hers. It surprised me how close I felt to her.

"I understand." She kept her head lowered. "You won't be in any danger, will you?"

"I won't seek it out and I know how to handle myself. Fortunately, I speak the language and have hired a guide who will take me where I need to go." Undoubtedly, there would be certain risks. There were in any travel, but I could get hit by a bus right here in Oceanside. I wouldn't allow fear to hold me back. Having traveled all over the world by this point, I had little doubt I'd be fine.

"Will the guide be with you the entire twenty-three days?"

"No. He'll drive me to Lake Titicaca toward the town of Charazani and beyond. I'll meet up with one of the locals there and stay with him in his home." Nothing could replace this kind of experience.

"How far is that from La Paz?"

That remained unclear. "Can't tell you in miles, but Reymundo, my guide, said the drive would take around six hours."

"Then what?"

"Then we walk."

"Walk? To where?" She was beginning to sound more concerned.

"It'll be fine. The whole idea is for me to document what's going on in the lives of the alpaca herders living in that area. Climate change has had a drastic impact on their lives and their story needs to be told."

"How do you know about this?"

That was a whole other story, one which I chose to condense. "I was on another shoot in South America, in Peru, and I met the son of one of the alpaca herders, who had recently returned from visiting his family in that area. He told me of his parents' plight and their struggles to make a living on the land that had sustained generations before him. I decided I wanted to see it for myself."

Willa grew quiet, and soon it was dark and the sky came alive with fireworks, raining down wild bursts of light and color. Bandit rested between Willa and me and trembled at the sound of the explosions. At one point he buried his nose under my thigh. Resting my hand on his spine, I dug my fingers deep into his fur, knowing he needed the comfort and reassurance.

Following the fireworks display, we all worked together cleaning up the beach.

Because Logan was at the beach with his mother, he volunteered to take Bandit back to his house. Kneeling in front of my dog, I looked him in the eye. "I'll be back."

Holding on to the leash, Logan led him away. Logan had

gone only a few feet when Bandit stopped and looked over his shoulder at me. "Go on," I called out to him. "I'll be back."

"He's going to miss you, too," Willa said, wrapping her arm around my elbow.

We waited until Logan and Bandit were out of sight before I walked Willa to her apartment complex, which was only two blocks off the beach. We stood in the moonlight and I wrapped my arms around her, knotting my hands at the small of her back. I breathed in her lavender scent as I rested my chin on the top of her head. For a long time, all we did was hold on to each other. She didn't speak and I didn't, either. We'd basically said our goodbyes earlier.

When we eased apart, I kissed her and promised to be in touch as soon as I landed in La Paz.

The heat is what hit me hardest when I set foot in the administrative capital of Bolivia. As soon as I was settled in my hotel room, I logged on to its Wi-Fi and sent Willa a text.

Here. Exhausted. Missing you.

There was so much more I wanted to say, but I'd been up for nearly twenty-four hours. What I needed most was something to eat, a hot shower, and bed, in that order.

I slept for nearly ten hours. When I woke, the first thing I did was reach for my phone. Willa didn't disappoint me. I read her message and frowned.

How come you never told me you played professional baseball?

I groaned. This wasn't something I wanted to get into when I was nearly six thousand miles away.

Who told you?

I was surprised with her speedy response.

Lucas. When he heard we were dating, he checked you out.

You mad?

She didn't answer, which I suspected was answer enough. I was tempted to call, prepared to pay whatever it cost me, when my phone dinged, indicating I had a text.

Not mad. I don't know why you felt you couldn't share this with me.

I wiped my hand down my face. She was right, I should have mentioned it long before now. For me, baseball was in the past; I'd moved on and put that part of my life behind closed doors. I wasn't that man any longer, and I hoped I wouldn't be again. Unsure how best to smooth this over, I went for the delay tactic. It wasn't my finest moment, but it was the best I could do until I could look her in the eyes and explain.

Can we talk about this when I get back?

I held on to my phone, staring at the screen, waiting for her reply, holding my breath the entire time. It took what felt like several minutes before she responded.

Okay.

I released a long, slow breath and felt like I'd dodged a bullet. Willa wasn't the type to anger easily or make a fuss. By not telling her, I realized I'd hurt her feelings; that had shaken her trust in me. When I returned, I'd do my best to explain and make it up to her. The one thing I didn't want to do was ruin what we had going. The relationship was fragile, still undeveloped, still taking shape. I'd hoped to build it on trust and realized I'd been the one who'd shaken that shallow foundation.

The following day, Reymundo and I met in the hotel lobby. I loaded my gear into his Range Rover. We traveled along the northern edge of Lake Titicaca to Charazani. The roads grew worse with every mile and the towns grew smaller. Earlier, I'd sent Willa and my parents an email detailing the next few days as best I could. I didn't want either to worry if they didn't hear from me for the next few weeks. I hoped I'd be able to connect at some point, but that remained doubtful.

At the end of the road, and I mean that literally, Reymundo and I were met by a man named Alfonso. We spoke in Spanish and he explained that he would take me to his house, which was just over the hill. Reymundo left and promised to return to collect me in twenty days' time.

Alfonso and I walked for four hours before we arrived at his small home and I met his wife, Carmen. She showed me to the room she had prepared for me. It consisted of a narrow bed and a rickety table. There was no running water and no electricity.

During the walk, I'd developed a killer headache. I knew it was due to the elevation. At this point we were almost ten thousand feet above sea level. I took two aspirin and hoped it would help.

Carmen served us a meal of quinoa soup and dried guinea pig. I welcomed the warmth of the soup and managed to eat the dried meat, which tasted even worse than anyone can imagine. Early on, I learned that being a photojournalist meant learning to eat anything placed in front of me and preferably not knowing or asking what it was.

That night and every night that followed, fog rolled in. Getting comfortable was impossible. I swear I could have frozen to death. I'd been to the Antarctic and not been this cold.

That morning and every one that followed, Alfonso and I were up before dawn. We spent every day together, working the herd. My headaches didn't ease up, despite the medication I took. I woke every morning in pain. I'd thought I'd adjust to the altitude change, but as time passed, I realized it wasn't going to happen. As best I could, I ignored the discomfort and listened to his stories.

As the weeks passed, I wrote what I'd learned and tried to understand how Alfonso's life and the lives of the other alpaca herders were changing due to weather and climate change. It was an education.

He explained that the differences in temperature and precipitation caused frequent large storms. We endured two while I was with him. The wind howled with thunder and lightning as rain pelted the earth. One result was less grass for the animals. The topsoil eroded with the storms. The thick ice meant the alpacas couldn't break through to eat the grass. Life was hard with or without climate change, but the challenges were more intense now than ever before. The herders were leaving, migrating into the cities, and what had once been their way of life was quickly vanishing from the landscape.

Each night as I crawled into my bed, surrounded by alpaca fiber and skins that were stacked in every spare bit of space in the tiny house, I dreamed of Willa and Oceanside. I'd never experienced a deeper sense of homesickness as I did on this trip. The primitive conditions and the constant headaches made the lure of home all the stronger.

Chapter 11

Willa

Sean had been gone ten days, and odd as it was, I felt like part of me was missing. I barely knew him, apparently even less than I thought I did. When Lucas excitedly announced Sean had played professional baseball, I'd been convinced it was a different Sean O'Malley. It had to be. This was something he should have, would have, told me. I assumed. Assumed wrong.

In all the lengthy conversations we'd shared, when we'd joked and laughed together, not once had Sean mentioned his time in the pros. Not. Once. For several days after I heard the news, I'd reeled, wavering between disappointment and hurt. This steady-dating business was new to me, and the fact that he was keeping secrets didn't bode well for a meaningful relationship.

Other than a few text messages and one email I'd gotten after he landed in Bolivia, I hadn't heard from him. He'd explained he'd be out of coverage and that I shouldn't expect him to email or text. The first few days I was upset and grateful he was away. I needed time to think this through.

My mistake came when I decided to look him up on the internet myself. The Sean O'Malley I found looked nothing like the Sean I'd come to know. I squinted at the photo and found it hard to believe this was my Sean. The photo was a classic baseball pose, with him leaning against a baseball bat. Everything about the picture spoke of arrogance. His look said it all: I'm talented. I'm handsome. I'm rich.

And you're not.

I must have been seeking ways to punish myself, because I went on a search to find what I could about his romantic entanglements. It didn't take much effort to dig up a photo of him with some girl named Nikki, who looked like a model. She was stunning. Not only was she beautiful, but tall, with a perfectly proportioned body along with boobs a stripper would envy. She knew it, too. Her cocky smile said as much. As far as I could see, they were a perfect couple.

When it came to men and relationships, I wasn't drowning in self-confidence. Anything but. Sean played in the majors. I wasn't qualified for Little League. Maybe not even T-ball. Finding another photo of Nikki with Sean's arm wrapped around her caused me to suck in my breath and wrap my thin sweater more tightly around me, as if suddenly thrust into below-zero weather.

Wanting to know what had happened, I found the video where Sean hurled himself into home base, collided with the catcher, and blew out his knee. I held a hand over my mouth and cried out when I watched the aftermath as the medical staff rushed to his aid. He'd been in horrific pain. A sports magazine followed up with an article about this being a career-ending injury. That must have been when Sean turned to photography. Naturally, I wondered what had become of Nikki, and then decided I'd rather not know.

Sean and his secrets weren't the only concerns that plagued me. Harper was scheduled to go into Seattle for her six-month checkup. We decided to drive into the city together, as Chantelle wanted us to look over the bridesmaid dresses she'd designed for the two of us.

"I want to do something different with my hair," Harper mentioned as we climbed in the car and headed for the big city. Alice and Shirley were covering Bean There. We scheduled the outing for Wednesday, as that was my slowest day of the week. Harper insisted on driving, and I was happy to turn the wheel over to her.

"What are you thinking?" I asked. Before cancer, Harper's hair had been gloriously long. It was as straight as a board and fell halfway down her back. After her first chemo treatment, she'd started to lose it, hair falling out by the handfuls. I'd shed more tears over it than Harper had. As the oncologist had promised, it came back, but strangely it had returned in tight curls. It was shoulder length and she often wore it up in a loose bun on the top of her head. She looked adorable and I hated to see her fuss with it.

"I'm thinking of cutting it."

"Okay."

Harper snickered. "Not asking your permission."

"I know."

"You're such a mother. You should marry Sean and have half a dozen kids."

My smile was decidedly forced.

"Don't give me that look. You'll be a wonderful mother. Look at all the practice you've had."

She wasn't wrong there. How I wished I could have been a normal, carefree teenager.

Halfway into the two-and-a-half-hour drive, my sister glanced over at me, shook her head. "Would you stop."

"Stop what?" I hadn't been doing anything.

"Worrying. You're like this every time I go in to have my blood tested. I'm feeling great. I've had three good years. If it turns out the cancer is back, then it's back. We'll deal with it the same as before and thank God for the extra years I had."

She was right. I'd been stewing about this upcoming blood draw for days. Learning what I had about Sean didn't help put my mind at ease, either.

"I'm always nervous when it comes to your blood tests."

"Remember when you gave me your bone marrow?"

That wasn't something I was likely to forget. "Of course I remember."

"We're about as different as any two sisters can be, and yet you were a perfect match. Your bone marrow saved my life. Doesn't that tell you something?"

"Ah, no, what is that supposed to mean?"

Harper's smile was huge. "I am as healthy as you are.

Now smile, we're going to have a fabulous day. We'll be in and out of the hospital in less than an hour, then we're meeting Chantelle for lunch and looking at dress designs. Personally, I can't think of a better way to spend my afternoon."

My sister was correct. I had no right playing the role of Atlas, carting the weight of the world upon my shoulders. Harper herself claimed she'd never felt better. I was smothering her natural enthusiasm for life with my worries, unable to hide them from her or from anyone.

"I love that she chose burgundy as her wedding color," I said, changing the subject to something more pleasant. "It's perfect for December." When I thought about Lucas and Chantelle marrying, my spirits lifted. It did me good to see my brother move forward with his life.

"I love it, too," Harper agreed. "Have you ever thought about what colors you'd want for your wedding?"

Good question. "I need to find a groom before I think about a color scheme." I could see Harper was about to say something. I cut her off before she did. "What about you?"

"Lilac. I've always loved that color and the flowers, too," she said dreamily.

"You'll make a beautiful bride."

"You too, big sister."

"Just not yet."

Harper sighed. "Not yet for me, either. One thing I know for sure. There's someone out there for you."

"And you," I countered.

She took the next exit and that was the end of our conversation.

Harper was right. It took far less time than I imagined for her blood draw. The waiting was the worst, and that took anywhere from three to six hours before we could get the results. If any abnormality showed, the doctor would phone that day. The longer we waited for a report, the less chance there was a problem.

Chantelle was sitting at a table when we arrived at the restaurant. She chose Mediterranean cuisine because it was healthy and tasty, and because Harper was a bit of a health nut and had been since her bout with cancer.

My sister had her phone on the outside of her purse. Despite all my efforts, I kept glancing at it every few minutes, willing it not to ring.

"I have the sketches of the dresses I designed for you," Chantelle said as soon as we'd placed our order. "While the colors are the same, I have a different style for each. My sister gave the go-ahead for her maid of honor dress. Once I get your approval, I'll start on yours."

She handed each of us a sketch to look over. My dress was a classic, floor length, with long sleeves and a deep V-neck. It was simple and beautiful, more of a deep rust-red than burgundy.

"What do you think?" Chantelle asked anxiously.

I couldn't stop looking at the design. "It's perfect."

Harper showed me her design and it was strikingly

different. Three-quarter length, full skirt, flaring out from her waist. The top was similar to mine, with small changes. Each dress fit our personalities to a T.

"Love it," Harper said.

"Then it's a go?"

"Oh yes." I hoped my brother appreciated how lucky he was to be marrying Chantelle.

The call with the test results came on the ride home. Harper's phone pealed as we neared Tacoma.

"Answer it," Harper said. "You can pretend you're me. The assistant won't know the difference."

"You're sure?" This was sooner than I'd hoped, which made me uncomfortable.

"Answer the damn phone," she barked.

"Okay, okay." I reached for it, my hand pressing so hard against the case that I feared my fingers would leave indentation marks. "Hello, this is Harper Lakey." I swear I held my breath for the entire conversation, which thankfully was brief. I got the report and set the phone down.

"Well?" Harper asked, her voice barely above a whisper.

She'd been as concerned as me, although she hadn't shown it until now. She'd fooled me.

"Everything looks good. There's no sign of leukemia."

Her sigh was strong enough to blow out all the candles on a retiree's birthday cake. "Told you," she said with a short laugh that I easily recognized as relief.

"Yes, you did," I said, unable to keep the happiness out of my own voice.

That night I slept better than I had since Sean left for

Bolivia. That didn't mean I missed him any less, because I did miss him terribly. Despite everything I'd learned, my thoughts were constantly wrapped up in him.

The following afternoon, I decided to check on Bandit. I knew Logan was taking good care of him. What concerned me was how, once again, Bandit had been abandoned by his owner. Just as he was beginning to adjust to his new home, everything had changed.

Teresa Hoffert's house was less than half a mile from my own, so I decided to head there after my walk along the beach. To my delight, I saw Logan out front, tossing a ball to Bandit and another mixed-breed dog of about the same size. I remembered Sean telling me that Keaton had given the boy a puppy a few years back.

"Hey, Logan," I called to him as I approached the front yard. "How's it going?"

He tossed the ball and then turned his attention to me. "Okay, I guess. Mom's home."

"Actually, I came to see Bandit."

Hearing his name, Bandit noticed me and immediately ran to the gate. Logan held it open for me to pass through. Bandit was on his haunches, looking up with dark, sad eyes.

"Oh Bandit," I whispered, and bent down to wrap my arms around his neck. "I miss him, too."

Bandit gave a low bark as if he understood.

"He hasn't been eating much," Teresa said, stepping onto the front porch.

I'd been worried how Bandit would handle having Sean away for this long. It appeared he wasn't doing any better than I was.

"How about a glass of iced tea?" Teresa offered. She was cordial, always welcoming.

I nodded, appreciating the offer. Sitting on the top porch step, I looked out over the area, silently inviting Sean's dog to join me. Bandit slowly wandered to my side and placed his head in my lap. I gently petted him and offered reassurances while Teresa went after the tea.

"Logan, bring out his food dish," I suggested, hoping Bandit would feel more like eating when he was with someone familiar.

Logan went into the house and returned with a silver dog bowl filled with dry dog food. He set it down on the pathway. Bandit briefly looked at the food and then returned his head to my lap.

"I wish I could bring you home with me," I whispered, running my fingers through his short fur. Harper and I were already risking being evicted by giving Snowball a home. A dog, any dog, no matter what size, wouldn't go unnoticed.

"Maybe you could stop by again," Logan suggested.

"I will."

Teresa brought out the cold drink and sat with me. We talked for several minutes and she mentioned she missed seeing me at Bean There on Wednesday.

"Harper and I were in Seattle." I explained the reason and the good news about Harper and my brother.

"How's your dad doing?"

Teresa had known my mother and what happened to Dad after her death. "The same. We don't hear from him much."

I'd reached out to Dad a couple of times since our dinner and left voicemails. I'd called with Harper's test results and hadn't heard back. I was afraid he was drinking again. That fear was always in the back of my mind.

Teresa nodded knowingly. I recalled she'd been married to a man with drinking problems. She understood.

"It is what it is," I said, knowing Dad would eventually sober up. That was his pattern. He'd go days and often weeks without a drink and then something would happen to cause him to reach for a bottle. I didn't need to guess what it was this time. He knew it was time for Harper to have her blood tested.

"I don't know what your family would have done without you," Teresa told me.

I chose to ignore the compliment. I'd done only what was necessary. Taking care of my family wasn't a job I sought or even wanted. Given the opportunity, I would have done anything to escape the responsibility.

Thirty minutes later I left Teresa and Logan with the promise to return soon. Bandit walked me to the gate and then followed the fence line as far as he could as I left. Seeing the sadness in his eyes nearly broke my heart.

Harper wasn't at the apartment when I returned. Snowball was sleeping on my bed. That cat refused to accept that she belonged to my sister, not me. I noticed that her food dish was empty and filled it.

The front door opened, and Harper called out, "Close your eyes."

"What?"

"You heard me. I won't come in until you turn around and close your eyes."

"Why?" If she'd brought another kitten home, I was putting my foot down.

"You'll see in a minute. Now do it."

Grumbling under my breath, I followed her instructions. "Can I look now?"

"Not yet."

She was giddy, almost as if she'd been drinking, which I knew she'd never do.

"Remember that I wanted to do something different with my hair."

"I remember."

"Okay, you can look."

Dropping my hands, I turned around to find my sister had done something different, all right. Her hair was a silver/lavender shade. My mouth hung open with surprise.

"Well, what do you think?" she asked, and then added, "John likes it."

I had no words and so I started to giggle.

"You don't like it?" Harper was hurt.

"I do like it. Harper, it's fabulous. I love it."

Her shoulders relaxed. "I knew you would. We should do the same for you as a surprise for Sean when he comes back."

I waved my hands. "Not happening, but on you it's perfect."

Sean. He couldn't return to Oceanside soon enough to suit me.

Chapter 12

Sean

My flight landed in Seattle and I couldn't get back to Oceanside fast enough. Who was I kidding? This was all about seeing Willa. I should be thinking about sleeping in my own bed, taking a lengthy shower, and eating food that was digestible. I didn't know that I would ever be able to look at guinea pigs the same way again. While the comforts of home certainly called to me, seeing Willa held far more appeal.

I hadn't texted or phoned her when I landed in La Paz or when I changed planes in Atlanta before catching the flight back to Seattle. Any conversation was sure to include my past, and that needed to happen when we were face-to-face. The hours it took to return from Bolivia were sluggish. I couldn't remember any twenty-hour period in my life that passed slower. I felt an urgency to explain myself, to clear the air, and prayed she wouldn't hold my reluctance to share my past against me.

When I arrived back in town, my first stop was where I knew Willa would be. By the time I got there, it was only five minutes before closing at Bean There. I parked the car in front of the coffee shop and sat looking inside the window for several seconds, unable to move. My heart raced at the speed of a bullet to the point that I felt light-headed.

Although desperate to see her, hold her, I was afraid. If keeping my past a secret ruined this relationship, I didn't know how I'd handle it. I needed Willa as part of my life. If I could explain how right I felt when I was with her, I would. Words escaped me. I was high on emotion, high on the sense she was the one for me. If I lost her due to my own stupidity, I would have no one to blame but myself.

When I could no longer stand to wait, I climbed out of the car and walked into the café. Happily, it was empty. Willa was busy putting what was left of the baked goods away for the night. When the bell above the door dinged, she glanced up and froze.

Immediately my name was on her lips. "Sean."

Neither of us moved for a few moments. I stood just inside the door and she remained on the far side of the counter. And then Willa raced around to the other side and leaped into my embrace. As soon as she was in my arms and I could hug her, I experienced my first sense of having arrived home.

"You're back," she cried, her arms around my neck, squeezing as if she never intended to let me go.

I was certain I felt moisture against my neck. Willa was crying.

"I came here first. I had to see you."

Leaning back, her hands cupped my face and her watery smile was my undoing. It was either kiss her or die. My mouth fused with hers and we kissed until we were both breathless. It seemed impossible to get enough of each other in a single exchange.

When we broke apart, she stroked my jaw with her hand and said, "Bandit didn't do well without you. The poor dog has abandonment issues."

Her gaze was holding mine as if she was actually talking about herself, not Bandit. It was selfish of me, but I had to know. "What about you?"

She answered with a weak smile and lowered her eyes as though she'd rather avoid the question. "I never knew twenty-three days could take so long."

Grinning, I kissed her again. "Me, either."

She slid down my front. I couldn't take my eyes off her. This was what I needed, what I'd craved, being with Willa, holding and kissing her. It felt as if I could breathe again.

"I know we need to talk," I told her, unwilling to let her go, "and I promise we will."

She swallowed hard and nodded. "We need to. Not today, though. You're exhausted. Tomorrow?"

"Tomorrow," I agreed. My mind had been composing what I wanted to say for the last three weeks. I hoped it would be enough to convince her that the cocky, self-absorbed idiot I'd once been was no more. With everything in me, I prayed she hadn't gone on an internet search and found pictures of me with Nikki.

"How was Bolivia? Did you get what you needed?" she asked, leading me to a table where we could sit and talk.

"I believe I did. I took about ten thousand photographs."

"Ten thousand?"

I would need to go through, sort, and analyze which ones would tell the story that I hoped would convey the lives of these herders. The project would demand countless hours in front of the computer. As tempting as it was to linger with Willa, I needed to collect Bandit, unpack, and get to work as soon as possible.

She must have read my mind. "How about I bring you dinner tomorrow night? You can tell me about Bolivia and show me some of the photos, and we can talk."

That was a perfect solution. I hadn't eaten a decent meal in weeks. "Yes. Please."

"What time should I plan to arrive?"

"Any time you want." I craved her company, regretted every moment we were apart, and was eager to settle matters between us.

By the time Bandit and I arrived home, I was bone weary and exhausted. I unloaded the car, unpacked my equipment, and tossed every piece of clothing from my backpack into the washing machine. When I finished, I was shaking with fatigue and nearly passed out in the shower.

"Okay, bed now." I didn't know who I was looking to convince. Nothing appealed to me more than a solid ten hours of sleep. Not food. Not work, which I was eager to start. Nothing.

In the morning I woke with a monster headache, barely able to lift my head from the pillow. Standing next to the bed, Bandit rested his chin on the mattress, looking to me to feed him and let him outside.

"I don't feel so great," I managed to say. Overtaken by chills, I shivered and pulled the blankets over my shoulders as I curled into a tight ball. I must have returned to sleep, because Bandit's bark woke me.

With effort I managed to let him out to do his business. I poured food into his dish and literally fell back into bed. My head pounded like someone had taken a jackhammer to it. Aspirin didn't put a dent in the constant, persistent ache. In all the travel I'd done over the years, I'd never returned from a trip feeling worse.

Lingering in bed, I forced myself to get up and get dressed around four, knowing Willa would arrive sometime soon. The chills wouldn't leave me. I walked around the house with a blanket tucked around my shoulders, cold and sweating buckets at the same time.

Willa arrived at four-forty-five. She took one look at me and her face instantly clouded with concern. "You're sick," she said.

"Looks that way." By all that was right, I should have warned her. It was selfish of me. My need to see her, to settle any differences between us, had overridden my common sense. "I should have called."

Taking the casserole dish into the kitchen, she looked at

me and frowned. "I'm glad you didn't. Let me help you; you need to be in bed."

"Will you join me?"

"Very funny," she said, taking charge. "Where do you keep your thermometer?"

Dizzy now, I stumbled into the bedroom. "Don't have one."

"Sean!"

She made it sound like I didn't keep toilet paper on hand. For all the traveling I'd done over the years, I had never needed one. I was young and healthy, and I wasn't foolish. I never drank water that wasn't bottled or hadn't been purified. I'd taken care of my shots and was careful of the food I ate.

Willa helped me into bed and pulled the covers over me. She started to leave.

"Don't go." I sounded like a big baby, but I couldn't help it.

"I'll be back, and if you aren't better by morning, I'm taking you in to see the doctor."

"I'll be better." I hoped this wasn't a case of wishful thinking.

I heard the front door close, and although I'd slept a good majority of the day, I felt myself drifting off again. It seemed like only minutes before Willa returned. I was in a fetal position. Chills wracked my body and my sheets were soaked.

Willa stayed with me. She wiped my face with a damp cloth, got me to drink some fluid, and freaked out when the thermometer showed my fever registered at one hundred and three.

"I need to get you to the clinic," she said, pulling back the covers, attempting to get me out of bed.

My head ached and my body felt like I'd been run over by a snowplow. "Tomorrow." The local clinic was closed and the closest one outside of Oceanside was Aberdeen. No way was I interested in leaving my bed and traveling to another town. Not with what I could only assume was a migraine and a high fever. What I needed most was rest and Willa watching over me.

"I don't understand it," Willa said, pacing my bedroom. "You seemed fine when I first saw you."

I didn't understand it, either. I would have talked more if I'd had the energy. It took everything I had in me to function when my entire body screamed with pain. The headache was the worst.

"If this is your way of getting out of us talking, then you're going to extremes," she said, wiping down my face. The rag felt cool and my eyes drifted closed. Willa stayed at my side, forcing liquids down my throat. She was on the phone and I didn't know who she was talking to until I heard her mention Harper's name.

When she finished, she placed her hand on my forehead. "I'm staying the night."

"This isn't exactly the way I planned to lure you to my bed," I mused, and must have said the words out loud, because Willa laughed.

During the night, Willa woke me every few hours. She took my temperature and forced me to drink some ugly-tasting fluid. My head continued to pound, and I doubted I slept more than a few hours. I was cold and sweating and unable to understand how that could happen at the same time.

First thing in the morning, she bundled me up and drove me to the clinic to see Dr. Annie. I'd been to a foreign country. I'd eaten the food, such as it was. The obvious conclusion was that I'd picked up a bug. Tests were run and I was given a prescription to kill whatever had infected me.

The office visit and following tests felt like they took half the day. I was weak and eager to get back home and in bed. Willa drove me, changed my sheets, and tucked me in. Again, she fed me broth and stayed at my side.

Knowing I was keeping her away from Bean There weighed heavily on me. As hard as it was to admit, I needed her. My temperature hovered at about one hundred and three for two more days, even with the antibiotics. Normally by now I would have checked in with my parents.

On the third morning, Willa called Dr. Annie. "This is something more, something worse," she said. "His fever hasn't gone down and he isn't getting any better. Something is terribly wrong." She sounded desperate and her voice wobbled with emotion. I realized she was afraid. Her fear fueled my own. Could I be dying? I'd never been this sick before, and I had to wonder.

Lost in my thoughts, I was unable to hear the rest of the conversation. The next thing I knew, Willa got me out of bed and into her car, explaining that we were headed to Aberdeen.

"Where are you taking me?"

"Dr. Annie called a friend of hers who's an infectious disease doctor. She's agreed to see you right away."

By this time, I was willing to do anything to end this constant pain and misery. If antibiotics weren't helping, I had to wonder what would.

On the ride into Aberdeen, Willa kept muttering to herself. "I should have followed my instinct that first night," she said angrily.

"I'm sorry, Willa." I hated that she had to see me like this. Frankly, I didn't know what I would have done without her.

"I'm not mad at you, Sean. I'm furious with myself. You're much too sick for this to be a minor infection. And you're not showing the symptoms of some easily killed normal bug. This is far and away more than that."

"Maybe not. I—"

"I'm no dummy," she said, cutting me off. "Do you even know how many hours I spent in the hospital with Harper? Of course you don't. From what I learned when she was sick with leukemia, I could be a consultant to the medical team."

If I'd had the wherewithal to respond I would have. When we arrived in Aberdeen, Willa shepherded me into the medical offices. As soon as she gave the receptionist my name, we were ushered into the exam room.

The infectious disease doctor gave me a thorough examination and drew my blood. I answered a hundred or more questions and she put me on a ten-day course of Cipro with warnings that this was a powerful drug that often came with dangerous side effects. While we still didn't have any answers, whatever bug I'd picked up wasn't something that could be handled with a Z-Pak.

This was serious.

Willa was silent on the way home. I'd infringed on her long enough. It was time to call in family. My chest tightened and I reached for my phone.

"Who are you calling?" she asked, as we neared Oceanside.

"My parents."

"Good idea. Do you want me to talk to them?" she asked, when she noticed how violently my hand shook.

"Maybe that would be best."

Willa got me into the house. After spending nearly four days in bed, it was the last place I wanted to go. "Let me sit up for a bit," I said, when she tried to steer me back into the bedroom.

"Okay." She set me down in the chair and brought an afghan to tuck around me before bringing me a cup of warm chicken broth. I was about to explain what I wanted her to say to my parents when the phone rang.

Caller ID said it was the Oceanside Clinic. I answered and put the phone on speaker.

"Sean, this is Dr. Annie Keaton. The test results came back from the stool samples we took."

"Is it a parasite?" I asked.

"No, Sean, you have typhoid."

Chapter 13

Willa

The news that Sean was dealing with typhoid fever was a shock and at the same time a relief. I'd felt something similar when we learned Harper had leukemia. First the shock, followed by a sense that at least we knew what we faced and could prepare for the battle.

What I didn't know was how serious this news was. Typhoid fever was nothing to fool around with. Dr. Morgan, the infectious disease doctor, recognized within a short amount of time that this wasn't your normal, run-of-the-mill infection. She'd prescribed Cipro with caution, explaining how powerful this drug was.

As he asked me to do, I contacted Sean's parents and spoke to his father. Within twelve hours of our conversation his parents were on a flight from Phoenix, where they are retired, to Seattle. I was with Sean the morning they arrived.

His mother burst into the house like a freight train shooting into a tunnel, nearly bowling me over in order to get to her son. "Sean Patrick O'Malley . . . typhoid fever," she cried.

Sean groaned and laid his head back against the overstuffed chair where he sat. "Mom, please, I'm fine."

Sean looked at me and I read the apology in his eyes. I understood better than he realized. Had it been my mother she would have reacted the same.

His father followed close behind, carting in two suitcases. "Patrick O'Malley," he introduced himself as he scooted past me.

"I'm Willa. Willa Lakey."

As if she recognized my name, his mother whirled around. "You're Willa?"

With a laser focus, she looked straight through me. I would have been uncomfortable if the stare hadn't been followed with a slow, easy smile that softened her tight features.

"You're Willa," she repeated, and then, without a word, gathered me into her arms and hugged me as if I was long-lost family. "I'm Joanna and I am happy to meet you. So happy."

"Mom. Dad—" Sean wasn't allowed to finish.

Joanna's worried face returned as she looked to me. "What's his temperature? When was the last time he ate? What do I need to watch for? Shouldn't he be hospitalized?" The questions came at me all at once, with no room for response.

"Mom," Sean protested. "Give Willa a chance to breathe, will you?"

"Perhaps ask one question at a time," his father inserted when he returned from setting the luggage in the spare bedroom.

"Sean might not look so great, but he'll survive, won't you, son?"

"I'll live to worry you another day," Sean assured his mother.

"Why didn't you call us sooner?" she demanded, as if offended. "Your father and I would have come immediately."

"I know—"

"Willa, we owe you," his father said.

"I was happy to be here."

"Can everyone kindly sit down," Sean barked, waving his hand toward the sofa. "It's hurting my neck to look up."

"He must be feeling better," Joanna said to her husband, and then turned to me and added, "Sean never was a good patient. You must have the patience of a saint to put up with him."

"He's been too sick to put up much of a fuss," I said, glancing toward Sean, who rolled his eyes at his parents. I sat on the ottoman next to him and he reached for my hand. His smile was indulgent and appreciative at the same time. He seemed to be telling me how grateful he was that I'd spent the last four days looking after him, and asking me to forgive his parents, particularly his mother, for rushing in like a herd of stampeding buffalo.

"Sean's temperature is down to a hundred and one," I said,

answering the most important questions. "And he ate some scrambled eggs and toast for breakfast, which is the first solid food he's been able to tolerate."

"You should have let us know sooner," his mother bemoaned.

Sean's hand tightened around mine. "Willa was here, and Mom, really, I was too sick. I don't know what I would have done without Willa. She stepped in and took care of me."

"Thank God." His mother still didn't look happy with him.

"I didn't want you flying in until we knew what was wrong," he added. "Now we do and I'm grateful you're here."

"Sean told us you have your own business," his father said, relaxing on the sofa. One leg was balanced across his knee and his arm rested on the back of the sofa and cupped his wife's shoulder.

I could see he was the calm one in the family, a good balance for his mother, who was in mama-bear mode.

It took me a moment to realize his parents were waiting for me to answer. "Yes, I have a small coffee shop on Main Street."

"She bakes, too," Sean threw in.

"Ah yes, I've heard rumors about your cinnamon rolls," Patrick said, and his eyes brightened.

It appeared Sean had mentioned me in more than passing. Knowing that flustered me. I tugged my hand free from Sean's and stood. "Now that you're here, I feel more comfortable leaving."

Sean started to protest and then, after a glare from his mother, stopped.

His mother stood and followed me to the front door. "We don't mean to run you off," she said.

"You aren't. I need to get back to the shop. My sister and her friend have been covering for me." Harper and Leesa had been wonderful. While Leesa took over Harper's yoga classes, my sister had worked beside Alice and Shirley. I'd never have been able to spend these four days with Sean otherwise.

"You'll be back soon, won't you?" Joanna asked, walking outside with me.

"Of course. Please don't hesitate to call me if you need anything."

Joanna followed me down the three short porch steps and to my car. She paused as if she wasn't sure what to say before she felt obliged to mention, "You mean a lot to our son."

I froze, unsure how to respond. "I'm surprised Sean mentioned me . . . We haven't been seeing each other long."

"Yes, I know . . . but Patrick and I knew you were special when he told us about you. We both took notice. You see, our son has had money and fame. He's dated a wide variety of women."

My heart sank and I lowered my gaze, not wanting to hear about all the beautiful women Sean had known and had relationships with over the years.

"But, Willa," she continued, "you need to know you're the first woman he's ever mentioned to his father and me."

My head shot up. "Really?"

"Yes. He asked his father how he felt when he first met

me. He wanted to know how soon Patrick knew I was the right woman for him."

"Oh." I could feel myself blush as color filled my cheeks.

"Naturally, I wanted to know why he was drilling his father about our courtship. Sean is private and I don't think he wanted to tell us. He did, though. He said he'd met someone who was the most genuine, caring woman he'd ever known. He said you fed a stray dog and he saw you give a warm drink to a drifter when the weather dropped. He said you have a kind heart."

I had no idea Sean knew about the drifter. I had mentioned I'd fed Bandit a time or two, and then blamed myself when the stray stole a customer's cinnamon roll.

"I'm . . . flattered he thinks of me that way," I managed.

"You proved it by looking after him through the worst of this fever."

"I did what anyone would have," I said, uncomfortable with her gratitude. No one would have ignored Sean, as ill as he'd been.

"Perhaps," she agreed, although she didn't sound like she believed it. "I hope you'll give us a chance to get to know you."

"I'd like that."

"Sean knew his father and I would come without question. He didn't want us. He wanted you—otherwise, he'd have reached out sooner."

Her words shook me. I didn't know what to say.

"Don't stay away just because we're here," Joanna insisted.

"I won't," I promised. Halfway into the car I paused,

settled into my seat, and looked up. "Do you mind if I ask you a question?"

"Ask away," Joanna said, dismissing my doubt with a wave of her hand.

"When Patrick met you, did he know you were the one?"

Joanna smiled, and I could see the answer in her eyes as she glanced toward the house. "I should hope so. We were married within six months of our first date."

"Did you know you would marry Patrick soon after you met?"

I might have been mistaken, but it seemed she blushed a little. "No. He was exactly what I didn't want in a husband. He was the college golden boy, king of the hill, so to speak. A sports legend, and I was this studious girl who took my education seriously. The teacher assigned us to the same study group. Patrick couldn't seem to get calculus and asked if I would help him. I learned later it was all a ploy to get to know me better."

"So you tutored him?" This was a romance-novel type of story, and one of my favorite plotlines.

"What you need to know," Joanna continued, "is that Patrick said almost the same thing about me as Sean told us about you."

For reasons I was uncomfortable exploring, hearing this unnerved me. I was anxious to get away and think over what she'd told me. "I'm sorry to rush off. I need to get back to my shop." That much was true. I'd been away far longer than I'd anticipated.

"No worries; I understand."

Stepping back, Joanna closed the door for me. "Don't be away long. I'm cooking and I hope you'll join us for dinner later."

"I'll be here," I promised.

"Good. No excuses now."

My first stop when I arrived in town was Bean There. Harper was behind the counter and doing a robust business. Several young men lingered in the shop, seemingly unaware that she was seeing a good deal of her climbing partner, John Neal. Watching my sister work her magic was a sight to behold. While I might attract customers with my baked goods, all Harper had to do was show up. Her silver/lilac hair suited her perfectly. She really was beautiful. I thanked God every day that she'd been spared. The world would be a bleak place without Harper. Her smile lit up a room. People were naturally drawn to her. I could be halfway across the floor and could feel her energy radiating, warming the area. I marveled at her ability to attract others like a bee to honey.

She waved her arm above her head when she saw me and called out, "You forgot your cell. Dr. Annie called." Meeting me halfway, she handed me the pink slip with the call information.

Thinking this might be related to Sean, I rushed to my office and returned the call. The receptionist answered and put me on hold. The seconds felt like minutes and my stomach knotted with concern. Thank goodness I had a short wait.

"Willa," Annie greeted cheerfully. "Thanks for returning my call."

"Of course. Is everything all right with Sean? Is there something I should be doing?" My brain was spinning, afraid there was more to this fever than typhoid. If so, wouldn't she be letting him know and not me?

"No, no. This isn't about Sean."

My relief was instantaneous.

"How's he recovering? Is his fever down?"

"It is. His parents arrived this morning."

"Great." She paused briefly. "The reason I called has to do with Relay for Life. I'm grateful you're my co-chair. I know how busy you've been and that you've already put in a lot of work, but time is getting short."

No question, I was all in with the fight against cancer. "You can count on me."

"Wonderful. I got word out on social media. The posters are up and the Chamber of Commerce is on board."

"I'll go back to the service clubs," I offered. I'd worked my contacts with the Rotary, Kiwanis, Friends of the Library, and several church groups.

We spoke for several minutes, reviewing our efforts for getting the community involved.

I'd been active with the local Relay for Life ever since Harper was first diagnosed with leukemia. As the signature fundraising event of the American Cancer Society, it united those suffering with cancer, cancer survivors, and the families of those who'd lost loved ones in the battle to find a cure for all forms of cancer. The event was fun and inspirational. I'd been involved every year, co-chairing with Dr. Annie.

Harper did her part as well and was instrumental in gathering volunteers. It was a twenty-four-hour walk, each person signing up to walk for an hour and collecting money for their efforts. The funds then went toward research and awareness.

My sister was a survivor and I considered it my goal to make sure she remained in remission. A job I would do everything within my power to fulfill.

Chapter 14

Willa

Sean's parents stayed for a week, and I saw them every day. His mother was a hoot, fussing over Sean, cooking night and day, filling his freezer with dinners. She took his temperature every few hours and fretted over him like he was a five-year-old. In contrast, his father was laid back and easygoing. In many ways Sean was the perfect combination of Patrick and Joanna.

While he complained about his mother's constant attention, I was grateful to know she had a handle on keeping him on track, taking his medication at the times prescribed, eating right, and drinking plenty of fluids.

Every afternoon, once I'd closed for the day, I stopped by Sean's house, staying three nights for dinner and into the evening. His parents faithfully watched *Wheel of Fortune* and *Jeopardy!* That gave Sean and me time to be alone. Because he'd been so seriously ill, we'd never discussed what I'd learned about him playing professional baseball. Instead we played board games and UNO, laughing and enjoying each other's company until he tired out.

Sean improved a little more each day. On the third day after the medication regime, he took a turn for the better. I could see it in his face and his energy level. He'd lost weight and didn't have much of an appetite, despite his mother's effort to get him to eat. She cooked all his favorite meals and wrote out the recipes for me to prepare after she returned home.

As soon as he started feeling more like himself, Sean started sorting through the thousands of photographs he'd taken. At first, he was able to work only an hour at a time; then two, then four. By the end of the week, Joanna, worried that Sean was pushing himself too hard, asked me to drag him away from his computer.

"He's been holed up in his workroom for nearly six hours. That can't be good for him," she complained to me over the phone. "He doesn't eat. Can you come?"

"Not until later." I sympathized with her. I was concerned, too. The way I figured it, Sean's ability to concentrate was self-limiting. He'd know when it was time to give it up for another day. Taking him away from his work wasn't something I wanted to do. No one appreciated being pulled from a project while in the groove.

"He was like this as a youngster, too," Joanna complained. "The worst was when he first got involved in baseball. He'd practice hitting the ball for hours, until he had blisters on his hands from holding the bat. From the time I can remember, he's always been driven. I worry about him."

"Watching him drive himself like that must have been hard on you."

"You don't know the half of it," she said and sighed. "All I ask is that you stop by the house as soon as you can."

"I will," I assured her. What I didn't tell her was that I was deeply involved in getting the event for Relay for Life organized. Every minute I wasn't at Bean There or with Sean, I was working on the event with Annie Keaton. The date was set for Friday, August 14. We had walkers willing to volunteer to circle the high school track for every hour except between two and three. The wee hours of the morning were always the most difficult to fill.

Mellie Young preferred those early-morning turns and chose to walk between one and two. Rather than let the following hour between two and three go blank, I penciled in my name. Since I was up early most mornings, it wouldn't be that much of a stretch.

Dinner was on the table when I arrived at Sean's. "I'm sorry to be so late," I said, "I got hung up working on the Relay for Life event."

"I've heard of that," Joanna said, setting food on the table. "A friend of ours was involved. She told me that although it's nationwide, it started in Washington State."

"That's what I understand."

"Everyone knows someone who has dealt with cancer. It's long past time to eradicate the disease."

"I couldn't agree with you more," I said.

Sean came into the kitchen, kissing my cheek and then his mother's before sitting down. He looked drawn, and I realized his mother had reason to be concerned. He was doing too much too soon, and I feared he might relapse.

His mother and I shared a look, and it was as if she'd silently shouted the words: *I told you so.*

"We leave first thing in the morning," Patrick told me, as we passed the fresh green salad around the table.

While aware his parents would be returning to Arizona, I was surprised by how much I hated to see them go. Spending time with Joanna reminded me of how desperately I missed my own mother. I hadn't talked to my father in weeks and he hadn't returned my most recent phone calls. Busy as I was caring for Sean and my efforts for Relay for Life, I hadn't reached out in the last week. Watching how Sean's family had gathered around him, I regretted that I hadn't tried harder with my own father.

After dinner, I helped with the dishes and then joined Sean on the back patio while his parents settled down in front of the television. The UNO pack was out, but I noticed he hadn't opened the box. Tired as he was, this wasn't a good night for games.

The evening was perfect. The weather was cooling down with a gentle breeze, wafting the scent of pine from the tall fir trees that surrounded Sean's property. He reached for my hand and I could see how tired he was.

"I've enjoyed spending time with your parents."

"I'm glad you didn't run for the hills," Sean joked. "My mother can be a bit much. It's the attorney in her; you should see her in the courtroom. I know judges who are afraid of her."

I could see Joanna fiercely defending her clients.

"Count your blessings you have your mother," I told him, feeling the loss of my own. I'd lost count of the times I'd have given anything to be able to talk to my mom. She'd been patient and wise, and oh, how I missed being able to share my concerns with her. She would have loved Sean and been a constant support when Harper had been so desperately ill.

"I am grateful," he said, "but to be frank, I'll be happy to not have her constantly hovering over me. This afternoon I was tempted to install a lock on my door."

I smiled, knowing in my heart that no lock would have kept Joanna out.

"It's my sister's turn next," he said. "Angie's pregnant and Mom is dying for grandchildren."

This eagerness to spoil grandchildren was something his mother had mentioned repeatedly. Joanna had dropped several hints at my feet. I pretended not to hear. This was far and away a subject I wasn't prepared to address. Sean and I had been seeing each other only a few weeks. It was much too early to say where this relationship would lead us.

"We never did have our talk," Sean said, his hand holding on to mine with more pressure than necessary.

I could feel his reluctance. To be fair, I wasn't eager to address the subject myself, although I knew it was necessary.

"I know I should have mentioned my baseball career, Willa," he said, his gaze locked on my hand in his. "It wasn't that I purposely hid it from you . . . I mean, I did in some ways. I guess I was afraid you'd think less of me."

"Less of you?" I found his reasoning odd.

"If you'd known me then, you wouldn't have wanted anything to do with me. The man I was back then"—he paused and ran his fingers through his hair—"I was arrogant and self-centered. I cringe every time I think of what a fool I made of myself. It embarrasses me, and I didn't want you to know I'd ever been like that."

"Oh Sean." I could see how difficult it was for him to talk about his past, and I cupped my hand over his.

"The women I dated back then . . ."

"Nikki?"

At the mention of her name, Sean froze. "You know about Nikki?"

"Not a lot. I saw a photo of the two of you. She's . . . gorgeous." It was hard to get the words out of my mouth.

He closed his eyes and shook his head as if to discard the memory. "I hate that you saw that photo or any photo of the women I once dated."

"Why?"

"Why?" he repeated, his voice raised. "Because it says far too clearly what I valued. Every woman I saw was empty spiritually and mentally. The fact is I was, too. It took hitting the bottom to realize what I'd become. When I was down and out, my career over, I had to take an honest appraisal of myself and my values. I detested what I saw."

His honesty cut straight through every negative thought I'd held on to since I first learned the truth.

"Can you imagine Nikki sticking with me while I dealt with typhoid fever?" he asked and answered his own question with a sarcastic laugh. "She'd have run for the hills so fast it would make your head swim."

He knew his former girlfriend better than me, so I didn't respond. One question had been eating at me, and I picked at the edge of my blouse. "Did you love her?"

He jerked back as if I'd punched him in the gut. He took several uncomfortable moments to consider his answer. "I won't lie to you. Idiot that I was, I thought I did. That says more about me than it does her. I sincerely doubt Nikki is capable of loving anyone but herself."

"You didn't introduce her to your parents." His mother had told me that I was the first woman he'd ever mentioned to her or Patrick.

"I was on the road a lot of the time and wasn't in contact with my parents a great deal. In retrospect, I think I subconsciously knew Nikki would be a big disappointment to them."

He paused and shook his head as if to clear his mind. "No, that's not right," he said, correcting himself. "I know they would have been disappointed in me, and I was looking to avoid that."

I hadn't meant for our talk to revolve around the women he'd once known and loved. Jealousy had prompted the question. The thought of Sean with anyone else made my stomach curdle. Of all that I'd learned about him, it was the part about his affairs that had plagued me most.

He turned to look at me, his eyes pleading with mine.

"Can we get past this, Willa? Are you able to put this behind us so we can move forward?"

"Is that what you want?" I asked, my heart in my throat. "For us to move forward?"

His shoulders rose as he straightened. "More than you will ever know." Taking my hand in both of his, he raised it to his lips and kissed my knuckles, all the while holding my gaze with his own.

Even now I wasn't sure what he saw in me that had interested him. I didn't mean to discount myself or my abilities, but the contrast between me and women like Nikki couldn't have been more blatant. When I researched her name I saw that she was a cover model, so there was plenty of evidence. I'd never considered myself beautiful or fashionable. Sean had been with a woman who was both. If he was looking for different, then that was me.

"You haven't answered my question, Willa. Can we start again?"

My heart was full, and I nodded.

"Thank you," he whispered. Taking hold of my neck, he drew me closer and kissed me and then braced his forehead against mine. "I can't thank you enough for seeing me through all this."

"You're pushing yourself too hard, working too many hours."

"I know. I'll ease up."

"Promise?"

He nodded. "Every day I feel more like myself."

"I'm glad."

"I'll recover faster now that I know you and I are okay. I've been worried about us having this conversation, afraid you were waiting until I was well enough to dump me."

His words shocked me. "I would never dump you . . . We might disagree from time to time, Sean. I'm not perfect, and while it might come as a shock, you aren't, either."

He grinned and then grew serious. "There's something you should know. I'm all in, Willa."

"What does that mean?" My lack of experience in romantic relationships made me unsure.

"It means there's no one else for me but you. If we plan to make something of this relationship, you should decide now if you're as serious as I am."

This was daunting. "I . . ."

"I don't mean to put you on the spot. I'm not asking for anything more than the assurance you care about me."

"I do care." That was never in doubt.

"And if some other guy asks you out or makes a play for you, what would you say?"

This seemed to be some form of test. "Well," I said, considering my response, "I guess I'd need to explain that I had a boyfriend who's all in and would object to me going out with someone else."

"Good girl."

"Depending on who it was, I'd probably add that my 'all-in boyfriend' was big and mean and didn't take kindly to other men flirting with me."

"Even better," Sean said and laughed.

"Now that we've cleared the air, I need to say goodbye to your parents."

"You know they love you already."

"Are they all in, too?" I teased, remembering his mother's less-than-subtle hints about grandchildren.

"You better believe it."

Before I left, I hugged both Joanna and Patrick and reassured them I would keep a close eye on Sean. He walked me to my car, kissed me again, and stood with his hands in his pockets as I drove away. I watched his figure fade from my rearview mirror.

Smiling, I realized I was in serious danger of falling in love with Sean. Serious, serious danger.

Instead of driving back to our apartment, I headed in a different direction. It was time I checked in on my father.

Chapter 15

Willa

I didn't know Dad's work schedule and took a chance he'd be home. The trailer park where he lived wasn't in a bad neighborhood, but it wasn't the best, either. Most of the yards were well maintained. Dad had a small patio with his space and had set out several potted plants. When she'd been alive our mother had maintained a large garden. It seemed our father had something of a green thumb himself. His tomato plants, heavy with ripe fruit, lined the small walkway leading up to the trailer.

Standing on the porch step, I knocked on the door. I'd been to his home only a few times. He discouraged company. Before, when I'd stopped by, it'd always been the middle of the day and I'd warned him in advance that I was coming. I silently prayed he wouldn't be upset at my unexpected visit and that he wasn't drinking.

"Who's there?" he called from inside the trailer. His voice, as well as his words, lacked welcome.

"It's Willa."

"Willa." Almost immediately the front door was thrown open and Dad stood there in a stained white T-shirt and jeans. He blinked as if he wasn't sure it was really me.

"Sorry to come this late. I should have phoned first." My impulsive visit seemed all wrong now and I regretted it, especially seeing how uncomfortable he was.

"Is it Harper?" he asked, worry sketched across his face. His eyes bored into mine and it seemed he braced himself for bad news.

"No, Dad, everything is fine."

Relief washed over his features before he frowned. "You're not just saying that, are you?"

"No, Dad. All's well."

Stepping aside, he motioned for me to come into his home. Dad had never been particularly neat; the years hadn't changed him. Dirty dishes lined the countertop and a couple of pans rested atop the stove. The furniture held discarded clothing and the top of the coffee table was obscured with old newspapers, unopened mail, and magazines. Our mother would cringe if she could see how unkempt he was.

Dad cleared a spot for me on the sofa. "Sit. Make yourself at home."

Home.

We'd lost so much more than our mother with her brain

aneurysm. Within a few years we'd lost our house to foreclosure and been forced to find other lodging. The father we knew and loved became a shell of the man that he'd once been.

In the years since Mom's passing, we'd all drifted like feathers captured in the wind, floating in different directions. Dad floundered from one job to another. Lucas had joined the Army. Thankfully, Harper and I remained close and shared an apartment. The time would come when we, too, would find our own paths in life and we would go our separate ways.

Dad rubbed a hand down his face. "Harper had her blood tested?"

Nodding, I said, "I called, and left a voicemail. You never returned my call."

"You know how I hate to talk on the phone."

That wasn't all he disliked. Apparently, listening to phone messages was also on his do-not-like list.

"We drove into Seattle to the Medical Center and got the results later that same afternoon." I relaxed against the sofa. "Everything looks good."

"Glad to hear it." His weak smile confirmed his words.

He wasn't the only one who was relieved. Dad hadn't always been like this, detached and emotionally distant from his children. True enough, it was bad after we lost Mom, but the bigger separation came when Harper had been diagnosed. The news was more than he could handle. Throughout the ordeal, Dad had been to the hospital only once or twice. It was as if the thought of losing first his wife and then his youngest child had crippled him. That was when the worst of the drinking had started.

The silence that followed was awkward, and, needing to fill it, I said, "While we were in Seattle, we had lunch with Chantelle."

"Ah yes, Lucas's girl."

"Fiancée," I corrected with overstated enthusiasm. "The wedding plans are in full swing. Harper and I are to be her bridesmaids."

Dad smiled and I could see that news lifted his spirits.

"Chantelle is designing the bridesmaids' dresses herself. She's really talented; they're going to be beautiful."

"Where's Harper now?"

"She's with a group of friends. That girl has more energy than ten teenage boys. You know she has it in her head to climb Mount Rainier, don't you?"

Dad frowned, clearly disapproving. "I'm not sure that's such a good idea."

"Tell Harper that." I'd tried without success. Even Lucas had mentioned he felt it might be too much for her, health-wise. Not that our concerns did any good. My sister had a mind of her own.

"Is she dating anyone special?" he asked.

"No. She was out last weekend with a guy named Travis, and then this morning she said something about meeting John for the conditioning session."

"Travis? John? Is that girl ever going to settle down?"

"She'll find the right one when she's ready," I assured him, just as I'd found the right one for me.

Hold on a minute. Where did that thought come from?

My relationship with Sean was in the infancy stage. I didn't know why, out of the blue, these thoughts were coming into my head. Then I did. When he'd been in Bolivia, I'd felt like a part of me was missing. I'd broken my arm as a freshman in high school and had to keep it in a sling. Handling life with one arm had been nerve-racking and frustrating, especially since I had taken over all the tasks that Mom had once done. Many of the same feelings I'd had that month were akin to how I felt when Sean had been out of the country.

When he'd returned seriously ill, I found it impossible to leave his side until his parents arrived. He'd asked me, just an hour or so earlier, if I was all in with this relationship. I hadn't answered him. I couldn't. Not because I wasn't sure. The truth was I was all in and that frightened me. It was too soon.

Conversations with my father were always short and to the point. After a few minutes he stood as if to announce it was time for me to go. If I didn't know him as well as I did, I would have been insulted by the way he hustled me out the door.

"It was good to see you, Dad."

"You too, Willa." He placed his hands on my shoulders and pecked my cheek.

Not until I was at the car did I realize that of the three of us kids, he'd asked only about Harper. It was expected; I didn't mind. Even before she developed cancer, Harper had been his favorite. I thanked God she'd survived, because I didn't know what would have happened to our father if she hadn't.

When I arrived back at our apartment, Harper was spread out on the sofa with Snowball asleep on her tummy. She seemed completely wrung out. Her face was red from exertion and her clothes clung to her body.

"Hey," she said, turning her head to look at me when I entered.

"Hey, back at you." I resisted the urge to mention how dreadful she looked.

"You're late tonight. Sean hasn't had a relapse, has he?"

I set my purse aside and walked into the kitchen and got a bottle of water. "Sean's recovering more every day. His mother is concerned that he's pushing himself too hard and I agree with her. I decided to stop off and see Dad after I left."

"How is he?"

"About the same." Same ol', same ol'. "And before you ask, I didn't see any evidence that he was drinking."

"That's good," she said with a sigh. "How long are Sean's folks staying?"

"They leave in the morning."

Sitting on the chair angled next to the sofa, I looked at Harper. Her face remained flushed. In all the times she'd been to these conditioning sessions I had never seen her take to the sofa afterward. I broached the subject carefully. "How was tonight's workout?"

"Brutal."

Unable to resist, I felt I had to ask. "Are you sure you're up for this?"

"Of course," she replied flippantly, as if it was a ridiculous question.

Her attitude alarmed me. "Harper, climbing Mount Rainier isn't a matter of life and death. If you don't make it this time, there's always next year. You don't need to kill yourself to make a point. We all know how mentally tough you are. You don't have anything to prove." I resisted asking her if John had suggested the same thing. As her climbing partner and a physician, he might well have shared my concerns.

Harper laughed as if she found my warning amusing. "I didn't come this far to back out now. A few of us are doing a practice climb this weekend. That will be the real test to see if we have what it takes."

"Am I hearing a note of doubt in your voice?" I asked. From the first moment she'd announced this summer challenge, Harper had been gung-ho. She was singing "Climb Every Mountain," the song from *The Sound of Music*, bragging to all who would listen about how she was a mountain climber. She'd been the one to talk a few of her friends into joining her. Not once in all these weeks had her confidence wavered. Although her words said otherwise, I sensed her hesitation.

"Promise me, after this weekend's practice, that if you feel it's too much you'll bow out."

"Nope. Not making that promise."

"Harper!"

"I'm all in."

Twice this evening I'd heard someone make that claim. I bit down on my tongue to keep from arguing. Anything more I said to talk reason would only cause her to stiffen her pride.

"It's summit or plummet."

"What?" I cried, thinking of the news coverage from last summer when a climber had fallen into a crevasse. Despite repeated attempts, the body had never been recovered.

"Don't even think that," I warned. It was bad enough that she'd voiced it.

"Chill, Willa," Harper said, laughing. Holding on to Snowball, she swiveled her legs out and sat upright.

When it came to my sister's welfare, "chilling" was a problem. My natural inclination was to worry about her. But I realized now that, having survived cancer, Harper wanted to live life to the fullest.

"Oh, before I forget, Chantelle sent a text," she said as she set Snowball down on the floor. "She wants to do a fitting for our dresses."

"Great. When?"

"This weekend. It should be on your phone, too."

I collected my purse to retrieve my phone. I hadn't looked at it in several hours. Sure enough, there was a text from my soon-to-be sister-in-law. "Saturday at noon." The note said Lucas would be coming with her. I hesitated. My weekend was already busy.

"I can't be here," said Harper.

"Did you let her know? We'll need to find another date."

"No way," Harper protested. "We're close enough to the same size. If the dress fits you it'll fit me. I don't want to hold up Chantelle."

I didn't feel good about trying on Harper's dress, especially since the design was different from my own, shorter; besides, Harper had bigger boobs than I did. If it didn't fit her at the wedding, I'd feel dreadful.

She must have read the hesitation in my eyes because she braced her hands against her hips and sighed heavily, as if I was being unreasonable. "Come on, Willa. You can do this one small thing, can't you?"

"Let me think about it." The timing wasn't great. Friday night was the Relay for Life event. Both Harper and I were deeply involved in that. Then on Saturday, Harper intended to do this practice climb. Another weekend would work much better for us both. I was surprised Harper hadn't suggested that.

With my phone in my hand, I sent Chantelle a text.

Need to reschedule. Is that a problem?

No more than five minutes later her reply came.

Nope. Connect later.

There. One simple note and it was all fixed. I told Harper, who frowned at me and headed into her bedroom. "I wish you'd talked to me first. You're making a big deal over nothing. I ask you to do one small thing and you blow it out of proportion, change everyone's plans. Did anyone ever tell you that you're a control freak?"

Stunned, I stood with my phone in my hand, my mouth

open. I didn't know what had come over my sister. We rarely argued, especially over something this petty.

"Are you feeling okay?" I asked.

Whipping around, Harper glared at me with eyes that would cut through a steel rod. "Do you know how often you ask me that question? Would. You. Stop," she all but shouted. She went into her bedroom and slammed the door.

At the sound of the door, Snowball leaped several inches off the ground and hid underneath the sofa.

I stood like a marble statue for several moments, unable to believe my sister had come unglued over something this trivial. I'd never thought of myself as a control freak. True, I worried about her health, but with good reason. My sister had nearly died. Even now I wondered if she realized how close to death she'd come.

Opening her bedroom door, she stood in the doorway, arms crossed. Her mouth was set in a thin line, and her eyes narrowed. "I'm moving out."

"Moving out?" I repeated, too stunned to say anything more.

"I've been thinking about it for some time now. Leesa and I want to get an apartment together."

My throat constricted and I swallowed hard. This had come out of the blue. "But . . . why?" We'd had differences of opinion before, but we'd always made up quickly. "I'm sorry if I—"

"It isn't you," she said, without a lot of conviction. "I need to find an apartment that allows pets. You're right. It won't take long for Snowball to become an adult cat, and we won't be able to hide her. Why risk getting evicted?"

"We can move," I said, feeling desperate now, unable to believe Harper had gotten this angry over something minor.

"Not we. Me. This apartment suits you perfectly. It's close to the shop. You're making enough to be able to afford the rent on your own now. If you're worried about it, then get another roommate."

I recognized the look in her eyes. Nothing I said would make a difference; her mind was made up. It hurt that my sister no longer wanted to live with me. Tears clouded my eyes and I blinked furiously.

"Okay," I whispered, turned, and retreated into my own room. All I could do was pray that by morning Harper would get over her anger and give up this idea of moving.

Chapter 16

Willa

Moonlight cast a golden glow over the track where I was set to walk my turn in the Relay for Life event. Mellie had finished her hour and walked the first lap with me.

"There's something about the stillness of these early-morning hours, isn't there?" she said.

We were fortunate, the weather couldn't have been any more perfect. We'd held the main ceremony the night before with a huge crowd in attendance. The atmosphere was festive. Our event was small compared to those in larger metropolitan cities. But we were dedicated and eager to do our part in the fight against cancer.

The walk was held on the track at the local high school. The school band performed, and the fence was lined with colorful balloons. Bean There had a booth, and we dispensed samples of Harper's special protein drink that she'd personally developed.

Dr. Annie kicked off the opening ceremony, reminding the community of our common goal, to cure cancer. We were asked to remember those who had lost the battle and to fight back against this disease that had brought grief and heartache to so many.

Harper led the victory lap around the field with other survivors from our community. I knew she was disappointed that John hadn't been able to join her. He'd been unable to take time away from the hospital, seeing that he would spend the weekend on Mount Rainier.

Cheers rose from the stands as those who had been blessed to beat this disease into remission walked and waved to their friends and loved ones while the band played.

The track was crowded as men, women, and children from Oceanside gathered behind the survivors after their victory lap. I was busy registering those last-minute attendees before I joined Shirley and Alice to hand out samples of Harper's special drink.

The most moving part of the evening was the Luminaria Ceremony, when white sacks with the names and often the photos of those who had succumbed to cancer were set with lights around the track. Dr. Annie read each name aloud and then spoke briefly, highlighting the latest research. Her words gave me reason to hope that the medical community would find the answer to wipe out cancer in our lifetime. Hope that no man, woman, or child would need to endure what Harper had in the fight for her life.

During the event, Harper had been in her element. Following her outburst from the night before, she'd avoided me. I hadn't seen her all day until we met at the high school field that evening. That she hadn't come into the shop after her classes told me she remained in a huff. I didn't know where this anger was coming from and it upset me.

"It's the quiet I appreciate most," I said, my mind circling back to Mellie, who walked at my side. The smell of the ocean was potent, especially at this time of morning. Other than the moonlight, the field remained dark. Two or three families had pitched tents in the center of the field. The colorful balloons that marked the border of the fence swayed in the gentle breeze.

"Do you want me to continue walking with you?" Mellie asked.

She had a young family, and while I appreciated the offer, I didn't mind walking alone. "I'm good. Thank you, though." My gaze went to the luminaria bags at the edges of the track. How grateful I was that Harper's name didn't appear there. I prayed it never would.

Before she left for home, Mellie and I hugged. With a farewell wave, she jogged toward the parking lot. I could walk more than three miles in that hour. In years past I'd brought along an audiobook or my music to help pass the time. Not this year. This rift with my sister continued to plague me, and I needed to think it through. Something was going on with Harper and I didn't know what it was or how best to deal with it.

During the ceremonies, no one would have guessed Harper was upset with me. She hid it well. I knew, though. When she looked at me, her smile was tight, and she hung with

Leesa instead of helping me the way she normally would. She did exactly what I asked of her and was friendly and affable to all. But I knew, and that was enough to put my mind to racing on what I did or didn't do that was the underlying problem.

As I continued to walk the track, I sorted through my memories, thinking hard over the last month. Going through the events of the weeks prior, I tried to think of what I might have done that Harper found objectionable.

Hard as it was to face, she was right when she accused me of being controlling, even if it was in minor ways. I'd never said she couldn't or shouldn't do any of the crazy things she was intent on doing. Half the time I didn't know until afterward and was thankful for it.

Selfishly I hated the thought of her moving out. I didn't want to live alone. We'd always been together, and close, more than ever since losing our mother and her leukemia.

A car door slammed in the distance, the sound echoing in the silence of the night. I couldn't possibly have been walking an entire hour. I checked the time and saw that I was only fifteen minutes into the time I'd promised. I walked two entire rotations around the track, caught up in my thoughts.

As I returned to the starting point, Sean jogged over to join me. "Morning," he said, and rubbed his palms together as if to chase off the morning chill.

I nearly stumbled in surprise. "What are you doing here?" I had to admit that wasn't the most welcoming of questions.

His grin was wide. "I can't let my best girl walk alone, can I?"

How he even knew the time slot I'd volunteered for, I didn't know. Perhaps I'd mentioned it in passing without realizing it. "You should be home in bed, Sean. You've been sick." He needed his rest, and this exercise couldn't be aiding his recovery.

"I'm feeling great."

Unsure if I should believe him, I muttered under my breath.

"You looked absorbed in your thoughts," he said, matching his steps to my own as we continued around the track. "You walked all the way around the track without seeing me."

That car door I heard closing had been Sean. He was right, I'd been deep in thought. "Harper's upset with me," I said, and explained the circumstances.

"It isn't like my sister to slam doors and make a big fuss," I told Sean.

"Sounds to me like an overreaction."

It was, and it'd taken me this long to unravel the reason. "I believe Harper's been wanting to break free and get her own place for some time now. This tiff is the perfect excuse."

Sean mulled over my words. "You're a wise and thoughtful woman, Willa. Are you going to let her do it?"

"Of course. I have no control over her life. Looking back, I think she tried to tell me what she wanted earlier when she brought Snowball home. I should have read between the lines then."

"You'll miss her."

"I will. She's right, though, she needs to be on her own. I'm more mother than sister," I said, even though it was difficult to admit, even to myself. The time had come for Harper to soar on her own without her big sister constantly looking over her shoulder.

"She's fortunate to have you." He reached for my hand, entwining our fingers.

The compliment was sincere. I wasn't sure I agreed with him, seeing how long it'd taken me to make sense of what Harper really wanted. My chest tightened at the thought of her moving out of our apartment. When she returned from her practice climb later today, I'd do what I could to smooth matters between us.

For the rest of the hour's walk, Sean kept pace with me and didn't show any signs of fatigue. We chatted back and forth, at ease with each other, joking and laughing. When we'd finished, what we both needed most was a hot cup of coffee. I was scheduled to do the baking that morning, as Shirley had the day off. I invited him to join me in the café's kitchen before I realized he might want to go back to bed.

"Unless . . . Listen, don't feel obligated."

"Coffee with my girl. Not turning that down."

His girl. I liked the sound of that.

Pastor McDonald, a family friend, was scheduled to walk the next hour. He arrived right on time.

Before I had a chance to introduce him, the pastor stretched out his hand to Sean. "Heath McDonald."

"Sean O'Malley."

The two exchanged handshakes.

"Pastor McDonald was a tremendous help after Mom died and again later when Harper was ill. I don't know what our family would have done without him." It gladdened my heart to know that Lucas and Chantelle had asked him to perform their wedding ceremony.

"I'm pleased to know you, Pastor."

"Heath, please. The minute people hear that I'm a pastor they clam up and are afraid to be themselves. The only one who calls me Pastor is Willa. I'd like to think of myself as more of a spiritual doctor."

"Thank you for doing this," I said. Pastor Heath was a gentle-spirited man with a giving heart. Without him and the help of the church, I don't know what would have happened to our family after Mom died. For months after her death, the women from church took turns coming to the house, teaching me to cook and clean. They'd loved my mother, too. The pastor had counseled Dad, until Dad refused to see him any longer, preferring to drown his grief in cheap whiskey.

Sean followed me to the shop. I arrived earlier than I normally would, which gave us time for coffee. The kitchen was dark and cold until I turned on the lights and put the coffee on to brew. I took the dough out of the refrigerator to let it warm and rise again before I baked the cinnamon rolls.

"What are those?" Sean asked, nodding toward the row of round cake pans resting on the counter.

"Cake," I explained the obvious.

"You don't sell cakes. Are you thinking of expanding into a bakery?"

"Nope, that's wedding cake. I promised my brother and Chantelle I'd bake the cake for their wedding. I'm trying out a few different flavors." I didn't mention that one of my stress-relievers was to bake. Rather than stew about Harper's plan to move, I'd baked four different-flavored cakes.

"Do you need a taste-tester?"

"Are you volunteering?"

He patted his flat stomach. "I did lose a few pounds while sick. Mom did her best to fatten me up. What she didn't try was cake. I'd love to be your taste-tester."

"You got it." Chantelle and Lucas would make the final decision; however, having Sean test out my practice runs would be a help.

Taking down four small plates, I dished up a thin slice of each cake, sans frosting. "I didn't frost the cakes," I explained. "I want you to taste the flavor without it being masked with frosting."

"Which one should I sample first?"

"Vanilla. I know it sounds boring, but vanilla remains the most popular choice."

"Okay." His fork slid into the moist cake. He chewed, swallowed, and nodded. "Delicious. It's going to be hard to beat that one."

"Good to know. Funfetti is next."

"Fun what?"

"It's called Funfetti, which is basically the same white cake mixed with colorful sprinkles. They melt in the baking process, so the cake looks like confetti."

"Looks good." His fork dipped into the cake and lifted it

to his mouth. He swallowed and nodded. "This one is equally good."

"Glad you approve."

He sipped his coffee to clear the taste from his mouth and then asked, "What's next on the agenda?"

"Lemon cake."

"I've always been fond of lemon anything." He tasted it and jiggled his eyebrows approvingly. "That's delicious. It's my favorite so far." He took another bite while I reached for the fourth plate.

"Now for the grand finale." With a bit of show, I set down the final piece of cake. "This is coconut."

He poured himself a glass of water before he tried the last sample. Each recipe had my own special twist. The vanilla and Funfetti cakes had been made from whole vanilla beans. The lemon cake had lemon zest and lemon juice in the mix. For coconut cake, I'd used coconut milk for the liquid. I was eager to see his reaction to this last cake the most. It was my personal favorite. I knew Chantelle liked coconut pie, which is what prompted me to add this to the list. I didn't remember if Lucas much cared for the flavor or not.

After the first forkful, Sean closed his eyes and moaned. "Willa, this is incredible. I don't know what you did to make it taste like fresh coconut. This is heaven in cake form."

"Which would you vote for?"

"Need you ask? Coconut," he said, and then added, "with the lemon cake running a close second. I'd marry you for the coconut cake alone," he teased. His eyes were bright with merriment before slowly growing more serious. "I'd marry you for far more than your baking skills, Willa."

At his comment, my heart felt like it was about to explode. "Don't be silly," I protested, my hand to my throat. "We barely know each other and—"

"I know everything I need to know," he said, reaching for me. His arms went around my waist, bringing him to me. I leaned down and our lips met in a kiss that was hot enough to sound the fire alarm. We were heavily involved in each other when I heard a noise behind us.

The outside door to the kitchen opened and Harper walked in. "Oh," she cried. "Sorry, I didn't mean to interrupt anything."

Sean and I broke apart as if caught in the middle of a bank robbery. "You weren't."

"You could have fooled me," Harper said with a wide grin. She was dressed for hiking, ready to meet her friends for the practice climb up Mount Rainier.

"Did you want to take your protein drink with you?" I asked, assuming that was the reason she'd stopped by.

She looked to Sean and a sly smile came over her before she said, "I was hoping to have a word."

Sean stepped away from me. "No, please, I was about to go."

"No need," Harper insisted, stopping him as he started to walk away. "This will only take a minute."

I was glad he didn't leave. I wanted to talk to my sister, and anything she had to say could be said in front of Sean.

Chapter 17

Sean

Harper turned her gaze to me. I had reason to stay but felt it would be awkward when it was clear Willa and her sister needed to talk. Nearly all our conversation that night had revolved around Willa's relationship with her sister. We laughed and joked, but then the topic would drift back to Harper and what was going on between the two sisters.

"I'll go. It's not a problem," I reiterated. "I can connect with Willa later." I hated the thought, but I didn't want to intrude.

"No, please stay." Harper stretched out her arm as if to block me from leaving. "I've come to apologize to Willa . . . and seeing that you are part of the reason, you should hear this, too." Her gaze flickered away from Willa to land on me.

"Did I do something?" I asked, uncertain what she could possibly mean.

Harper's eyes sparkled with mischief. "In a way, you're to blame for my decision."

Me? It was hard to know what role I'd played in the drama between the two of them.

"Not in a bad way," she rushed to explain. "Seeing that you and Willa are together now, I realized she wouldn't be nearly as upset if I decided to get my own apartment. If anything, I should thank you." Turning her attention away from me, she looked to Willa. "I'm sorry, Willa."

"Harper, it's fine. I—"

"It isn't fine." She walked over to Willa and hugged her. "I behaved like a five-year-old brat who didn't get her own way and I apologize."

Willa's arms squeezed her sister. She didn't need to say anything for Harper to know her little temper tantrum had long since been forgiven and forgotten.

Exhaling, Willa eased away, her hands gripping the sides of Harper's shoulders. "I know you've wanted your own apartment for some time now. Only it took me a while to figure it out. You should have said something sooner."

Harper lowered her eyes and appeared speechless. She didn't deny or disclaim Willa.

"If you're looking for my permission, you have it. You don't need it, Harper. You're over twenty-one and it's time for you to spread your wings and fly on your own. You don't need me; you've always been your own person."

Harper shuffled her feet. "You can be such a mother, you know."

Seeing that that was the role Willa had been cast into after their mother's death, it wasn't a surprise that Harper said that. Her cancer had cemented it.

"I didn't mean to smother you . . ."

"You didn't always; mostly, it's been the last three years," Harper said quickly. "It's like you're waiting for something else bad to happen. I feel that once I have my own place, you can be my sister instead of acting like a mother." Harper sucked in a breath. "That didn't come out quite right."

Although I could see how hard it was for Willa to hear this, she managed a weak smile. "I get what you're saying. You're right. It got bad after your cancer, didn't it? I got even worse."

"It isn't all your fault. The family desperately needed you after Mom. Dad fell apart, and Lucas, being Lucas, was more comfortable pretending all was well and good. And for him, it was. Little changed. He had three square meals a day. His laundry was done. He was able to participate in sports and continue on as if her death was a minor blip in his life."

"That's not true," Willa argued, defending her brother. "He missed Mom, too, just not in the same way as you and I did."

"Yes, I suppose. With Lucas, though, it was easier to pretend everything was fine when it felt for us as if our entire world had gone into a tailspin."

Willa didn't argue, and I suspected she knew Harper was probably right. I'd never met Lucas, so it was hard for me to understand her brother. From what little Willa had told me about him, he seemed to have his head on straight. In one of our conversations about her family I remembered Willa telling me that the military had done her brother a world of good. He'd come out disciplined, clearheaded, mature beyond his years, with the resolve to make his own life.

"He made up for it later," Harper said. "When I was sick, he was a great support."

"To both of us," Willa chimed in, stiffening her shoulders, as if reluctant to return to their earlier conversation. "Getting back to our tiff," she continued, "I realized as I walked the field this morning that this need to get your own place with Leesa has been brewing for some time."

"It has," Harper agreed. "We've been talking about it for a couple of months now."

"Why didn't you say anything?" Willa asked, frowning. "I would have understood."

Once more Harper looked uncomfortable, kicking at an imaginary spot on the floor. "I needed to wait."

"But why?"

She exhaled. "I wanted to be sure the blood tests were okay. It didn't seem like a good idea to make plans to move out if there was a possibility the leukemia was back."

"Right. That makes sense."

Willa glanced my way as if to say she should have figured that out earlier.

"So you're looking at apartments with Leesa," Willa said brightly. I could see she was doing her best to be encouraging and supportive.

Harper's eyes instantly lit up and she nodded. "We are. I've been saving up for the deposit, and Leesa has, too."

"What's your timing?"

Harper was quick to answer. "September first if we can find the right place, one that's convenient for us both and at a price we can afford. The fifteenth at the latest. That won't be a problem, will it?" She studied Willa, seeking her approval. "I mean, if you don't feel that you can make the rent on your own—"

"It won't be a problem," Willa rushed to reassure her sister.

I had to wonder if she was as okay with this as she said she was. Willa had been her little sister's advocate from the time Harper had been born. Freeing Harper to move out was a huge step emotionally for her. I could only imagine how bereft this decision made her feel.

"Will you get a new roommate?" Harper asked, as if she worried what would become of Willa without her. Her gaze flickered to mine. I nodded, hoping she understood I wasn't going anywhere. When it came to Willa, I intended to be around for as long as she'd have me.

"A new roommate," Willa echoed, as if only now considering the option. "Possibly. I haven't thought that far ahead."

"I need to find a place that will allow pets," Harper said absently, and for the first time, she noticed the cake pans that lined the counter. "You baked cakes?" she asked with some surprise.

"For the wedding. Four different flavors."

"I did a taste test," I volunteered. "The coconut is my favorite, with the lemon cake running a close second."

Harper grinned. "You were serious about baking Lucas and Chantelle's wedding cake, then?"

"Of course."

Harper hugged Willa and started toward the door. "Wish me luck today."

"Luck?" I asked. Clearly she was up to something, to be awake this early on a Saturday morning.

"I'm doing a practice climb up Mount Rainier with the whole group," Harper explained. "It's a big deal. We're scheduled to make the full climb next weekend. This will be my first time to meet the guide."

"Harper has been conditioning all summer," Willa explained. "She intends to impress the guide with how fit she is."

"So you're ready?" I asked.

"I'm as ready as I'll ever be."

Seeing that she taught yoga and fitness classes, this news came as no surprise.

"This is more than a practice climb," Harper explained, gripping her hands together. "It's a strength and endurance test, too. Anyone who can't make it to Camp Muir will need to withdraw from the group."

"That'll be like a cakewalk for you."

"Should be," Harper agreed, looking eager to be on her way. "Gotta scoot. We're okay, right?" she turned back to ask Willa.

"Of course. Have fun today."

"Will do." Harper looked happy and far more relaxed than she had when she'd first arrived.

"We can talk more tonight." Willa blew her a kiss.

Harper waved on her way out the door.

As the two had been talking, Willa had rolled out the dough for the cinnamon rolls and placed them on a large sheet to rise again. They looked amazing. I had to wonder if any of this got old. She worked with practiced hands, almost without thinking. Yet I could see the love that went into her baking. It was the secret ingredient that kept drawing customers back. Me being one of them.

I'd put off discussing my news long enough and decided it was best to tell her now. "I have something in the works myself," I said, slipping back onto the stool. Watching her turn a second batch of dough onto the counter, I waited until she glanced up before I explained.

"Did I mention the opportunity I have to shoot marine life on a few of the islands in the Philippines?"

Willa's hands stilled. "Maybe."

"I've been waiting for months to hear if the shoot was a go and I would be chosen as the photographer."

"And?"

"And word came late last night. It's happening and I'm in."

This was big. I'd won the bid over a dozen other photographers, many of whom had far more experience than I did. This was a career coup and I was doing my best to tone down my excitement. Blood rushed through my heart at the thought of what this assignment would mean for my career.

Willa went still while I waited for her congratulations.

When she spoke, her voice was soft and small. "You're leaving again?"

"Yes, this is what I do, Willa. You know that."

She bit into her lower lip as if holding back her disappointment. "So soon after Bolivia?"

"It happens like that sometimes." I could see how badly she wanted to argue with me.

"But you've been desperately ill."

"I'm much better. My last blood tests proved as much. This doesn't mean I'll be flying out right away. It'll probably take a few weeks to get everything sorted out."

She held my gaze and I could see the effort it took for her not to say anything more.

"You don't need to worry," I said, wanting to reassure her. I was excited and disappointed that she didn't share my enthusiasm. My hope was that she'd recognize how fortunate I was to have gotten this plum assignment. This wasn't something that had come together at the last minute. I'd been waiting for weeks, hoping for this opportunity.

"Don't tell me not to worry," she said, attacking the dough with her hands, kneading it with such force I took a step back.

"But . . ."

"Telling me not to worry guarantees that I will worry."

"Willa, please."

"Please what? 'Please understand. Please be happy for me. Please put this out of my mind and be the sweet little girlfriend who waves you off with a smile.' "

"Yes." That was all I could think to say.

"Which one?" she demanded.

"All of the above," I stated calmly. To be fair, I'd expected her to complain it was too soon after being ill or to argue that I should give myself more time to heal properly.

Her shoulders slumped forward and her hands stilled. "Just how long will you be away this time? Three weeks? A month? Two?"

"I don't know. It could be up to two months."

She lifted her forearm and wiped it across her forehead. "Will it be dangerous work?"

I opened my mouth to assure her I'd be as safe as a baby tucked in his mother's arms. As much as I wanted to make light of any dangers I would likely encounter, to claim otherwise would be misleading. Any excursion into a foreign country came with certain risks. The polluted drinking water, various insects, and snakes were only a few of the threats I'd likely face.

"I'll be careful," I whispered. Unable to keep from touching her any longer, I stepped behind her and wrapped my arms around her middle, hugging her and resting my chin on her shoulder.

"Will . . . Will you be able to stay in touch?"

Most likely it would be hit and miss with a whole lot more misses than hits. The areas where I'd be working were remote, and any chance of finding an internet connection was unlikely. With an assignment this lengthy, there would be opportunities to travel into town for supplies. Depending on the location, we might be fortunate enough to find an internet café. When it came to guarantees, I couldn't give her any.

"Your silence says it all."

Willa continued working. Neither of us spoke as she rolled out the dough and spread the sugar, butter, and cinnamon over the top before securing it. She cut each roll into one-inch slices with surprising accuracy, never needing to measure before she placed them on the sheet to rise next to the first sheet.

Earlier Willa said it had taken her time to understand what Harper had been trying to tell her for weeks. She needed space from the sister who had been more mother than sibling. It hurt her to let go of Harper.

Willa used the back of her hand to wipe the moisture from her face.

Turning her around so I could look at her, I saw that tears had filled her eyes, threatening to spill down her cheeks.

"It's too much," she whispered. "First Harper wants to leave me, and now you."

"Baby," I whispered, drawing her close. I kissed the top of her head. "Harper's not leaving you any more than I am. We'll both be right here."

"You'll be half a world away," she argued.

"My heart won't be. That will be with you."

She chuckled and slammed her palm against my shoulder. "Do you think a few pretty words are going to make me feel better?"

"I can hope, can't I?" Drawing in a deep breath, I felt I had to ask even when I wasn't sure of her answer. "Do you want me to turn down this assignment?"

She pulled away and looked me in the eyes as if to gauge the sincerity of my question. "Are you serious? Would you actually turn it down if I asked you to?"

I was serious and nodded, holding in my breath, fearing that was what she wanted. If she did, I wasn't sure how I'd respond. Years ago, I heard a television attorney mention how important it was to never ask the witness a question when they didn't know the answer. Perhaps I should have taken a lesson from that.

If Willa asked me to give up this assignment, I wasn't sure I could do it, no matter how strong my feelings were for her. It would possibly be the beginning of the end of our relationship.

"No," she said after the longest moment of my life, "I would never ask that of you."

Relief flooded through me and I released a long pent-up breath. "Thank you, Willa."

To have her hit my shoulder with far more force than she had before came as a surprise.

"Don't you dare get sick. I swear, if you return again with some tropical disease, I will never forgive you."

It wasn't like I intended to shop around for some deadly fever. "I'll do my best to stay safe and healthy."

"And I expect to hear from you as often as you can manage it."

"Done."

"You better miss me."

"Every hour of every day."

The beginning of a smile touched her lips, making her

irresistible. Before she could make any further demands, I bent down and kissed her, letting her know how important she was to me.

Yes, this was an assignment of a lifetime and I was fortunate to get it. Nevertheless, that paled against what I'd found with Willa.

Chapter 18

Willa

I didn't hear from Harper following her practice climb. That wasn't a shock, although I'd hoped she'd at least call. She'd mentioned that she'd be staying at a cabin near Mount Rainier that night with her friends. No worries. There was sure to be a big party after the climb, and checking in with my sister wasn't high on my priority list, given the busy day I had and my lack of sleep the night before. When she didn't show Sunday afternoon, I decided she was flexing her independence and didn't feel the need to connect with me.

Since she'd made a point of letting me know she didn't appreciate my mothering her, I didn't text or phone her, either. I worried plenty, but no way was I going to hunt her down to be sure she was okay. Harper would hate that. At any other time, I would've been on the phone so fast it would burn up the line.

Sunday afternoon Sean stopped by the apartment with

Bandit. I packed us a light lunch and we headed to the beach. Tourists crowded the oceanfront. Kids raced up and down in the sand. Sean built me a sandcastle with the help of four or five kids. He was great with them. Spending time with him helped take my mind off my sister.

After we ate, he threw a Frisbee for Bandit. We laughed, watching his dog leap into the air to catch the round disk. Children gathered and applauded. Sean let them toss it several times and there was fun all around. We tired out long before Bandit did.

When we returned to the house, we were both exhausted. Sean stayed for dinner and we watched a romantic comedy, snuggling together on the couch.

"Any word from Harper?" he asked.

"None. She's going out of her way to show me what she really wants from me is to be her sister." I'd failed her in that way and planned to do whatever was needed to show I'd taken her words to heart.

"Are you worried?"

"Not really," I lied.

His smile was all too knowing.

"All right, maybe a little. She's fine. If anyone was ready to conquer that mountain it's my sister." Harper had been climbing mountains her entire life, each one higher and more challenging than the last.

On Monday morning, when I still hadn't spoken to Harper, my confidence wavered. I battled the urge to contact one of her climbing partners. If I did, I knew she'd never let me live it down. It wasn't until I checked her bedroom that I discovered she'd made it home after all. Her bed was mussed. She must have arrived home late, because I hadn't heard her. That morning, she must have snuck out early. By now it was apparent she was avoiding me.

Snowball wasn't happy, either. Her food dish was empty. Before I left for Bean There, I fed Harper's cat and refilled her water bowl. For the life of me I couldn't imagine what was going on with my sister.

She didn't show up between her yoga and fitness classes for her special protein drink, either. Now I really was concerned.

"Is everything all right?" Shirley asked me during a late-morning lull.

"Sure. Why wouldn't it be?"

"You tell me," Shirley shot back. "You haven't been yourself all morning. What gives?"

Shirley was a no-nonsense kind of woman and wouldn't ignore my obvious distress. "I haven't heard from Harper since she left for Mount Rainier last Saturday."

To her credit, Shirley looked as stricken as I felt. "She didn't call?"

"No. She's been home," I rushed to explain. "Her bed wasn't made this morning, so I know she returned at some point last night." To be fair, I'd been completely worn out after Sean and I had spent the day on the beach. Being in the sun did that to me. I'd fallen asleep halfway through the movie. Sean had to wake me before he left and saw me to bed.

"She can't avoid you forever." Shirley was ever sensible.

"Why would she avoid me in the first place?" I asked, not expecting an answer. Yes, we'd had a minor disagreement earlier, but we'd sorted everything out Saturday morning. I'd assumed we had. Perhaps I'd been wrong. I'd felt good about the progress we'd made. It was rare for us to fight. I was grateful Harper had sought me out before she'd left. If there remained trouble between us, I wanted it settled. I didn't know what it could be, though.

When I returned to the apartment after the shop closed, I found Harper curled up on the sofa, a blanket wrapped around her, although it was one of the hottest days of the summer. She had her head buried under the quilt.

"Harper, are you ill? What's wrong?"

She peeked her head out and looked my way. Unhappiness radiated from her face and she swallowed hard, as if she couldn't bear to speak the words.

This was so unlike my sister that I was immediately alarmed. Easing myself down on the far end of the couch, I searched for a plausible excuse. "Are you still angry with me?" That was the question that plagued me most. I couldn't bear it if she was.

"No." Her voice sounded like it took every ounce of energy she possessed to get it out.

"Did you and Leesa have a falling-out?" Perhaps her hopes of sharing an apartment with her best friend had fallen through.

She shook her head.

Not knowing what else to do, I placed my hand on her leg. "Won't you tell me what's wrong?"

She heaved in a huge breath as if rising from the water after holding it in as long as she could manage. "I didn't make it."

"Didn't make what?"

"To Camp Muir," she snapped, as if that was obvious.

That made no sense. She'd been ready to tackle that mountain. Not once did I consider that she wouldn't reach past the tree line.

"I couldn't make it even halfway up."

"What?" I found that hard to believe. "That's not possible. You're in terrific shape."

"That's what I thought." She leaned forward and pressed her forehead against her bent knees. "The only other person who couldn't make the climb was a fat disc jockey. I don't think he's done a day of exercise in his entire life."

This probably wasn't the time to laugh, but I couldn't help it. The mere idea that Harper hadn't been able to outdo an overweight disc jockey was beyond the scope of my imagination. It didn't add up.

"The guide said this sort of thing happens now and again. People who've trained all summer choke up. I feel like I let down John and everyone else, myself included."

Harper didn't choke. She tackled life with the same intensity that she'd used to take on every challenge.

"How far were you able to go?"

She buried her face again. "Obviously not far enough. It

was humiliating. I was huffing and puffing like I'd been smoking a pack of cigarettes a day for the last forty years."

If she hadn't been able to make the climb, I was afraid it was something physical that had stopped her. With her medical history, this was nothing to mess with. "I'm going to make an appointment with Dr. Annie."

"No," she practically shouted. "Don't you dare. Stop. Just stop. Why do you think I didn't tell you right away? I knew this was exactly what you'd do, and it's the last thing I want."

"Harper . . ."

"The air was thin; others had trouble, too."

But the others had been able to make the climb, despite the altitude. She must have read the doubt in my eyes because she blasted me with "There's nothing wrong with me. You do this every time. How many times do I have to tell you I don't want you hounding me about my health?" Her eyes blazed with anger.

I raised both hands like she'd pointed a gun at me. "Okay."

"I choked," she said, calmer now. "It happens," she insisted. "You make it sound like I'm going to fall over dead any minute."

I narrowed my eyes and let that comment pass. "You aren't having any trouble breathing while teaching your yoga and fitness classes, are you?"

"None." Again, she was vehement.

Rubbing my hand across the back of my neck, I debated how much I should or shouldn't say. One thing was certain: Harper didn't want me making more of this than she felt was warranted.

"I know you're disappointed."

"That's not the half of it. I've been working toward this climb for months. I thought I was ready. Everyone else in my training group will make it to the summit next week and I won't be with them." Her voice wobbled, and I could tell she was close to tears.

"I'm so sorry, Harper. I know how much this meant to you. Maybe next year?"

"Maybe," she muttered, and lowered her forehead to her knees. After a moment, she brought the blanket over herself again.

I didn't have any other words of comfort. In her present mood, I doubted she wanted to hear them, anyway.

Harper's dark mood continued for the remainder of the week. She was a bear to live with. I did my best to ignore her melancholy state and go about my own business, pretending all was well. Not once did she show up at the coffee shop between her classes for her special drink. Obviously, she was doing everything possible to avoid me. With no other choice, I let her.

Her friends from the training group who made the entire climb up Mount Rainier invited Harper to the victory party. It surprised me when she decided to attend. I should have known she would. Although she was bitterly disappointed, Harper put on a bright smile and celebrated with her friends, going out of her way to congratulate them.

Finding an apartment within her and Leesa's budget was

proving to be more difficult than either of them had imagined. Every afternoon for the next week, the two girls went out on the great apartment search, finally seeing one that they could easily swing, rent-wise.

"How was it?" I asked.

Harper groaned. "The entire building should be condemned."

"That bad?"

"Worse."

"I'm sorry."

Sinking onto the sofa, Harper let out a discouraged sigh. "I never dreamed it would be this difficult."

I sympathized, but there wasn't anything I could do. Leesa lived with her parents, and I knew she was desperate to get out on her own as much as Harper was.

In the middle of Harper's angst, Sean was busy getting ready to travel to the Philippines. Not knowing how long he would be out of the country, I made a point of seeing him every day. He worked ridiculously long hours, sorting through all the photos from his trip to Bolivia and getting them ready to submit for publication. For these two trips to land almost on top of each other had stretched him to the limit. His ordeal with typhoid had set him back two weeks, and he worked every spare moment to make up for the time he'd lost.

With Harper out of sorts and Sean still recovering and working all hours of the day and night, I felt like the peanut butter between two slices of bread. Both seemed to need me. Harper would rather bite off her arm than admit it. I know she was disappointed with missing out on the mountain-climbing adventure. Her struggles to find a decent apartment depressed her further. She felt off in other ways, too, and I found myself stressing about her health. I didn't dare mention it. Far be it from me to let her know I was worried!

Bandit seemed to know Sean was about to leave. He moped around the house and lost his appetite. I wasn't in much better shape myself. The closer the day came to when Sean was scheduled to go, the lower my spirits were sinking. I tried to hide how I felt, but Sean easily saw through me.

Two weeks after he announced he'd gotten the assignment, we dropped Bandit off with Logan to dog-sit until Sean returned. Then I drove him into Seattle to catch his flight. My chest felt like there was a huge knot in it as we drove, increasing in size the closer we got.

After we parked, he'd checked in his luggage, carrying with him as much of his camera gear as the airlines would allow. His equipment was expensive. It went without saying that his biggest fear was that the airlines would lose it.

We sat outside of security and had coffee, neither one of us speaking.

"You'll let me know when you arrive?" I asked, swallowing around the lump in my throat.

"Of course."

"I'm going to miss you."

He reached across the table and wove our fingers together. "I'll miss you more."

"No, you won't. You'll be busy taking pictures and will barely have time to give me a thought."

He snorted as if that was impossible. "Wrong."

62

DEBBIE MACOMBER

I so badly wanted to believe him.

"Besides, you'll be busy preparing for Lucas and Chantelle's wedding."

Chantelle and Lucas had come to visit the weekend before. Harper and I had been fitted for our bridesmaid's gowns, both of which were stunning. Then they'd done their own taste test and couldn't agree on which cake they liked best. The issue was settled when I agreed to bake two cakes. One lemon and one Funfetti. I had no idea my brother detested coconut. According to him, he'd rather eat earwax than coconut.

When we couldn't delay Sean's departure any longer, I walked him to the security line.

"The weeks will fly by," he promised, turning me into his arms.

I rested my head against his shoulder. "Yeah, right." I hugged him so hard I was afraid I might have injured his ribs. He kissed me and then reluctantly released me. I remained where I was until he cleared security.

Waving at me, he walked backward, then turned and raced toward his gate, knowing he would probably be the last passenger to board the plane.

The drive home seemed to take forever. I didn't know how Seattle commuters could deal with this traffic. My heart felt heavy in my chest and didn't ease as I neared home. Sean had left me with a key to his house and asked if I would collect his mail and water his plants.

Instead of going back to the apartment, I stopped off at his place to make sure everything was as it should be. Sean was part of my life now, and I didn't know how I would manage without him. I hated that he never seemed to take assignments that were close to home—well, other than the mural one over in eastern Washington. I didn't know why it was necessary for him to travel to developing countries for a story.

If I loved Sean, I knew I would need to accept that this was his life, part and parcel of this man who had come to mean so much to me. This was what he loved. I couldn't ask him to change any more than he would make that request of me.

The apartment was dark when I returned well past the dinner hour. I wasn't hungry and hadn't stopped to eat. To my surprise, Harper sat in the dark in the living room, Snowball on her lap.

"Hey, do you want me to turn on the lights?" I asked.

"No."

Something was drastically wrong. I heard it in the lone word. Fear. Anxiety. Doubt.

I sat down next to her. "Harper," I said, and reached for her hand.

Her fingers grabbed hold of mine in a punishing grip.

"What is it?" I asked gently.

"I have a rash."

I swallowed hard, remembering that before she'd been diagnosed with leukemia, it had started out with hives. I was about to explain it all away, assure her that she was fine. The blood work had come back negative. There wasn't anything to worry about. The words never made it to my lips.

"My chest hurts, too."

Now it was my fingers that crushed hers.

"I made an appointment with Dr. Annie. Will you come with me?"

I couldn't respond verbally, couldn't get any words out from the anxiety that clogged my throat. That was like me, though. My mind immediately went to the worst-case scenario.

"I'm sure there's a simple explanation," I insisted, determined to be positive. What made my heart nearly stop was the fear I sensed in Harper. Determined not to jump to conclusions, I forced myself to think positively. A rash. A little trouble breathing. Just how bad could it be?

Chapter 19

Willa

Harper and I sat in the waiting room of Oceanside Walk-in Medical Clinic for our turn to see Dr. Annie. Mindlessly, I flipped through the pages of a six-month-old *People* magazine. Many of the names and faces were unknown to me. Their affairs, marriages, and divorces held no real interest. Harper had her legs crossed and was nervously swinging her foot back and forth. This morning she seemed to be more positive. I didn't think it was a front.

Within ten minutes of our arrival, Harper's name was called. We were directed into the small room. The nursing assistant took Harper's vitals. Becca was someone Harper had gone to high school with, although she was a year younger. The two women chatted.

"You're engaged?" Harper commented, noticing Becca's diamond engagement ring.

Becca blushed and nodded. "Alex Freeman."

"Alex?" Harper sounded surprised. The name meant nothing to me.

"I know, I know. He was such a nerd in high school. I hardly knew he was alive. We stumbled into each other on the WSU campus. He's a nuclear scientist now. Anyway, it was good to see a familiar face; he asked me to coffee and, as they say, the rest is history."

Harper's smile was genuine. "That's great. Congratulations."

"Thanks." Becca finished taking Harper's vitals, and after writing down the details, she left the room.

"Wow," Harper said, "I can't believe Alex and Becca are engaged. He was such a nerd and she, if you remember, was the yearbook editor and class president. I would never have seen the two of them together."

My memories of high school were vague at best. My main concern at the time was holding our family together. "Mom always said to forget the sports heroes and take more notice of the nerds instead. She claimed they were the ones who were destined to make something of themselves."

"Good advice," Harper murmured, just as the door opened and Dr. Annie entered the room.

Reading over the chart, she sat on the stool before looking up and giving us both a big smile. "Well, Harper, what seems to be the problem?"

"For starters, I've got a rash again."

"I've seen my fair share of those this summer," she said, crossing her legs and relaxing. "The heat, the sand, the moisture. Better let me look at it."

Harper unfastened her blouse so Annie could examine

her side. From what I could see the rash was minor, just a little red, but probably annoying. Despite remembering that her first diagnosis of leukemia had started with hives, I was convinced we were overreacting. It was a summer rash. Big deal, right?

"This looks like a heat rash, nothing serious," Annie said, confirming my suspicion. The stress eased from between my shoulder blades. Harper seemed to relax, too, as we both released the tension we'd held on to for the last several hours.

"You mentioned some chest pain?" Annie asked, looking down at the notes Becca had taken.

Harper nodded.

"When did that start?"

My sister glanced at me and then away. It was the same look she'd had when she was younger and knew she'd done something wrong. "A few weeks ago."

Last night was the first time she'd mentioned anything about a tightness in her chest. "Harper," I said, my mind whirling. Suddenly, it all made sense. This was the reason she hadn't been able to make the climb to Camp Muir on Mount Rainier. "Was that the problem with the climb?"

Harper shrugged. "My chest barely hurt then, but it does now."

"Let me take a listen," Annie said, and placed the stethoscope against Harper's chest.

My heart raced as Annie instructed Harper to breathe in deeply and then release, repeating the request twice more. Then she reached for the digital chart and scrolled up, read something, and her face relaxed. "Good report on your latest blood work. That's great."

Both Harper and I waited for her thoughts, almost leaning forward at the same time, eager for the diagnosis.

"I think what we're dealing with here is walking pneumonia," Annie said. "I'd like to order an X-ray. You can have it taken right down the hall."

My relief was instantaneous. Walking pneumonia made perfect sense. My mind had automatically gone down dark alleys with monsters lurking behind every door, ready to pounce and take my sister from me.

Annie wrote out a slip, handed it to Harper, and directed us to the diagnostic imaging unit across the hall from the clinic. No appointment was necessary, so Harper went up to the desk and handed the receptionist the paper Dr. Annie had given her.

"You can head home if you want," Harper said to me. She looked greatly relieved. It all sort of added up. Harper hadn't been herself for a while now, moping around, depressed. It seemed as if everything she'd planned and worked for had fallen through. Nothing felt right with her, and it hadn't in some time. While she hadn't said anything to me, she'd been worried. Afraid. She'd refused to deal with this, held back by fear, choosing to hope it would all go away on its own. Only now that the pain in her chest had worsened did she take the necessary steps to face the future.

I should have known. Should have paid more attention, especially lately. I'd been doing my best to play by Harper's rules and be the sister she wanted instead of mothering her. In the process I'd pushed my concerns aside and concentrated more on how much I missed Sean.

"I'd like to stay, if you don't mind."

"Sure." Most likely Dr. Annie was right about the diagnosis, but it made me feel good that Harper still wanted me by her side.

After a few minutes, Harper was taken back for the X-ray. While I waited, I reached for my phone, eager to see if I'd heard from Sean. A text message from him came up right away.

Arrived. Miserably hot and tired. Missing you.

I read his few words and placed my hand over my heart. I missed him, too. How quickly he'd become an important part of my life.

For several minutes I considered how best to reply. I wanted to tell him that Harper was at the doctor's getting an X-ray, but feared that would alarm him unnecessarily.

Miss you, too. Be safe.

His reply came quickly.

Always.

It didn't take long for Harper to reappear. We were instructed to return to Dr. Annie's office, where once again we sat in the clinic's waiting room. Harper smiled and I realized how long it'd been since I'd seen my sister genuinely happy. A while. It hurt that she hadn't felt free to share her concerns with me. I wondered if she'd shared any of this with John, and hoped that she had.

The waiting room was empty, and we sat for several minutes, discussing what we wanted for dinner. My sister suggested vegetarian pizza, but I was more in the mood for Chinese takeout. Neither of which was especially great, health-wise, something we wouldn't normally consider. This was to be a celebration. Dr. Annie would write out a prescription and we'd return home, our minds free from worry.

Finally, Becca called us back into the same exam room where we'd been sequestered earlier. Dr. Annie followed directly behind her. She had her laptop with her, and she wasn't smiling as she looked over the X-ray. I could see there would be no pizza or chicken chow mein tonight.

"What is it?" I asked, breaking into the silence.

"The X-ray shows a shadow," Dr. Annie said.

Puzzled, Harper and I looked at each other, both of us shocked into silence. I found words first. "What does that mean?"

"It could mean all sorts of things." She looked to Harper. "Because of your medical history, I want you to head to Aberdeen, to the ER. This late in the afternoon, it'd be impossible to get you into a doctor's office."

Harper reached for my hand, her grip punishing.

I waited until we were outside before I spoke. "Let's not panic. Remember, your blood tests showed you were in perfect health. We need to think positively. Like Dr. Annie said, it could be any number of things. This doesn't necessarily mean it's cancer."

For the life of me I don't know how we made the forty-minute drive in one piece. I barely remembered getting into the car, traveling into the city, and locating the hospital. Neither of us spoke. Not a single word during the entire drive.

When we walked into the emergency room, I paused,

shocked to find the entire room was crowded with the sick and injured awaiting their turn. After checking in, we were fortunate to locate two seats together. A baby coughed next to me and the man sitting directly across held a towel around his bleeding hand.

An hour passed. Then another before Harper was called in for a more detailed look at her lungs. Waiting for the results seemed to take an eternity. I connected with Shirley and asked her to fill in for me at Bean There the next morning. Alice would cover the front and I was grateful. Before long I'd need to hire a replacement, as the teenager would be leaving for college in a couple of weeks. So many thoughts spun through my head, colliding with one another.

Just after midnight, we were given the results. From the physician's sober look, I knew it wasn't good. The scan revealed a tumor on Harper's lung. It was cancerous.

Less than a month after the lab results showed my sister to be in robust health, the leukemia was back in the form of a rare chest tumor.

A choked gasp filled the room before I realized it had come from me. "No," I whispered, panic rising in me. "It can't be. Her blood work showed no signs of cancer a month ago."

"I'm sorry," Dr. Echols said. "Is there someone you'd like me to call?"

If he meant a priest or a family member I didn't know. All I could manage was to stare at him, unable to answer.

Harper was the one who came to her senses first. "Thank you. What should we do next?"

"I'm going to admit you."

"Now?" I asked. He wouldn't do that if this wasn't serious.

"Yes. I'm reaching out to University of Washington Medical Center. That was where your sister was treated earlier, correct?"

With my throat completely dry, it was impossible to answer.

"Yes, that's where I was treated the first time," Harper answered. She was the adult in this. Not me. I was in shock, unable to put together a coherent thought.

I remained in a stupor; it felt as if someone had zapped me with a stun gun. I was frozen, hardly able to function.

We waited until three that morning before a bed was available. Dealing with the shock of it, I knew I was incapable of making the return drive to Oceanside. Once Harper was given a gown and had a bed, the nurse handed me a pillow. Fortunately, the chair could be made into some semblance of a bed, not that I expected to get much sleep. Harper drifted off and I suspected she'd been given a sedative. Frankly, I could use one myself.

As dawn approached, the shadows leaped about the walls in the room like demons sent to torment me. My head was full of all my sister had endured in her first fight against cancer. I remembered how deathly ill the chemotherapy had made her. The loss of her beautiful blond hair. She lost so much weight I barely recognized her. Here we were again.

Round two.

Harper would need to deal with it all one more time. My heart was sick. I couldn't wrap my head around it. Not again. Oh God, please not again.

Knowing Lucas would be up early, I slipped out of Harper's room and went down the hallway to a waiting area. It wasn't quite five yet. Sitting in the chair, near the edge of the cushion, I stared down at my phone. My throat clogged. A minute passed before I found the courage to push the button that would connect with him.

"This better be important," Lucas barked into the receiver. My brother never had been much of a morning person.

"It's Willa," I choked out.

"I know who this is. Is it Dad again?"

Dad? I hadn't thought to call him. The fear of what this news would do to him felt like someone slammed a hard fist against my chest, knocking me off-center, losing even more of my precarious balance.

"No. It's not Dad."

The silence was heartbreaking.

Finally, Lucas spoke, his voice a husky whisper. "Is it Harper?"

For the life of me, I couldn't answer. With a sudden surge of uncontrollable emotion, I burst into sobs. Covering my mouth, I tried to stop, to regain control of myself. I knew what we faced.

"Willa, tell me."

My brother's words broke through the fog of shock and fear that all but suffocated me. Sucking in a deep, controlling breath, I waited until the shaking stopped and I could breathe normally once again.

"It's back," I managed. No need to explain further.

The line went silent.

"Where are you?"

"Aberdeen. I'll know more when I talk to the doctor. He said something about sending Harper back to Seattle. It's where she wants to go, as her friend John is an attending physician there."

"I thought the blood work was good?" His disbelief reflected mine. This couldn't be happening. We should have had more of a warning. Only a few weeks ago everything had been perfect. Our fears had been vanquished. All was well.

Only it wasn't.

"She has a cancerous tumor on her lung."

"I'll call you later this afternoon." Lucas was a take-charge kind of man. "You can tell me what you know then."

How calm and in control he sounded.

I was a wreck.

"We can do this," he told me.

The confidence in his voice settled over me. I needed that, desperately.

"Harper can do this," he added. "We'll be there with her. She got through this once; she can do it again."

We ended the call. The nurse, who must have heard my sobs, brought me a cup of coffee and sat with me for a few minutes. Before she returned to her station, she gently squeezed my shoulder. It was almost as if she knew I was going to need all the internal fortitude I could muster.

Chapter 20

Willa

We had three days at home. Three days before Harper would check back into the University of Washington Medical Center. Three short days to prepare ourselves for the battle. Harper was strong, far stronger than I was. I did my best to hide my anxiety, without much success. My sister was the one assuring me, the one lifting my spirits. That she would need to go through the entire horrific process of chemo again seemed outrageous and grossly unfair.

I wasn't sleeping well, barely eating, dreading every minute, but gearing up for the fight. I refused to let Harper go through this alone. Like before, I intended to be at her side, her advocate with the medical team. It went without saying that Lucas would be with us, and Chantelle, too. I was fortunate to have Shirley, who was willing to take over for me at Bean There. Leesa would supplement at the counter after Alice left for college, which was a relief as well.

Lucas and Chantelle's engagement party was coming up. Harper and I were attending, and then Harper would go directly from the party to check in at the hospital. We convinced Lucas not to tell Chantelle about Harper until after the party, for fear it would put a damper on everyone's mood. This was Lucas's and our soon-to-be sister's time, and Harper was determined not to do anything to ruin it. I agreed with her decision.

It was left to me to tell our father the news. At first, I toyed with the idea of keeping Dad in the dark for fear the news would send him spiraling back into the bottle. In the end I decided my father was an adult. Harper was his daughter. His favorite. He was responsible for his own actions. I would do what I could to help him, but my priority was Harper.

Before we left for Seattle, Harper went out for the evening with Leesa. I was grateful she had such a supportive and encouraging friend. Knowing they would be gone for some time, I invited Dad to join me for dinner. I cooked his favorite meal, pork chops and fried potatoes with onions. No matter what I cooked, he almost always had an excuse for why he couldn't come to dinner: He was scheduled to work. He had someplace he needed to be. He was meeting a friend. I'd heard it all before.

Something in my voice must have alerted him to the fact that this wasn't a run-of-the-mill invitation. This wasn't the time to come up with a convenient excuse. I sincerely doubted it was my pork chops that persuaded him.

Dad arrived a half hour after Harper left with Leesa for

a night on the town. I wouldn't begrudge my sister this. To my way of thinking, she should have all the fun she could now, especially with what lay before her.

"Hi, Dad." Holding the screen door open for him, I stepped aside so he could enter the apartment.

Like a whirling dervish, Snowball, a ball of white, raced from the living room and into the kitchen.

"When did you get a cat?" Dad broke into a huge grin.

"I didn't. Harper did."

Amusement brightened his eyes. "She's a little fluffball, isn't she?"

I grinned as I carried our plates to the table. "She certainly is." I had no idea what we would do with this kitten while Harper was in Seattle. It seemed a shame to leave the poor thing on her own for days on end.

Dad sat across from me at the table. "This is a nice surprise. Where's Harper?"

I lowered my gaze, fearing he would be able to read my worries. "She's out for the night."

He reached for his fork. "She's turned into a beautiful young woman, hasn't she?" Then he turned his attention to me. "When are you going to find yourself a young man, Willa?"

This wasn't the direction I wanted our conversation to go, but decided it was as good a time as any to mention Sean. "Actually, Dad, I am seeing someone. His name is Sean O'Malley and he's a photographer."

"Really?" Dad's eyes widened, as if he was surprised by my news.

"He's currently on assignment in the Philippines."

Impressed, Dad arched his brows.

"Would you like to meet him?" I asked.

"Of course, when the time is right." He grinned and I could see that he was pleased.

Dad attacked his meal with gusto. I suspected he didn't often eat a home-cooked meal. He didn't lack for meals. Working at the casino, he had access to several restaurants. I noticed he'd gained a middle-aged spread since he'd started his job as a blackjack dealer and hoped it was from food and not alcohol. When he finished, he planted his hands on his stomach. "I can't recall the last time I enjoyed dinner more."

"Thank you, Dad."

"You cook for that young man of yours and he's sure to stick around."

Smiling, I said, "I'll do that." Standing, I cleared away our dishes. Without asking, I poured us each a mug of coffee and carried them into the living room, silently inviting my father to join me.

Dad claimed the sofa and I took the chair. Leaning forward and placing both of my hands around the mug, I looked to my father. "I wish there was an easier way to say this." I swallowed hard.

"Willa? You in trouble?" Instantly he stiffened.

I shook my head.

"You need money for that coffee place of yours? I don't got much, but I'll give you what I have."

His unexpected offer, his concern, touched me, and tears

welled in my eyes. If only it was that easy. If only all it took was a bank loan to cure my sister, how much simpler life would be.

"It's not me, Dad," I said, struggling to get the words out. "It's Harper."

All the blood drained from my father's face, and for half a second I feared he would drop the mug or pass out. He opened his mouth to speak and then closed it. Tears welled in his eyes.

"The cancer's back?"

I nodded. "There's a tumor on her lung. It's a rare form of leukemia."

"Oh Willa, no. No."

Setting aside my coffee, I joined Dad on the sofa and the two of us hugged. His tears fell against my shoulder as we clung to each other.

After he broke away from me and composed himself, he asked, "Where is she now?"

"With friends. She needs this time away. It would be hard for her to see you this upset."

Nodding, Dad sniffled and ran his forearm beneath his nose. "Last time . . . I failed you and Harper. Lucas, too. I want to help. I want to be there for all of you. What do you need me to do? Tell me. If you want me at that hospital with you, I'll find a way, no matter what. If you need anything, anything at all, you call me."

That did it for me and I broke into tears. My father had floundered, taken to booze when the family needed him most. From the determined glint in his eye I knew he would do his best to not abandon us again. We needed him. Harper needed him, but so did Lucas and so did I.

"Is there anything I can help you with now?" he asked.

Snowball appeared, racing across the floor, chasing some imaginary foe. "Actually, will you take care of Snowball?" I asked. It would help not to worry about Harper's silly cat, and it would make my dad feel like he was contributing, which he was.

"Of course. You don't hesitate to call me, you hear? Any time you need me, I'll find a way to be there."

"I will, Dad." We hugged again.

"I love you, baby girl."

"Love you back," I said, my arms tightening around him. I couldn't remember the last time I told my father I loved him or heard those words from him.

"Come on, Willa," Harper urged. "Let me paint your toenails, too."

"Not lilac," I protested. We'd been in a flurry getting ready for Lucas and Chantelle's engagement party, hosted by her sister, who was to be the maid of honor.

"The lilac matches my hair." Harper's smile briefly faded.

If her last experience was any indication, my sister would be losing her beautiful silver/lilac-colored hair within a few weeks. In her first bout with cancer she'd been completely bald, although, ill as she was, her hair was the least of her concerns.

"How about blood red for me," I said, needing to turn her thoughts away from what awaited her.

"Got it," she said, dipping her hand into the plastic basket at her side and pulling out a bottle of deep red nail polish.

I pulled my foot out of the basin of hot water and reached for a towel to dry it off. "So what's with the gift?" I asked. Harper had returned earlier with a brightly wrapped gift box and set it down by her purse. She'd said it was for the happy couple. "It's an engagement party, not a shower, you realize."

"I do, but I don't know that I'll be able to attend any of her wedding showers, so I decided to give her my gift now."

"Which is?" I couldn't help being curious.

Harper jiggled her eyebrows. "Something Lucas is going to love."

"Harper!" I could well imagine my sister picking out skimpy black lingerie for Chantelle. Rolling my eyes, I finished drying off my feet so my sister could paint my toes.

"Have you heard from Sean?" she asked, as she unscrewed the top off the polish.

"Not much. He's out in the boonies, but it sounds like it's going well." Sean had explained this assignment to me before he'd left. It had something to do with the effects of climate change in the ocean waters in that area of the world. From the last brief email that arrived, it sounded like the project had proved to be more involved with the changes they had already found due to the drop in the water temperature, which affected nearly every aspect of life on this tiny island.

Keeping her head lowered, Harper continued to spread red polish across my big toenail. "Did you mention . . . tell him about me?"

"Not really." With Sean half a world away, it didn't seem

right to dump this news on him, seeing there was nothing he could do. He couldn't fly home, and if he did try to make such arrangements it would leave the entire project in a bind. Leaving could hurt him professionally, and I refused to be party to anything that would damage the career he'd worked so hard to build.

"What did you say?"

"Just that you were undergoing some tests and there wasn't anything to worry about." Sean hadn't questioned me further, and for that I was grateful. I doubted I could have continued with the lie.

"Good."

"I thought it was for the best."

Harper went silent before she said, "I think so, too. He's good for you, you know?"

I shrugged, not wanting to discuss Sean; that only made me miss him more. He'd been away a little more than a week and I already felt lost without him. A zillion times a day I'd think of something I wanted to tell him, something I wanted to say. Instead of moping and feeling bereft, I'd taken to writing him long letters, sort of like a journal. I wrote about my worries and fears for Harper, about this battle we were about to engage in and how surprised I was by my father's determination to help. I told him news from Bean There and how grateful I was for my staff and their willingness to lean in and give me the space so that I could be with my sister. At the end of each entry, I wrote how much I missed him and that I was quickly falling in love with him.

"You're going to have beautiful babies," she added.

"Stop."

"I'm serious."

"Harper," I protested, "you're getting way ahead of yourself with Sean and me."

"Mark my words!"

I held up my hand, embarrassed and uneasy to be talking about the future, especially knowing that there might not be one for Harper.

We left for Seattle the following morning. Harper had a small bag packed with essentials while at the hospital. A meeting with the team treating her had advised us that following two rounds of chemo she would need a lymphocyte infusion to fight the tumor, since her white blood cells were depleted and unable to aid the body's fight against the disease. The good news was that Harper would be able to leave the hospital between the chemotherapy sessions, although she would need to remain close by. We were fortunate that Lucas had a two-bedroom apartment and we would be able to stay there.

Harper's spirits lifted when she learned that John, one of the men she'd trained with for the Mount Rainier climb, was part of the medical team that had been assigned to her. I remembered how her face lit up when she first mentioned him.

With the dire news that the cancer was back, I'd been paying close attention to my sister. It may well have been my imagination, my fears leaping to the forefront of my mind; nevertheless, I noticed a decline in her coloring and in her general appearance, as if she'd recently recovered from a bad case of the flu.

Harper gripped my hand hard enough to capture my attention. "I want you to promise me that if I don't come out of this, you aren't going to mope around, bemoaning my fate."

"You're going to make it, Harper." I refused to listen to anything that suggested otherwise.

"I know you, big sister, and how you are. You seem to think your resolve alone will pull me through. You're strong. So am I. We're going to fight this together, but if the worst happens, I want you to deal with it, got me?"

"Who's mothering whom now?" I jested.

"You're going to do fine without me," Harper whispered.

That was the first note of defeat I'd heard in her voice since we got the news. Part of me wanted to argue with her, insist she needed to have a better attitude. She was right, though: As much as I would have liked to, I didn't control the future.

I double-checked my suitcase to be sure I had everything I needed for the next month. Lucas had cleared out the second bedroom in his apartment so I could stay with him. He and Chantelle would take over in the evenings and on weekends as needed. That would give me a chance to return to Oceanside to check on my little café.

Harper's bag was half the size of mine. She brought a few personal items. A photo of our mother, her Bible, and lip gloss, along with socks and a knitted shawl. The chemo often left her chilled, shaking with the cold, and she wanted to be prepared.

"What about a wig?" I asked.

She shook her head. "Not this time. Bald is beautiful."

The engagement party was fun and exactly what both Harper and I needed before we checked into the hospital. We played silly games, drank wine and spiked punch, and stuffed ourselves with a variety of appetizers and cupcakes, artfully displayed in the shape of a wedding dress.

Lucas had promised to tell Chantelle after the party where Harper and I were headed and that I would be living with Lucas for the foreseeable future. My sister insisted she didn't want anything to interfere with Chantelle and Lucas's wedding plans. The date had been set and the arrangements made. No matter what the future held for her, she wanted them to go through with the wedding whether she was there as a bridesmaid or not. I felt she was being a pessimist again but didn't want to waste her energy or mine arguing.

Once we left the party, Lucas drove us to the hospital. He dropped us off at the front door while he went to park the car.

Harper and I stood frozen in the hospital foyer, unable to move.

My sister was the one who propelled me forward. "Let's do this," she said.

I nodded and followed her to the reception desk.

We were prepared and ready for battle.

Chapter 21

Sean

The heat of the Philippines was the most intense I'd ever endured. The assignment was multifaceted. Our mission was to look first at the offshore fisheries and then later, if time allowed, the mangrove forest, seeking to document the damage done by climate change. I was working with an entire team of scientists and naturalists.

The days were long, and my thoughts continually drifted to Willa and Oceanside. Long before I boarded the plane that would take me halfway across the world, I knew I would miss her, but I had no clue how strong those feelings would be.

The frustrating part was my inability to connect with her. My guess was that she was working too hard, not caring for herself, because she felt it was her duty to take care of everyone else first. With her brother's wedding coming in a few months, I could imagine she was doing all she could to make the wedding cake of the century. Curious, I wondered which of the four flavors the couple had chosen. I was hoping for coconut.

Exhausted after a morning-long session of photographs, I returned to our campsite to download the photos I'd gotten earlier. I'd promised Willa I'd be safe and thanked God she couldn't see some of the crazy chances I took to get the perfect shot.

This was an important assignment, my most prestigious to date. In the oppressive heat of the afternoon beating down on me, I faced the naked truth. I was scared to death of failing. From the moment I joined the rest of the team, I'd been driven by the fear of failure. I was willing to do most anything to get the picture, and that included putting myself at risk. Danger can be an aphrodisiac for some. Not me. All I could think about was how furious Willa would be if I returned home injured or sick again. The thought made me smile. How important Willa's opinion had become to me.

Sweat rolled down my back as I bent over my computer, downloading hundreds of photographs. Working in the middle of the day was nearly impossible. The light was best in the early morning and late afternoon. Dawn and dusk. My afternoons were spent downloading and editing, napping when I could, writing, trying to keep cool, and missing Willa. Missing home.

Doug, the leader of our team, returned to our camp, mumbling under his breath about the necessity of a trip into the nearest town. More of a village with dirt streets and a few minor businesses. I barely remembered seeing it when we first arrived. Whatever it was he needed went straight over my head. All I heard was what mattered to me. Small as this village was, there might be an opportunity to find an internet café. Even the smallest of towns would sometimes boast of one. I was desperate to connect with Willa and check in with my family, too.

When my mother learned I was taking another assignment on a remote island in the Philippines, she nearly blew a gasket. She's always been a worrier, and my leaving again so soon after suffering with typhoid sent her on a rampage. I was surprised she didn't connect with Willa and demand that the two of them do whatever they could to stop me from leaving. For all I knew, Mom might have done exactly that.

Three of the five-man team opted to take the hour-long ride into town. The road, such as it was, was unpaved and filled with potholes big enough to swim in. Thankfully, Doug was an experienced driver and managed to avoid the hazards.

At one point we got behind a farmer herding ten head of cattle down a narrow section of road. We were forced to follow him until the path widened enough for us to get past.

While Doug and Larry went about their business, I found a hole-in-the-wall restaurant with internet access, if you could call a few mismatched tables and chairs on a dirt floor a restaurant. Knowing it would be appreciated if I made a purchase, I ordered a coffee, found a seat, and opened my computer. In my eagerness, my hand trembled. Two weeks, fourteen mere days, out of communication with Willa and I shook like an addict, needing a fix.

Once I was able to log in, I scanned emails until I saw

Willa's name. The first message was brief. After a few words asking about my welfare and wishing me success, she casually mentioned Harper was in the hospital. All Willa had mentioned earlier was that her sister was undergoing a few tests. Whatever the results were couldn't have been good. I frowned as I scanned her email a second time, hoping to read between the lines. I knew Willa worried incessantly about Harper's health. Seeing that she didn't elaborate led me to believe there was more to this than what she was saying.

Perhaps it was the flu? Or a cold? But those rarely led to hospital stays unless they had developed into something far more serious. I pondered her brief message again, remembering Harper's troubles in making the climb she'd prepared for all summer.

In the space of a single heartbeat it came to me. Could it be that Willa was telling me Harper's cancer had returned? I didn't want to leap to conclusions, but my mind refused to let go of the possibility. I felt my chest tighten, and for the next moment it seemed as if my heart stopped. The first bout had nearly claimed Harper's life. She'd recovered, but I didn't think Willa ever had. She'd lived in fear of her sister's future.

After a few deep breaths, I debated how best to respond as I scanned down to her most recent email. I hurriedly read her message. Again, it was short, as if she was afraid of saying too much. She told me she missed me and how she longed for me to hurry home. I felt the angst in those two lines, the fear and tension. Her next words confirmed my worst suspicions.

I'm staying with Lucas in Seattle while Harper is in the hospital. Please, my love, hurry home.

For the life of me I didn't know how I was going to tell her that it didn't look like we were going to be able to wrap up this assignment in the time allotted. Already Doug was talking about a two-week extension. From six weeks to eight. Maybe longer.

The one bright spot in her entire email was that she called me "my love."

I answered her, typing as fast as my fingers could manage, before Doug and Larry returned and I would be forced to leave. I let her know how sorry I was to hear about Harper and how desperately I wished I was there with her. I spoke of the job and what we were doing, the progress we'd made, and how much there was yet to be done.

Looking to take her mind off Harper and her current situation, I described the local people we'd met and worked with, their beauty and willingness to do whatever we asked, their generosity of spirit. I mentioned some of what I'd learned about the culture and how I spent my days and nights.

Hoping a long email from me would help ease her mind, I outlined what a typical day was like for me and the rest of the crew. I mentioned my fears and the importance of this assignment to my career and how most days I felt like I had failed until I was able to review the shots I'd taken. At night, when sleep came, I generally felt like I had the best job in the world. That said, it didn't nearly compensate for how desperately I missed her, how anxious I was to get home. I assured her I would do anything in my power to get back to Seattle as quickly as I could manage.

I pushed send and watched the message disappear. If only I could hear her voice. If only . . .

Checking my watch, I saw that it was a little after five in the afternoon. Seattle time was around two in the morning. I hated to wake Willa and toyed with letting her sleep, but what if this was the only chance I had to connect with her the entire trip?

Taking the chance, I logged my phone on to Wi-Fi and called her. It rang four times and I was afraid it would go to voicemail before I heard her groggy voice.

"Hello?" It was more question than greeting and laced with concern.

"Willa, it's me."

"Sean. Oh Sean." After saying my name, she immediately burst into tears.

"Baby, baby, what is it?" The pain in her voice broke my heart.

It took several moments for her to control the hiccupping sobs enough to speak. "Did you get my email?"

"Yes, that's why I'm calling. I'm in this village and only have a few minutes. Tell me. What's going on? Why is Harper in the hospital? What were the test results?" I pounded her with questions, not giving her a chance to answer one before I asked another.

"Her earlier blood work was good and we assumed everything was great. It isn't. She got another rash and then she complained about chest pain. When we went to see

Dr. Annie, we all assumed it was walking pneumonia. After a round of X-rays and more tests at the hospital we learned there's a cancerous tumor on her lung."

She drew in a deep breath before she continued.

"It's bad, Sean. Worse than before, and I didn't think that was possible. On a positive note, John is working closely with her oncologist. Harper's in Seattle for treatment now . . . the chemotherapy is supposed to be one of the best available. I was with her today when it was administered, and the nurse checked the dose twice. She said she'd never seen this dose before and wanted to be sure she was following the doctor's instructions."

"Oh Willa. I am so sorry. How's Harper holding up?"

"She's doing great. She never complains. The nurses and doctors are wonderful. They all love her. Everyone does. John is with her as much as his schedule allows. He's been wonderful."

"What happens after the chemotherapy?"

"This is only the first session. After this week she'll stay with me at Lucas's apartment until her white cells are built up enough for her to proceed with the second round of chemo." She hesitated before she could continue. "It's killing her, Sean, killing her. She's desperately ill, worse than before . . . I don't know how she does this day after day. It's more than I can bear, seeing her like this."

"What can I do?" I asked, desperately wanting to be there for Willa and her family.

"Come home when you can. That's the best thing you can do."

I could feel how badly she needed me at her side. Willa was only so strong, and she needed me to lean on, to comfort and support her. I hated that it wasn't possible, and coward that I was, I didn't mention the extension, and left her to read it in the email I'd sent earlier.

I knew it wasn't only Harper who required Willa's support. "How's your father dealing with the news?"

"Dad is doing better than ever . . . which is a surprise. When I told him that Harper's cancer was back, he said he'd do everything he could to be there for all of us, and he has. He calls every day for an update and has been talking to Pastor McDonald, praying for us all. Snowball is with him and seems to have adjusted to her new home."

That was good news. "And you?"

She paused and sniffled. "Oh Sean, I'm so afraid. Harper has had a horrible reaction to the chemotherapy. She's constantly sick and is already losing her beautiful hair. She barely eats and is losing a pound a day if not more. She looks . . ." She stopped and sobbed into the phone before she was able to continue. "She looks like death."

"Oh baby, I wish I was there with you."

"Lucas and Chantelle are thinking of moving up their wedding date. It means making a big adjustment on their part. We talked about it this evening, and Chantelle is going to talk to the hotel about the possibility. If it can be arranged, we'll do it in the time between the two treatments."

I closed my eyes, hating like the devil to tell her, but I refused to give her false hope. "I'll miss the wedding."

Silence.

"Our job is taking longer than anyone anticipated," I admitted, my words heavy with reluctance. "If I could, I'd fly home tomorrow. But there's only one vehicle, and the most common form of transportation here is oxcart. I don't have a choice but to stay with the team and see this through."

"I know." Resignation coated her words. "I know."

"As soon as I can, I'll get the first flight out, I promise."

She seemed to be drawing on a source of inner strength, because when she next spoke her voice was calm and controlled. I couldn't sense any anger from her. Perhaps a little disappointment, if that.

"I understand. This is important work and you're needed there."

I would forever love her for her understanding. Guilt at letting her down was eating at me like piranhas in a feeding frenzy. If only I could be in two places at once.

"Lucas and Chantelle have been wonderful. I spend my days with Harper and then Chantelle relieves me after work so I can get something to eat. Lucas comes and sits with us in the evenings until Harper can rest."

"What about Bean There?"

"Shirley, God bless her, is filling in, and Leesa and a couple of Harper's other friends are taking the morning shift. All have some bistro experience from their college days, so I don't worry as much as I would otherwise.

"Originally, I intended to drive back to Oceanside once a week, but I can see that will be impossible. At least not now. Maybe after this round of chemo I'll be able to manage it."

I covered my forehead with my free hand, feeling wretched to be away when Willa and her family needed me.

"Sean?"

"Yes, my love?"

"I need to tell you . . . something." Her voice trembled and lowered to a mere whisper. She paused, as if she found it difficult to get the words out.

"What is it, love?" I asked, sensing that whatever she was about to say was important, more important than anything else she'd said to this point.

"I have this feeling, this gut feeling that won't go away. I . . . I haven't said anything to Lucas or Chantelle or anyone else. I can't. I won't. But that doesn't change what I know in my gut . . . in my heart."

"You can tell me," I whispered.

Just then Doug burst into the café. "You ready?" he demanded, eager to return to our camp before we lost daylight.

"Give me a minute," I pleaded.

Naturally, Willa heard the exchange. "You need to go."

"Tell me what you want to say," I urged.

"Sean," she said, her voice full of tears. "I'm getting a vibe from the nurses . . . no one has come right out and said it aloud, but I've heard whispers. John is worried. He hasn't said it. It's a feeling . . . The nurses, even John . . . they don't think Harper will be well enough to leave the hospital between her chemo sessions. I'm afraid they don't believe Harper will ever go home again."

"You don't know that," I countered.

"I refuse to believe it. I can't. We need to remain positive. She beat cancer once. She can again . . . only it feels much different this time. Worse, somehow, and I didn't think that was possible."

Chapter 22

Willa

Ten days after hearing from Sean, it was exactly as I'd feared. When the chemotherapy was completed, Harper remained too sick to leave the hospital. The short break between chemotherapy sessions, when we'd hoped she would build up her strength and white blood cells while staying at Lucas's apartment, wasn't possible. Harper was far too sick. I'd prayed that once the infusions stopped, her appetite would return. It didn't. She ate less and less.

Chantelle thought if she brought Harper her favorite pizza that would be incentive enough for her to eat. She did her best, nibbling at a single slice, but couldn't manage more than what a bird would peck at. It said much more than any of us could bear to say aloud. She was going downhill quickly, far faster than we ever dared dream.

"Stop looking at me like I'm on my deathbed," Harper insisted. "I'm getting better; be patient. This stuff takes time.

Ask John . . . You're all looking so gloomy. You're being ridiculous."

"Am not," I muttered.

"Are too," Harper countered in banter, like we were children. Then, as if she was eager to change the subject, she asked me about Sean. "Have you heard from him lately?"

I shook my head.

"You know he'd contact you if he could."

"I know." Everything would be easier for me if he was here. I needed him, if for nothing more than to rest my head against his shoulder and let him hold me. He would absorb my fears, comfort me, and help me maintain a positive attitude.

"John's been wonderful," Harper whispered, already weakened by our short conversation. "I could love a man as caring and gentle as he is."

I strongly suspected Harper was already in love with the physician. She held her feelings close to her heart and never spoke of her feelings for him to me before now.

"Did you know his mother died from breast cancer when he was in his teens? It was because of her that he chose a career in medicine."

"He certainly has the heart for it."

"He does." Her words were a mere whisper, as she was already tired out from the effort to carry even a short conversation. Squeezing her hand, I left the room, fearing I would make everything worse if I allowed her to witness my tears.

Chantelle joined me a few minutes later. "She's doing her best to put on a brave face through this."

Leaning heavily against the wall, I exhaled, trying to forestall the tears. Emotion was close to the surface and had been ever since Harper had entered the hospital.

Wouldn't you know it, the brief time I was out of the room the physician in charge of Harper's case along with John came in to discuss the latest round of test results with her. This was how our day went: We hung on to the hope that her bone marrow would produce the necessary white blood cells to ignite Harper's immune system and fight off the leukemia.

Despite our prayers, every day the results were disappointing. It was hard to hold on when it was bad news followed by more bad news. We were left to watch Harper grow weaker and sicker every day.

It shocked me how quickly my sister had declined. She was bald now and wore a cute lilac-colored bow on the side of her hairless head.

"Leesa and Carrie are coming on Saturday," I remembered. Their visit was sure to raise Harper's spirits, and mine, too.

"Any more word from Sean?" Chantelle asked.

I shook my head. Although our conversation had been brief, Sean and I were fortunate to have had those few minutes. Remote as he was, I didn't expect to hear from him again. I kept my phone tucked away on silent at the bottom of my purse, checking intermittently. If Sean had phoned during the day, I would have missed his call. Because it came in the middle of the night, we'd been able to talk.

"Did you hear back from the hotel?" I asked, knowing Chantelle had been waiting to hear about the possibility of changing the wedding date. It would be difficult at this point, seeing that the invitations had already been mailed out. That Lucas and Chantelle were willing to consider rescheduling their wedding said a lot about the kind of people they were.

Chantelle's eyes immediately skirted away from mine. "The hotel is booked solid. I've checked every other venue in Oceanside and there's not one available. I've looked in Seattle, too. Unfortunately, this late in the game, it's impossible."

After much discussion in the end it was decided that it would be best to keep the original early-December date.

As hard as I tried, I couldn't make myself entertain the notion that Harper wouldn't be alive come December. The words nearly stuck in my throat; nevertheless, they needed to be said. "I don't know if Harper will be up to participating as a bridesmaid."

"Are you suggesting I make contingency plans?" Chantelle asked.

I bit into my lip so hard I was afraid I'd drawn blood. "I . . . think that might be best." Although Lucas and Chantelle did their part to support Harper, I was the one who'd spent the most time with her. Seeing her decline a little more each day, I feared the worst while doing my utmost to remain positive.

"We need a meeting with Dr. Carroll and John," Chantelle announced, wanting to hear for herself what we should expect.

My mind was stuck on the fact that the lab results had showed no improvement. Harper seemed to be losing ground, when we'd fully expected her to be gaining. After the first chemotherapy session, we all accepted that Harper was far too weak to endure another round. Everything that could traditionally be done to help had already been tried.

Chantelle walked over to the nurses' station and spoke to the supervisor. When she returned, she said, "Dr. Carroll has asked to meet with all of us tomorrow afternoon. John will be with him."

By "all of us," I knew she meant that Harper would be in on the meeting. That made sense, although I'd prefer to keep her in the dark for as long as possible. If the news was debilitating, then I'd rather she not hear it. I felt it was my duty to protect my sister from as much of the negative as I could. She'd hate it if she knew that was what I was doing. She'd insist I was mothering her again, and I was. I couldn't help myself.

Wednesday afternoon, Lucas got off work early and met Chantelle and me in Harper's hospital room. She had a private room, which was decorated with cards and gifts from family and friends. Our father had found a stuffed white kitten so Harper would have Snowball by her side. It sat by her head, next to her pillow.

As we awaited the two physicians' arrival, Harper's phone rang. When she answered, a smile came to her.

"Hi, Daddy."

Our father had talked to Harper only a few times. He checked in with me every night to ask for an update. When it came to Harper, he found it painfully difficult. I knew this was hard for him, and I loved him even more for making the effort.

"Better, I think." She listened for several moments while Dad spoke.

She was still on the phone when John and Dr. Carroll came into the room.

"Sorry, Dad, I need to go. The doctors are here. Thanks for calling. Love you, too." She disconnected and set the phone aside. Seeing that she was sitting up in bed was a good sign. It seemed a bit of her strength had returned. That was an encouragement when we badly needed one.

Dr. Carroll, unlike John, was middle-aged, probably early fifties, tall, slim, with warm blue eyes. Over the course of the time Harper had been hospitalized I'd had numerous conversations with him, and even more with John, as he was closely following Harper's treatment strategy. Although Dr. Carroll was in charge of Harper, it was John who spent most of the time caring for her, although he wasn't the physician in charge.

Ignoring the rest of us, John's gaze immediately went to Harper, and he smiled. As I watched the two, I realized how strong his feelings were for my sister. It showed in the way he looked at her, as if he didn't notice that she was bald and shockingly thin; he saw her as the beautiful woman she was. In that instant I fell a little in love with him myself.

"Dr. Carroll, this is my family. You've met Willa." Harper motioned toward me. "This is Lucas. He's usually here after you've left for the day. And this is his fiancée, Chantelle. You've probably seen her around now and again."

The men exchanged handshakes. We all returned to our seats. Dr. Carroll stood next to Harper's bed, his expression kind but serious. A knot formed in my throat, fearing what we were about to learn.

Lucas led the conversation. "Doctor, from what I've been hearing, the lab results aren't showing the improvement in Harper's white blood cells we'd hoped to see."

"To this point, that's true," he agreed.

"You mean you believe they will?" Lucas's voice rose marginally with hope.

I sat up a bit straighter myself.

"I'm optimistic. Her body is fighting hard and we're doing everything humanly possible to give Harper every chance available. Hopefully, with a bit more time, we'll see better results."

Lucas reached for Chantelle's hand. "Our wedding is coming up soon and Harper is a bridesmaid. We're wondering if we should"—he hesitated and glanced at Harper—"if we should arrange to be married earlier than originally planned."

"Harper is an important part of our wedding, so we really want her to be there." Chantelle paused and looked at my sister. "Even if she needs to be in a wheelchair."

"Do you think that's possible?" Lucas asked.

The question hung in the air like a bomb ready to explode. The silence was eerie, filled with expectation. Dread. Fear. It seemed we all leaned forward, anticipating his response.

The two physicians exchanged a look. Dr. Carroll took

his time answering. John looked at Harper and his eyes gentled.

"Of course I can't make any guarantee; no medical professional would in good conscience," Dr. Carroll said. "However, our hope is that Harper will be able to be part of your wedding, but I can't say that one way or the other."

"What needs to happen?"

For the next fifteen minutes, Dr. Carroll updated us on the next steps planned to build up Harper's immune system. In the three years since her first battle with cancer, the advancements in treatments were truly astonishing. Although much of what he explained was lost on me, his words offered hope, and that was something we all desperately needed at this point.

"Told you," Harper said with a hint of triumph in her voice. "You're all so full of gloom and doom."

"Are there any other questions I can answer for you?" Dr. Carroll asked, ever the professional.

Lucas and Chantelle held hands and I watched as Chantelle brushed a tear from the corner of her eye. "We're good."

"Thank you, Dr. Carroll," I said as I stood. "This means everything to my family."

"Absolutely. Don't hesitate to call me anytime."

"Thank you, we will."

The atmosphere was much lighter than it had been before his arrival. Chantelle hugged Harper and then she hugged me. Lucas did the same. "This calls for a celebration," my brother declared. "A big one, with champagne and—"

"Naked male dancers," Harper inserted, and then grinned at the shocked look that came over me.

"Honestly, Willa, you can be such a stick in the mud sometimes. I was only joking."

"Maybe so, but I think John might object to you being around a lot of naked men."

To my surprise, Harper's face filled with color. "He probably would. He's been wonderful. Did you know he comes and sits with me every morning before he goes on shift? He gives me strength and encouragement. I don't know what I'd do without him."

I didn't know about his early-morning visits, but it didn't surprise me. John gave my sister all the incentive she needed to fight, and for that I would be forever grateful.

Over the next few days Harper and I had long talks. She slept a lot of the time but when she was awake, she told me about her and John's conversations. He thought of himself as an introvert who worked hard and didn't have time to date. His mother's death changed him. He was determined to do everything within his power to heal cancer patients.

Although Harper tired quickly, she encouraged me to talk about Sean and the possibility of our future together. Not being able to communicate with him was hard, although he was never far from my thoughts.

On the weekend Leesa and Carrie arrived, bubbling over with news. They brought coloring books and fancy pens and sat and colored with Harper. It was a bit awkward for me, so

I went to the hospital cafeteria for a bite to eat. Seeing that most of my meals came from the cafeteria, I was on a first-name basis with the staff.

It was hard for me to stay away from Harper's room, knowing that while well-intentioned, the arrival of her two BFFs was sure to quickly tire my sister. Sure enough, when I returned, Harper was sound asleep, a coloring pen in her hand. The book lay open in her lap. I noticed very little on either page had been colored in.

Leesa and Carrie sat silently at her bedside, coloring away, as if nothing was amiss.

"How long did she last?" I whispered, not wanting to wake Harper.

"Only a few minutes," Leesa whispered back.

Seeing the question in their eyes, I asked, "Are you okay?" I knew Harper's appearance had shocked them. She was a shell of the vibrant, outgoing, fun young woman she'd once been.

Tears filled Leesa's eyes and I noticed that Carrie struggled to hold back her own.

Leesa nodded. "I barely recognized her when we arrived. At first I thought we had the wrong room." She wiped her hand across her face, her mascara raining black streaks down her cheeks. "How could this happen so quickly?"

"It was like this when she first got leukemia," I assured both friends. "I should have better prepared you. It's bad before it gets better. She's sick now, but the turning point is coming. Think positively. That's my mantra. Believe. Hold on to hope."

I understood what Leesa and Carrie were saying. It had all come on so quickly. It shocked me that my sister had functioned so well for as long as she had, teaching yoga and fitness classes while ignoring any symptoms she might have had.

I accepted part of the blame myself. I should have paid closer attention, should have watched for the signs. In thinking back, I speculated that deep down, Harper must have somehow known. I remembered the phone call I'd had with my brother earlier that summer, mentioning all the crazy things Harper had been doing: bungee jumping and everything else. This sudden desire to climb the largest mountain of the entire Cascade mountain range. All of that had come out of the blue. It was as if my little sister's subconscious had told her to squeeze in as many life experiences as she could manage.

"She's getting better," I said again, wanting desperately to believe it myself. Dr. Carroll had given us hope and I was holding on to the thin thread with both hands, refusing to let go.

Leesa and Carrie left shortly after our conversation and I returned to my e-reader. Harper slept most of the afternoon.

Drained from her friends' visit, my sister remained asleep when Chantelle arrived. Lucas followed a short while later.

"How'd it go?" Lucas asked.

He didn't need to explain the question. Harper had talked about Leesa and Carrie driving all the way from Oceanside from the minute she'd learned they were coming. It meant a great deal to her that her friends were willing to take the long drive through heavy Seattle traffic to see her.

"I should have prepared them for the changes in Harper," I admitted, regretting that I hadn't.

"Have the test results come in for today?" Lucas asked.

Come to think of it, I hadn't heard, which was unusual. I stepped out of the room, prepared to ask the nurses, when I saw Dr. Carroll. He acknowledged me, and then came over to where I stood.

"Did I see your brother and his fiancée arrive?"

"Yes, they're here. We didn't get the test results back today."

"Yes," he said slowly, sadly. "I'm wondering if it would be possible to speak to you and your family privately?"

I swallowed down the shock of his question and nodded. "Of course."

I raced back to Harper's room to get Lucas and Chantelle.

Dr. Carroll led us to a private room and closed the door. His face was sad and somber. Lowering his eyes, he blinked and murmured, "I was hoping to see a rise in her white blood cells. This is the point I would expect her body to respond, which is why I said what I did about her participating in the wedding. The tests that came back this afternoon showed a rapid decline, worse than anything I anticipated." He drew in a harsh breath. "It might be best if you considered holding the wedding sooner rather than wait."

A cry escaped my lips before I could hold it back.

Lucas placed his hand on my shoulder.

"We have to believe," I insisted, stiffening. "We can't give up hope. It might look bad now, but it could get better, right?" My eyes pleaded with Dr. Carroll.

"That's what we all want, Willa," he assured me. "More than anything, I want Harper to recover."

"Is there something you're not telling us?" Lucas asked.

"Not at all. I'm simply being honest with you. Of course, my hope, the hope of the entire staff, is that there will be a turning point. All I'm saying is that it would be best to remain positive, but to prepare for the worst."

"You can prepare for the worst, but I am clinging to hope." The hot fire that burned inside of me eased. I refused to allow anyone near my sister who didn't believe she had the will and the mental fortitude to survive.

Chapter 23

Willa

Chantelle was the first one to recover. "I believe we should follow Dr. Carroll's advice. We'll move up the wedding date," she said.

Lucas looked uncertain. "What about—"

"I've got this," she said with a certainty that left both Lucas and me speechless.

"We'll get married next Friday or Saturday . . . don't worry, I'll take care of the details. Leave it in my hands."

Dr. Carroll didn't pull any punches, looking us all straight in the eye. "The sooner the wedding can be arranged, the better."

For my part, I remained stunned. As hard as I fought against it, I was left feeling as if there was no hope left. None of what was happening added up. Harper had been diagnosed only a few weeks ago. How was it possible that a girl who had been ready to climb Mount Rainier could be close to death a measly six weeks later? I clung to the memory that my sister had pulled through before and she could again. For one wild moment, I found it impossible to breathe. I was numb, lost in my thoughts. It felt as if I was fighting every step of this journey, slogging my way up an impossibly steep hill.

"Where will we hold the wedding?" Lucas asked, shaking his head at Chantelle. "Only a few days ago you told me you'd searched every hotel and venue in the city. It would be impossible to pull off a proper wedding in a matter of a few days."

Chantelle placed her hands on both sides of my brother's face, her gaze holding his. "Oh ye of little faith. Don't you know where there's a will there's a way?"

My thought exactly, especially when it came to Harper. We all needed to stop with the doom and gloom. We had to help Harper, stand with her. Fight with everything in us.

Overwhelmed, Lucas shrugged. "All right, woman, you tell me where and I'll be there in a tuxedo, ready to swear my love to you for the remainder of my life."

Two days later, I got a text from Chantelle asking me to phone her as soon as I could. Harper was resting. I let her sleep as long as she wanted to, believing her body needed as much rest as possible. I stepped out of the room and called my soon-to-be sister-in-law.

"Hey, what's up?" I said, fully prepared for Chantelle to admit defeat. A part of me wanted her to fail so that when the day came for the wedding set in Oceanside, I could believe Harper would be there, well on her way to recovery.

Also, I thought Chantelle had taken on an impossible

task. No way would she be able to put together a wedding on the spur of the moment, unless we all trudged over to the King County Courthouse and stood before a judge. It went without saying that wasn't the kind of wedding Chantelle or my brother wanted. She'd worked far too hard creating her wedding dress and our bridesmaid gowns. A wedding before a judge would be a cheap imitation of what had been already set into place.

"How's Harper?"

"She's resting."

"Good. She's going to need all the strength she can muster for Friday afternoon."

"You found a venue for the wedding?"

"It's the perfect place for Harper, and for Lucas and me, too."

"Where?" I gasped the question, shocked that Chantelle had managed to pull this off.

"Have you ever sat in the courtyard outside the hospital cafeteria?"

I had. Many times. The space was lovely, with greenery flowing over waist-high planter boxes. Picnic tables dotted the area. It was an oasis in the middle of the hospital. Fresh. Green. Thriving. Alive.

"You and Lucas are going to be married . . . here?" Although I had asked the question, it was more of a statement. Just as Chantelle had promised, it was perfect for Harper. I'd fretted endlessly about her ability to dress and then be transported with her IV pole and wheelchair into town, or wherever Chantelle had found.

"Pastor McDonald is driving your father with him into town for the ceremony. My parents and the rest of the wedding party are all on board. I've got all the details handled."

"How . . . I mean, what made you think of holding it here?" The suggestion was brilliant.

She was quick to give credit where it was due. "John came up with the idea. I called him to ask about the risk of transporting Harper. As we were discussing what would need to be done, I realized how difficult it would be. He said it was too bad we couldn't hold the wedding in her room. That got me thinking about an area in the hospital that would work."

"Chantelle, it's perfect."

"It's a great solution," she agreed proudly.

"Do you have a time set?"

"Yes, well, that was the tricky part. As you know, the patio is a popular area at lunch and dinner. The best time we could arrange is three o'clock in the afternoon. The space will be cordoned off and decorated with streamers and balloons. The florist is supplying an archway for Lucas and me to stand under to exchange our vows. I've arranged for huge baskets of white roses on each side. It'll be every bit as good as what I'd planned for the ceremony in Oceanside."

"What about—"

Chantelle didn't let me finish. "Lucas and I decided we won't cancel the original date, seeing that the invitations have already been mailed. Instead of the wedding, it will be a dinner and reception."

It only made sense they would keep the original date. Making sense, however, was something that seemed to have been lost on me since our last meeting with Dr. Carroll. I was afraid, scared out of my wits that we would lose Harper. The thought was crippling me emotionally.

We ended the conversation a few minutes later, after Chantelle had filled in a few more of the details.

When I returned to Harper's room, I found my sister awake. "Hey," I said, "I've got great news. Lucas and Chantelle are going ahead with their wedding. It's going to be here at the hospital on Friday."

Harper blinked and I assumed she hadn't heard me. Then I realized she had, and understood, perhaps for the first time, the implication of why it was necessary.

"That's wonderful." Tears filled her eyes.

"Hey, hey. You're going to kick this, Harper. You and I both know it, right?"

"Right," she agreed, without a lot of enthusiasm.

"What's important is that Lucas and Chantelle want us both to be part of their wedding."

She smiled then. "I only hope my dress still fits, seeing how much weight I've lost." That was something Chantelle had already taken into consideration. Briefly, before we ended the call, she told me she'd altered Harper's dress so that it wouldn't hang on her.

We started getting ready for the wedding at about noon on Friday. Chantelle arranged for a hairdresser to come to the hospital. She even supplied a wig for Harper that was the same thick lilac/silver her own hair had been before she started chemo. With makeup and her wig, she looked almost as good as she did before the cancer and the weight loss.

John stopped by in the middle of the preparations to check on Harper. The excitement and adrenaline gave her a boost of energy that she was going to need to get through this day.

I noticed how gentle he was with my sister, how tender and kind. I wanted to hug him. Seeing him with Harper made me miss Sean with an intensity I'd never experienced. He'd been away long past the time he'd originally hoped. I hadn't heard a word from him since his phone call. Not a text, an email, or a call. I understood how important this assignment was to his career, and at the same time I longed for him to be with me, especially today, for my brother's wedding.

It seemed wrong that he would be on the other side of the world. He had no way of knowing what was happening. I couldn't blame him for not being with me, but that idea brought home what our lives would be like if we continued with this relationship. That gave me pause. I needed to rethink things. Not now, though. Later, when my head was clear and I wasn't fighting this battle.

Chantelle's sister checked in with Harper and me just before the ceremony started.

"Your dad is here. Is it all right if he comes in?"

"Yes, please," Harper answered before me.

She left and the hospital room door creaked open before my father's head appeared.

"Come in, Daddy," Harper whispered.

Dad was dressed in the same suit he wore for Mom's funeral. When he found Harper sitting upright in the wheelchair, he knelt on one knee on the floor next to her. I noticed his lips trembled with the effort to hold back tears.

"Even now you're so beautiful . . . Your mother would be so proud," he whispered, and turned his head to look up at me. "Of both of you. I don't know what I did to deserve such amazing children. I am blessed beyond anything I could ever have imagined." Tears leaked down his face.

Gently, Harper wiped them from his cheeks. "I love you, Daddy."

"Love you, too, baby girl, with all my heart."

A knock sounded against the door. It was time. To my surprise, John appeared, dressed in a suit and tie instead of his normal white lab coat. He went behind Harper's wheelchair, and with one hand holding on to the wheelchair and the other on her IV pole, he rolled her out of the room. Dad and I followed behind.

Once we were assembled in the cafeteria, the florist handed Harper and me floral bouquets tied in burgundy-colored ribbon. Looking onto the courtyard, I saw that the picnic tables had been removed and that two rows of chairs had been set angled before the flower-covered archway.

Chantelle's mother, along with her godmother and husband, were seated on one side. Dad and the wives of my brother's two best friends sat in the opposite section. I was escorted down the aisle first by Ted, Lucas's Army buddy, followed by Harper, pushed in the wheelchair by John. Harper stretched her arm over her shoulder so she could place her hand on his. Bill, another of my brother's Army friends, walked next to her. Chantelle's sister followed, and then, after a long pause, Chantelle walked down the aisle with her father.

Her wedding dress was stunning, but no more so than the bride. She beamed with a beauty I found difficult to describe. The dress was a simple creation, and it fit her like a dream, floating out from the waist. She held the same white roses that made up my own bouquet, only hers trailed with lily of the valley. Seeing her and the look that came over my brother as he spied her stole my breath.

His eyes filled with love, Lucas stepped forward to greet his bride. Chantelle kissed her father's cheek and placed her hand in Lucas's. Together they moved to stand before Pastor McDonald.

I noticed that while there was only close family in attendance, a small crowd had gathered inside the cafeteria to watch the ceremony. They stood by the windows, looking onto the patio. Doctors. Nurses. Staff. Even patients and visitors.

The day couldn't have been more perfect, with the sun shining down on the bride and groom, God's blessings from above. Birds circled overhead, while the subtle music swirled around, enveloping us all.

Lucas and Chantelle had written their own vows. I listened as best I could, caught up in my own thoughts. Love. Honor. Respect. Cherish. Sickness and health. Those words took on an entirely new meaning.

I glanced at Harper, who was looking up at John, their

eyes connected. It was as if they were exchanging these words, as if they were the ones promising to love and cherish each other.

My heart ached for Sean, wishing he was at my side to share this moment. I had no idea when I would see him again. I felt his absence more strongly than I had at any other time since his departure. Standing there, my brother with his bride, Harper with her doctor, and me alone. Rarely had I ever felt lonelier.

Each person present was connected to someone else. Everyone but me. Closing my eyes, I refused to feel sorry for myself. If I was going to become involved with Sean, I would need to learn to accept his intermittent travels, and the dangers he put himself in to advance his career. It was part and parcel of the man I was falling for. Asking him to change wasn't fair and might ruin the closeness we shared.

As soon as they exchanged their vows, Lucas kissed his bride. I could see that Harper's energy was quickly evaporating. Asking our father to hold my bouquet, I prepared to return her to her hospital room.

John stopped me. "I'll do it."

"But—"

"Stay," Harper insisted. "Let John escort me back."

I smiled and locked eyes with his. He winked and I nodded, letting my sister have her way. She was in good hands.

Before she left, Chantelle and Lucas each gave Harper a gentle hug. The moment was touching, and I noticed a photographer snap a photo. Harper smiling, John standing tall and handsome in his suit behind her. Chantelle and my brother thanking her and loving on her. Seeing the smile on my sister's face and the joy radiating from my brother and his bride was probably one of the most beautiful moments of my life

"She's beautiful, isn't she?" Dad said, coming to stand at my side.

Chantelle was stunning. My brother was a lucky man; I had no doubt that he was keenly aware of his good fortune. "Chantelle is beautiful inside and out. How she managed to put an entire wedding together in only a few days is a minor miracle."

"Indeed, she is," Dad concurred, "but I was talking about Harper."

Wrapping my arm around my father's elbow, I smiled over at him. "Yes, she is."

"And that doctor friend of hers?"

"He's a good man," I assured him. "He's doing everything he can, along with Dr. Carroll, to keep her alive."

My father hesitated and swallowed hard. "God bless him and give him success."

"Amen," I whispered, believing with all my heart there was hope, a reason to believe.

Lucas and Chantelle were surrounded by their guests and other well-wishers. The doors from the cafeteria opened and the group that had gathered to watch the ceremony spilled onto the patio.

Chantelle cut the small, bakery-supplied cake to be shared and enjoyed by all. My plan to bake their wedding cake felt like a million lifetimes ago, but I was determined to bake the original cakes we had chosen for their reception.

Dad and I sat next to each other, eating a thin slice of the rather boring cake, when my brother joined us.

"It was a lovely ceremony," Dad told Lucas.

"Thanks, Dad. Glad you could be here."

"I wouldn't have missed it for the world. Now, when are you going to give me grandchildren?"

At the stricken look that shot across my brother's face, I burst into giggles. It took me a moment to realize it had been a long time since I'd found a reason to laugh.

Chapter 24

Sean

The assignment was complete, although it had taken longer than any of us had anticipated. All of us were eager to get back to the States, to our families and all that was familiar and comfortable. Now I would need to sort through the thousands of photos I'd taken, and get started writing the story to accompany them.

I'd packed up our camp and was ready to head back home at last. To Oceanside. To Willa. Ever since our conversation, I'd been worried and distracted.

Traveling to the Manila Ninoy Aquino airport had been a challenge, and we were fortunate to make the flight. There was only one direct flight to the States. The thought of missing that plane and spending an extra day trapped in an airport had the entire team on edge.

Because of the traffic and the late start, we ended up racing to our gate and were the last passengers to board.

Once on the plane, I collapsed into my seat, breathing heavily, thanking God we'd made it. I'd planned on connecting with Willa at the airport. That unfortunately wasn't going to happen. I ground my teeth in frustration as I fastened my seatbelt and listened to the flight attendant review the safety instructions. Los Angeles would be my first opportunity to reach her.

The flight was long, nearly sixteen hours. Logging on to my computer, I worked as best I could, hoping to get a head start on sorting through the thirty thousand photos I'd taken. Doug and I would collaborate on the article, but my work was just starting. It would take weeks to review all the pictures I'd taken.

At some point in the flight, I fell asleep, waking only long enough to close my computer. Finally, the plane touched down in Los Angeles, bouncing against the runway and jolting me from a light sleep.

From this point the team that I'd been living and working with all these weeks would head in different directions. I would fly into Seattle and Doug would head to Chicago and the others to Phoenix.

As soon as I cleared customs, squared away my luggage, and got to my next gate, I reached for my phone. *Eager* didn't begin to explain how anxious I was to speak to Willa. Not having been able to communicate with her in the weeks since our last conversation, I was desperate for news.

My hand shook with nerves and anticipation until the call went through. It rang and rang. With each unanswered ring, my frustration mounted until the call went to voicemail.

Part of me was tempted to hang up and try again later. After hesitating, I decided to leave a message.

"Willa, it's me. I'm in L.A., about to board my flight. Give me a call when you get this." Given no choice, I disconnected. Disappointment settled in my stomach like acid. After weeks of going without hearing her voice, I was near desperate.

While waiting, I connected with my parents and assured them all was well, that I was in the States and would arrive back in Oceanside soon.

"By any chance have you heard from Willa?" I asked, hoping they might be able to fill me in on what was happening with her sister. My thoughts bounced from one scenario to another, not knowing what was worse.

My mother was on the other end of the phone, with my dad listening in. "Not a word. Has something happened?"

"It's her sister. Shortly after I left, Willa learned that Harper's cancer had returned."

"Oh no. I'm so sorry, Sean, but Willa didn't reach out. Did you expect her to?"

"No, but I was hoping."

We didn't talk long; I was in a hurry to get off the phone, anxious to try phoning Willa again. Although I loved my parents and was happy to hear their voices, the person I needed to speak to most was Willa.

When my flight was announced, Willa still hadn't returned my call, although I'd tried twice more. The two hours I was in the air flying into Seattle felt like the fifteen and a half hours it took to fly from Manila to California. Each minute felt like a year. The wheels had barely touched down when I reached for my phone, turned off airplane mode, and tried her yet again.

The results were the same and I groaned in frustration. I paid a king's ransom at the airport for a car service to drive me to Oceanside.

By the time I arrived, I was mentally and physically exhausted. I felt like I could sleep for a week, but I needed to collect Bandit. After everything my dog had been through, he must believe I was another human who had abandoned him.

When I drove up to the Hoffert home, Bandit was curled up on the porch, snoozing. At the sound of my car door closing, he lifted his head. Seeing me, he leaped up and raced to the fence, his tail swinging so hard and fast it slapped against the sides of his body.

After opening the gate, I got down on one knee and Bandit licked my face as I gave him the attention he craved. When Teresa and Logan came out of the house, I thanked them both for looking after Bandit and explained why I was away longer than I'd expected. I was grateful knowing Bandit was being well cared for.

Then, because I was anxious to find out what I could about Willa and her sister, I asked Teresa, "What's the word on Harper Lakey?"

Teresa's face fell. "We haven't heard much. Just that she is in that cancer hospital in Seattle."

"What about Willa?"

"She's in Seattle, too. Friends of theirs are keeping her coffee place going. Everyone misses Willa, though. It's not the same without her. Don't imagine her being away this long is good for business."

The last thing Willa needed on top of everything else was for Bean There to fail on account of her absence.

With Bandit resting in the backseat, I drove home. I unpacked my camera gear and my computer, fed Bandit, took a shower, and crashed. My bed had never felt more welcoming. Tense as I was, I wasn't sure I'd be able to rest. To my surprise, I fell asleep almost immediately.

A persistent sound like a church bell played in my sleep, droning on and on until I realized this was no dream. It was my phone. I nearly fell out of bed in my eagerness to answer before it went to voicemail.

"Hello," I said, my voice sounding more like a croaking frog than myself.

"Sean?"

"Willa. Willa. Thank God." The relief I felt just hearing her voice was nearly my undoing. "I lost count of how many times I tried to reach you. Did you get my messages?"

"Where are you?"

"Home. Oceanside."

"Oh Sean," she gasped, sounding close to tears, "you don't know how much I've missed you."

"Same goes for me. It's been hell being unable to be with you, especially now." A stampede of questions raced through my mind and I almost didn't know where to start, so I went with the most important: "How's Harper?"

She hesitated, as if she wasn't sure how to respond. "The same . . . Maybe a bit worse. We need to get her white cell count up and it isn't happening, and now . . . now . . ." She paused and seemed unable to continue.

I knew next to nothing about the treatment for cancer. "What's happened?" I asked, when she didn't finish.

"Dr. Carroll has her on oxygen. She hates the mask, but she needs it. I keep telling her it won't be for much longer. I have to believe it won't be long before she's better, but it's getting harder every day when I see her declining."

"Dr. Carroll is her physician?"

"Yes, but John Neal is with her every day, too. He's been wonderful. They're in love. He's doing everything possible to keep her alive."

That sounded hopeful. "When can I see you?" I asked, needing to take her in my arms, hold her close, and breathe her in. As much as possible, I longed to relieve her of this burden.

"I'm in Seattle . . . Oh, did you know Lucas and Chantelle are married? A little more than a week ago. I'll explain everything when I see you."

"I landed only a few hours ago. I'll get what sleep I can and drive into the city first thing in the morning. I've got a million things I need to do, so I won't be able to stay long; I'm sorry, love. I hope you understand." Any time with Willa would be worth the drive, even if it was for only an hour or two.

"Sleep, then. Call me before you leave and then when you're close."

"Do you want me to come to the hospital?"

"Yes, please. Oh Sean, you have no idea how badly I need

you . . . how I have longed to lay my head on your shoulder and have you hold me. I don't know how much longer I can last without you."

For Willa to be this vulnerable told me everything I needed to know. My strong, resilient woman was close to the breaking point. Sitting on the edge of my mattress after we hung up, I ran my hands over my face, debating leaving right then. I stood, and to my shock nearly collapsed. Driving, I decided, wouldn't be a good idea. Instead I climbed back into bed and slept for another eight hours straight.

I left for Seattle as soon as I was dressed and had a mocha. My bags remained unpacked, my seven-plus weeks' worth of mail still at the post office.

The drive into Seattle took nearly thirty minutes longer than I'd anticipated, with traffic stopped dead due to an accident on the freeway. As Willa requested, I called when I was close to the hospital. She told me the best spot to park and then said she'd meet me in the lobby.

The first thing that hit me when I saw her was how pale and drawn she looked. My girl was hanging on by a thread. As soon as she saw me, she hurried forward, nearly falling into me. The instant my arms were around her, she broke into sobs. Her cries tore at my heart.

I half carried her to a seating area, grateful we could have a few minutes alone. She sat on my lap and my hand cradled the back of her head as she sobbed into my shoulder.

"I'm here, baby, I'm here." Knowing I would need to leave

again soon tore at my heart. Now wasn't the time to tell her that only part of the assignment had been completed.

Holding her as I was, I could tell that she'd lost a considerable amount of weight. It was as if she believed that her will and might alone could keep her sister alive. She'd told me when Harper had first developed leukemia three years before that she refused to allow anyone to suggest, think, or even hint at a negative outcome.

"Is she still needing the oxygen mask?" I asked, silently praying that had been only temporary.

Willa's shoulders sagged as she nodded.

I hated to ask but needed to know. "Did she need oxygen the last time she had leukemia?"

Willa sniffled and shook her head. "It's . . . It's worse this time, but I'm trying not to read anything into this latest development."

"Don't let your mind go there," I said, wanting to be encouraging.

"I'm trying not to. I should get back. I hate to be away from her for too long. She likes me to do everything for her myself other than what's necessary for the nurses to handle."

"What about Lucas and Chantelle? Are they helping?"

"Yes. Lucas stops by every day after work and takes over for me on the weekends . . . but lately Harper only wants me."

"Can I come with you?"

She nodded, slipped off my lap, and reached for my hand. As we started toward the elevator, she stopped, her shoulders stiffening. "Before you see her, I need to prepare you. Leesa and Carrie came to visit not long ago . . . I'd tell you when, but the days all run together. They were shaken when they saw how far she's declined. She's bald and she's lost a lot of weight . . . and"—she paused, hiccupping a soft sob—"she's very sick."

It was all I could do not to wrap my arms around Willa again. It hurt me to see her struggle to maintain her hope, her belief. I'd give anything to take her away from all this, but I knew she would never leave her sister. Saving Harper meant everything to Willa. It terrified me to think what would happen to her if Harper lost this battle with cancer.

"Are you ready?" she asked, after we came out of the elevator. Her hand was clasped in mine.

"Ready," I said, and walked at her side to Harper's room.

Silently she opened the door and looked inside. "Harper," she said gently, "you have company. Sean is here."

Although she'd prepared me, I nearly gasped with shock. Lying in her hospital bed, Harper was curled in the fetal position, an oxygen mask over her face. When she heard my name, she opened her eyes, which were dull and lifeless. I could see she was making an effort to smile and all that it cost her to do so.

"She's not having a good day," Willa said, stepping over to the bed. She gently touched Harper's face.

Even though it was difficult, Harper smiled.

Willa moved closer to the bed and took hold of her sister's hand.

Harper lifted the mask so she could speak. "Take care of Willa."

"Of course," I said.

"For me," she added.

"Harper," Willa said with a forced laugh. "Why would Sean need to take care of me? Dr. Carroll told me he's getting the okay to try an experimental medication that shows promise."

Harper's eyes were closed, and it looked to me as if she was asleep and hadn't heard a word.

We didn't stay long. I hadn't eaten and my stomach growled. Knowing Willa probably hadn't had much herself, I suggested we go to the cafeteria. She had yet to tell me about Lucas and Chantelle's wedding.

The decision seemed hard for her to make. "We won't be away long, will we?"

"No," I promised. "Only a few minutes."

"I'll let Harper's nurse know where we are so she can come for me if there's any change."

"Sure."

Willa barely spoke on the elevator to the cafeteria. "I don't like to leave her for long," she reminded me.

"Don't worry, I won't order a four-course meal."

That produced only a semblance of a smile. Willa ordered coffee and I grabbed a premade sandwich and bottled water.

We were at the table only a few minutes, and I had yet to take more than a few bites, when we were interrupted.

An orderly approached our table. "You're Willa?"

"Yes." Immediately she pushed back her chair and was on her feet. "What?"

"Dr. Carroll asked me to come for you."

"I'll be right there." Willa didn't wait for me but started for the elevator, her steps urgent.

I left my sandwich and hurried after her. When we got back, the physician I could only assume was Dr. Carroll stood outside Harper's room, talking to John. Both looked troubled. He turned when he saw Willa and me.

"What is it?" Willa demanded. "What's happened?"

The physician Willa had hung all her hope on wasn't able to meet her eyes. His shoulders slumped and I could see the dread written all over him. My stomach pitched. Whatever it was he had to tell her couldn't be good.

"Harper's vomiting blood."

Chapter 25

Willa

The next two days were an emotional roller coaster as we dealt with this latest development in Harper's declining condition. I was at her bedside constantly until I was ready to drop from the emotional and physical strain. Within forty-eight hours Harper was stable and I could breathe again.

Lucas and Chantelle must have said something to Sean, because he drove to Seattle to collect me, claiming I needed a break. At first I refused to leave Harper, until my sister all but banned me from the room. Dr. Carroll and John insisted that a few days away from the hospital would do me good. Chantelle agreed to stand in for me and promised to be in touch if anything new developed with Harper. Leaving my sister for even a day was hard, but in the end, I capitulated and left with Sean.

Since Harper and I left for Seattle I hadn't been back to Oceanside. In the time I'd been away my business had taken a dramatic turn for the worse. My thoughts were leaping from one crisis to another. Although Bean There was the biggest investment of my life, I'd left it on the back burner while I was with my sister.

My mood was sullen as we headed back to Oceanside.

"You okay?" Sean asked, once we left the heavy Seattle traffic.

"No. I shouldn't have left Harper."

"Willa, you're exhausted. You need this."

"I need this?" I cried, both frustrated and angry. I bit down hard on my back molars to the point I feared they might crack. "What gives you the right to tell me what I need? You've been halfway around the world doing whatever it is you do. What right do you have to tell me anything?" It was unfair to resent him for not being around when I needed his support, but I couldn't hold back a minute longer.

My words were met with a silence that grew as thick as a London fog.

Hanging my head, I closed my eyes and whispered, "I'm sorry . . . I don't mean to take my frustration out on you." I chanced to look at Sean. He reached over and took hold of my hand and gave it a gentle squeeze. I relaxed and leaned my head against the passenger window and closed my eyes. No more than a few minutes later, I was asleep.

When we arrived in Oceanside, Sean gently shook my shoulder. "Willa." He spoke softly, stirring me from my slumber.

Sitting upright, I blinked a couple of times. "Where are we?"

"At your apartment."

Straightening, I wiped the sleep from my face and looked over at Sean, regretting being cross with him earlier. "I slept . . . almost the entire way," I whispered, surprised at myself.

"You needed it."

Sean got out of the car and came around to my side, opening the passenger door. I started to climb out, forgetting the seatbelt. Leaning over me, Sean released it and then offered me his hand. "Come on, Sleeping Beauty, I'll walk you to the door."

I paused in front of my apartment. Ridiculous as it seemed, entering the home my sister and I had shared suddenly felt daunting. Overcome and hesitant, I asked, "Would you come inside with me?"

Sean glanced at the time. "I can't stay long."

"I know." He was just back himself and had yet to catch up with his own affairs. I appreciated that he'd taken the time to come and collect me from Seattle. The crux of the matter was that I didn't want to be alone. I didn't want to look inside Harper's bedroom and find her things scattered about while she was back in Seattle battling for her life.

"Stay with me," he said, standing behind me, his hands on my shoulders.

The need in me was strong, weighty. It didn't take me long to decide. "Yes, please. I want to."

We collected a few personal items from the apartment that I would need for the night. Sean led me back to the car and helped me inside. Neither of us had anything to say as we rode to his place.

As we came through the front door, Bandit leaped up with a bark, excited to see Sean and me, tail swishing from side to side with carefree abandon. I crouched down and rubbed his ears. "Good to see you, too, buddy," I whispered, as my arms circled his neck and I pressed my face against his.

Sean's living room was a disaster. His bag was only half unpacked, with clothes dumped on the sofa. Newspapers and mail cluttered the top of the coffee table. After weeks of grueling work and the long flight back to the States, Sean was as exhausted as me, only in a different way and for different reasons.

"I apologize for the mess," he said, hands in his pockets, embarrassed.

"No mind," I said on the tail end of a yawn. "This is what Harper's room has looked like from the time she was five."

Although we made an effort to eat dinner, all either of us could think about was sleep. Without needing to point out the obvious, Sean led me to the spare bedroom. I followed behind him, looking into a room that had only the essentials: a bed, a nightstand, and a dresser. The bed seemed sterile and uninviting, like one I might see at the hospital.

"Would you mind terribly," I said, my voice trembling slightly, "if I slept with you? . . . I don't want to be alone tonight." I wasn't asking him to make love to me. What I wanted, what I needed, was a warm body, a healthy one that I could cuddle against and forget what awaited me in Seattle.

"Yes, of course. I didn't want to assume . . ."

"Just sleep."

"Frankly, at this moment, that's all I'm capable of myself."

It was late; we were both tired. Stepping into the spare room, I slipped into my pajamas before I returned to his bedroom and folded back the covers.

"Right side or left?" Sean asked.

I shook my head. It didn't matter.

We climbed into bed together and Sean gathered me in his arms so that my head rested on his shoulder. Neither of us spoke. I closed my eyes, savoring the warmth of his embrace, needing his touch, the feel of his skin against mine. His heart beat strong and steady in my ear. Listening to the even beat quickly lulled me to sleep.

At some point during the night, I must have rolled onto my side, away from Sean. I woke with him cuddling me, his arm around my waist, securing me firmly against him. For the first time in weeks, my initial thought on waking wasn't about Harper, what she needed, how I could best help her, who I needed to talk to, what should be done. Instead I was wrapped in warmth and comfort. Every cell in my body wanted to escape that hospital. If I never stepped into a medical facility again it would be too soon.

We woke after eight. Eight! This was the first night of solid sleep I'd had since I couldn't remember when. But eight? I'd planned on being at Bean There when it opened. Apparently, I'd slept through my alarm. Sean had, too.

The moment I saw the time, I tossed aside the covers and scurried out of bed. Forgetting my clothes were in the spare bedroom, I ran around the bed, searching for something to wear.

"Sean," I cried, waking him.

He sat up and stretched his arms above his head. Yawning, he announced the obvious. "We slept in."

Well, duh. That was putting it mildly. "I need to get to the café."

"Give me a few minutes," he said, sounding far too calm.

Couldn't he see how panicked I was? I should have been at the shop hours ago. Instead, Sean stilled me, brought me into his arms, and hugged me close.

"Good morning, baby," he whispered, and kissed the side of my neck.

His touch and kiss calmed my racing heart. I drank in his strength, his calm, wondering how long it would be before I would have the opportunity to be in his arms again. Breaking away from him was hard.

"Dad is coming for me at noon," I said, not that Sean needed the reminder. The sooner I could return to Harper, the better I'd feel.

I was about to ask Sean when I would be able to see him again when he volunteered his plans for the day.

"I've got to unpack, do laundry, deal with the mail, and make my flight arrangements."

Flight arrangements.

His words fell like lead weights into the center of the room.

"You're leaving? Again?" The words stuck in my throat to the point that releasing them was painful. I was convinced I hadn't heard him correctly. Surely there was some misunderstanding. Why would he need to leave again when he'd so recently arrived home? It made no sense.

He held me at arm's length, only it felt as if we were worlds apart. "I need to go to Chicago, where Doug lives. The two of us are working on the article for *National Geographic*." He spoke slowly, succinctly, as if I should already know this.

I shook my head to clear my thoughts.

"I won't be gone long," he promised. When I didn't comment, he added, "Trust me, I'm not excited about leaving you again, especially now."

Swallowing became difficult. Speaking was impossible. It felt as if I'd been sucker-punched.

"It isn't something I want to do, Willa. But I have to see the rest of this assignment through . . ."

I was frozen in place; it was all I could do to take in a breath.

"I don't want to leave," he said, looking miserable. "I tried to get an extension, have the magazine hold the article until the following month, but the editor refused."

Heading back to the bedroom, I reached for my clothes, dressing with my back to him, eager to leave.

"I realize the timing is bad. If I could put this off, I would."

"So you said," I managed, eager to be on my way before I lost control and said something I'd regret.

"Please, Willa, don't be angry . . . I probably should have said something sooner. I'm sorry, sorrier than you know."

"It's fine," I said, doing my best to hide my feelings. "You have no obligation to me or my family. We've only been dating a few months. This situation is with my family, not yours."

As far as I was concerned, we were finished. This was his life, his profession. He left for weeks on end to places any sane person would avoid, risking his health and his safety. His camera was his mistress. The time had come for me to wake up and accept the truth. This relationship was not going to work for me. Perhaps I was a coward not to break it off right then. The temptation was strong, but I didn't want to lash out impulsively. When we next talked, I'd be able to think and speak without emotions clouding what needed to be said.

As soon as I dressed, Sean drove me into town. The silence between us was as heavy as a concrete wall.

When we arrived at Bean There, I climbed out of the car and leaned into the open window on the passenger side. "Thank you," I said stiffly, letting it go with that. He started to say something, but I turned away before he had the chance.

"Call me once you're back in Seattle," he called after me.

I ignored him and headed toward my shop.

I entered Bean There and felt a collective sigh from both the staff and the customers. Everyone wanted an update on Harper, but no one had the courage to ask.

"I left Harper yesterday afternoon in good spirits." That was a bit of an exaggeration.

Shirley gave me a hug. She looked tired and I couldn't blame her. Since I'd been gone, she'd carried the weight of responsibility for the baking and bookkeeping, plus everything else: schedules, payroll, customer service, ordering supplies, and morale.

"How are you holding up?" she asked, automatically handing me a cup of coffee and a breakfast roll.

"Okay." That, too, was an exaggeration. Worse now that I'd mentally ended things with Sean.

Shirley had emailed me the ledger entries so I could keep track of how the business was doing. Revenues were down, which was to be expected, I suppose. She suggested we add pecan rolls to the menu and commented that pumpkin spice was the current bestseller in the flavor category. We discussed a few strategies that would boost sales when I was away. While with Harper, my attention hadn't been on the business. I wasn't paying near enough the attention I should have been.

After about a half hour, Shirley asked what had to be her most pressing question. "Do you know how much longer you will be in Seattle?"

I didn't know and admitted as much. "I . . . can't say." I realized my being away from the business had gone on far longer than anyone had anticipated.

"The thing is," she said, looking down at her hands, "I don't know if I can continue filling in for you. I'm working all hours of the day. I want to help, Willa, you know that. But it was never my intention to come on full-time." Reluctance weighed down her voice.

"You've done far and above anything I could have asked." One option would be for me to close the business until matters with Harper were settled. No one else was capable of stepping in for me other than Shirley. It had been seamless with the two of us working in tandem, her filling in two days a week. I couldn't continue to ask her to work as many hours as I did. When I'd hired her, it was for twenty hours a week, not fifty to sixty.

"Can you manage for another couple of weeks?" I asked, my heart in my throat.

She hesitated and then nodded. "I suppose, but no longer. I'm really sorry, Willa."

"Don't be. I understand."

Shirley's face betrayed her regret. "What will you do?"

I shrugged. My options were few. "I'm not sure. Winter is slower anyway, so it makes sense to close for the time being." I hated to do it; financially, it would be devastating. But what choice did I have?

Mentally I reviewed my savings account. I'd need to make rent for both the shop and the apartment. I'd started to build a small nest egg, hummingbird-size, that would carry me one month, possibly two.

A huge knot cramped my stomach with the reality of my situation. While I could be optimistic, in every likelihood I would need to close Bean There for good. Immediate tears filled my eyes and I blinked them away.

Shirley reached for my hand and gave it a squeeze. Maybe it was time I moved away from Oceanside. Maybe I should think about living in Seattle. The girl who worked the hospital cafeteria did a horrible job with the lattes. I could get a job there and . . .

Joelle, a longtime friend of Harper's, knocked against the office door. "Sorry to interrupt," she said. "Dr. Annie heard you were in town and wondered if you had a few minutes."

"Of course."

Patting my hand, Shirley stood. "I'll leave the two of you to talk."

266 , DEBBIE MACOMBER

Shirley returned to the kitchen and Annie came into the office. "Willa," she said, and exhaled as if she'd been holding in her breath. "It's good to see you. Can you update me on Harper's condition?"

As best as I could, I replayed the events of the last few weeks, Lucas and Chantelle's wedding being the highlight. I told her about John and his determination to help Harper. For the first time that morning, I smiled, relaying the obvious devotion the doctor and my sister had for each other.

Annie listened intently, nodding now and again, frowning at other times. When I finished, she asked, "How are you holding up?"

"I'm fine."

She shook her head as though she didn't believe me. "How are you really?"

"Fine," I said again, and burst into tears. It was too much. I was losing my sister and my relationship with Sean had reached a dead end. He didn't know it, but the handwriting was on the wall.

Annie stood and wrapped her arms around me, holding on to me tightly. "That's what I thought."

"I want to believe Harper will beat this. She did the first time, but it's much, much worse now."

"I hope you realize you can't keep her alive by the force of your own will," Annie whispered.

Someone else had said that and I'd ignored it, refusing to believe I wasn't the one keeping Harper alive by wishing and believing it. That was nuts. I held no such power over my sister's cancer.

Or did I?

Annie was able to stay only a few minutes, as she'd left patients waiting at the clinic, but she'd wanted a personal update when she heard I was in town. Not knowing how long I'd be around, she took the chance I was available.

After Annie left, I talked to the two girls who manned the front of the shop. Joelle had worked for me before she started at Oceanside Fitness. She was taking classes to become a physical therapist. Working part-time for me while Harper was in Seattle had put a lot of stress on her. I thanked her and Leesa, who backed her up.

Dad arrived just after noon. He looked good. Better than he had at any time that I could remember since we'd lost Mom.

"You ready?" he asked.

"I am." I reached for my purse and my overnight bag and headed to the car.

I looked longingly at the ocean. "Would you give me a minute?" I asked my father.

"Sure. No problem."

I walked over to the beach, removed my shoes, and dug my feet into the cool October sand. Walking along the beach had always had the power to help me clear my mind and soothe my soul. Breathing in the briny scent of the wind, I held it in my lungs, comforted by the familiar smell and taste of it. A wave crashed against the shore, wiping out my footprints. The ebb and flow of change, of letting go, of moving forward and seeing everything wiped away like that single wave beating against the sand.

Knowing Dad was waiting for me, I stayed only long enough to find my center before I brushed the sand from my feet and slipped on my shoes. I hurried back to Dad, who stood waiting by the car.

My stay in town was brief but telling. So telling, especially when it came to my relationship with Sean. With my heart in my throat, I wondered how much longer I would be able to hold myself together.

Chapter 26

Willa

On the long drive back to Seattle, Dad was in a talkative mood. He had nearly two months' sobriety and was feeling good about himself.

Being that I had been the one to look after Dad when our mother died, I was afraid what might happen when he saw Harper. He'd seen her only one time since she'd been admitted, and that was for Lucas and Chantelle's wedding. Harper had declined since then, and I didn't want it to shock him.

I thought to prepare him, but couldn't get a word in, as he talked nearly nonstop, filling me in on his life. I'd never known my father to be chatty or this open. Despite my heavy heart, I enjoyed seeing him this way. His chatter helped me keep my mind off Sean, Bean There, and what we faced with Harper.

"I've been eating better, too," he said, "healthy stuff.

Harper told me about this drink she concocted with all those seeds and germs and spinach. Sounded dreadful. Told her if she added beer I might be interested." He laughed at his own joke. "Tried it without the beer and it isn't half bad. Even ate nonfat Greek yogurt and a salad for lunch last week."

"Good for you, Dad."

"I've been getting extra hours at the casino, too."

I was pleased to see him taking an interest in his well-being.

"I'm putting a little money aside, so if you ever need help, you let me know."

"I'll do that." As tempting as it was, I wouldn't take his money to keep Bean There open. Whatever my father had managed to accumulate probably wouldn't be enough to keep me solvent for longer than a week or two. I didn't want to make my problems his. This was my business, and its success or failure was on my shoulders and no one else's.

As we drew closer to Seattle and got tangled up in the heavy flow of traffic, dread settled over me. I hadn't realized how depressed I'd become until we neared the hospital. With everything in me, I wanted to remain outside; breathe in the fresh air, look at the sky, forget that my sister was inside, battling for her life.

Dad found a good parking spot and we walked together, side by side, toward the bank of elevators. My steps were sluggish, but if Dad noticed, he didn't comment.

"Dad," I said, stopping him just before he pushed the button to call for the elevator. "I need to warn you . . . Harper is very sick."

His eyes dimmed and he reached for my hand, taking it in his own and squeezing. "I know. Lucas has been giving me regular updates."

That was all well and good, but hearing and seeing were two entirely different things.

"Don't worry about me," he said, giving my hand another squeeze. "I'm stronger than I look."

I hoped he was right. It wasn't like I could keep him away, not that I would want that. Protecting him as I had in the past had done more harm than good. As Harper had so often told me: I was such a mother.

Before we entered the hospital, I texted John and told him we were on our way to Harper's room. He met us in the hallway outside her room, his expression revealing nothing about what had transpired in the time I'd been away.

I asked Dad if he remembered John.

"Of course," Dad replied. "You're the handsome doctor who escorted Harper down the aisle at the wedding." He offered his hand. "Good to see you again, Doctor."

"You, too." They exchanged handshakes.

"You ready, Dad?" I wrapped my arm around his elbow, unsure who would need the support more: him or me.

"Ready," he said.

I pushed open the door to find my sister curled up on her side. Apparently, she no longer needed the oxygen mask, because it was gone. I looked upon this as a good sign. When she saw it was me and Dad, she smiled. How pale she looked. So sick and so determined to be brave.

"Baby girl," Dad said, as he pulled the chair up alongside her bed.

Harper extended her arm to him and Dad gripped hold of her hand, raising it to his lips and kissing her fingers. For a long time, he said nothing. Then he pressed his forehead against her hand. When he straightened, he looked to me.

"I'm grateful you're here, Willa. I have something to say and you both need to hear it."

"Of course, Dad."

"You know how deeply I loved your mother." His eyes filled with tears, which he managed to hold at bay.

Seeing how he grieved, we knew Mom had been his soulmate. He'd floundered badly without her.

"We met when I was in the Army, stationed at Fort Lewis, and she worked as a waitress at Denny's, putting aside her tip money to take college classes. The minute I saw her it was like I got struck by lightning. Knew right then this was the girl I'd marry."

He stopped, rubbed the side of his face, and chuckled. "Thing was, it took some time to convince her we were meant to be together. She was determined to graduate college and teach English. Oh my, how that woman loved to read. She could rip through a book in a day, swallowing up all them words like it was nothing."

Harper's eyes found mine and we grinned at each other. That was the perfect description of Mom. She'd read to us from the time we were infants. One of my first memories was Mom giving me a book. I could remember sitting in her lap as she read to all of us each night. Books were her world.

"When we first met, Claire wasn't interested in dating anyone in the military," Dad continued. " 'Here today, gone tomorrow' is what she said. I ate at that Denny's every night for a month before she'd agree to go to dinner with me."

"Don't tell me you took her to dinner at Denny's," I said, joking with him. I loved hearing the details of Mom and Dad's courtship. We all knew our father had been in the military and that he'd met Mom while stationed at Fort Lewis, but not how they'd met or how long it'd taken him to convince her to date him.

"No, I took her to a little seafood place by the ocean."

"Oceanside?"

He nodded. "Seeing how much she enjoyed being on that beach, I said if she'd agree to marry me, I'd move us here."

"Dad, you mean to say you proposed on your first date?"

He chuckled. "Yup. That woman had my heart wrapped around her little finger. If she'd wanted to move to the moon, I'd have found a way."

"How long did it take for you to convince her to marry you?"

He grinned as if proud of himself. "In less than six months she had my engagement ring on her finger. We waited until I was released from the Army and she got that degree she wanted so badly, and then we married. I found work in Oceanside and she taught at the junior high until Lucas was born."

He grew serious then, his eyes sad. "I always thought we'd grow old together. I assumed I'd be the one to die first; it generally happens that way, me being five years older and all."

"One never knows," Harper whispered, her breath wispy.

"It was always my job to provide for the family. Your mother wanted to be at home with you children. I encouraged it. Oh, how she loved you; she took such pride in each one of you. When she died"—he stopped for a moment, but was able to continue—"I felt that I'd somehow failed her. It was my job to care for her. To see to her needs, to be her protector. That's what a loving husband does. It was why I found solace in a bottle after we buried her. I'd failed her, failed all of you. Countless nights I sat, wondering if there was something I'd missed, something I should have seen before that aneurysm."

"Daddy . . ."

"No, please let me finish."

Seeing how hard it was for him to speak of our mother, I moved closer and sat in the chair next to his. Seated, we were eye level with Harper.

"After we buried your mom, it didn't seem more than a blink of an eye and we learned Harper had leukemia. Getting hit with that news was too much for me to take. I'd failed Claire and then I'd failed Harper."

"No . . ." Harper stopped him. "Don't say that."

"It's a father's job to see to the welfare of his family. First Claire and then my sweet baby girl and I could do nothing. I let you all down, and honey, I am so sorry. Can you ever forgive me?"

"There's nothing to forgive," Harper whispered.

"Willa, you carried the load that was mine. I was selfish and unfair, a weakling when you needed me to be strong. If it wasn't for you our entire family would have imploded."

My throat was thick. I leaned toward our father, and he wrapped his arms around me and squeezed.

"I'm here," he said. "You need me, you call, and I'll come. You two girls and your brother are my world. I'm nothing without you. I'll never touch a bottle of liquor again; you have my word on that."

"Dad."

"No, I mean it. I went back to AA and have a sponsor. I can't do this alone, and I know it. I've got God on my side and a whole meeting full of men and women who have made it and are here to help me along the way. I'm finished burying my pain in the bottom of a bottle. The only thing alcohol has given me is more grief, more self-pity, more headaches, and more wrong turns. I'm on the right path now. I'm ready to be the father I should have always been."

"Love you, Dad," Harper said.

"Love you," I repeated.

He nodded. "Lucas and I had this talk a while back, said I'd give the same one to you two. Told him to love his wife the same way I loved Claire and he assured me he already did."

He stood then, and, leaning down, kissed Harper's cheek. "Rest well, baby girl. I'm meeting Lucas and Chantelle for dinner." He looked at me. "Join us, Willa. Your dad's treating."

"Thanks, but I think I'll stay with Harper a while longer."

This was the best conversation I'd had with our dad in more years than I could count. Maybe ever.

I could see that his visit had exhausted Harper, and she quickly drifted off to sleep. I welcomed the solitude and settled back in the comfortable chair, tucking my feet beneath me. My head swam with gratitude for the turnaround our father had made. His steps toward making restitution showed his determination to carve a new path. Knowing and loving him, I was convinced he was sincere and hoped he would pull through, no matter what the future held.

Seeing that Harper was resting comfortably, I left the hospital around nine. Lucas agreed to come get me. Before I headed back, Dr. Carroll found me and said Harper was talking less and seemed to tire even more quickly in the last couple of days. I wasn't sure what that meant and was too afraid to ask. Lucas and Chantelle were talking to Dad when I entered the apartment. They were happy, animated, chatting away. They greeted me warmly when I arrived.

"Did you pick up dinner at the hospital?" Chantelle asked.

I nodded. By the time I'd gone down to the cafeteria, the choices were few. I'd ended up with an apple and a cup of lukewarm vegetable soup. It was plenty.

"How's Harper?"

"Sleeping."

The call came in the middle of the night. It must have been around two. I didn't bother to check the time when I reached for my phone, noticing only that it was the hospital.

"Yes," I said, instantly alert.

Because Dad was sleeping in the spare room, I was on the sofa. As if aware a call in the middle of the night wouldn't be good news, both Lucas and Chantelle came out of their bedroom.

Chantelle tied the sash around her silk robe and Lucas

stood bare-chested in flannel bottoms, listening, their eyes steady on me, waiting.

My eyes held theirs as I listened, gasped, and covered my mouth, holding back the confusion and fear.

"I was with her only a few hours ago," I argued. What could possibly have happened to change everything so quickly?

The nurse made no sense. Her words were plain enough, but I couldn't take in what she was saying.

"Yes . . . thank you for letting us know." I ended the call.

Dad stood in the doorway leading to the spare bedroom. "Willa," he said, "what's happened?"

It took me a moment to answer as I mentally reviewed the short conversation. "When I left, the nurse told me Harper was stable and resting comfortably."

"That's what you said earlier," Dad reminded me.

"She's being moved to ICU."

"What?" Lucas asked, finding it as hard to assimilate as I had.

With no time to lose, I grabbed my jeans.

"You're going to the hospital?" Dad asked. "Now?"

Nodding, I shoved my legs into my pants as quickly as my body could move. "Harper asked that I come right away."

"I'm going with you," Dad insisted.

I was in a hurry. "Then I suggest you get a move on, because I'm not waiting for you."

"I'm coming, too," Lucas added, racing back to his room.

"I'll drive," Chantelle offered.

Twenty minutes later, we rushed through the hospital doors. All these weeks, I'd held on to the hope that my beautiful, vivacious sister would recover. Reality hit me in the face as we headed to the intensive care floor. The doors swung open and I paused, breathless and afraid of what awaited me on the other side.

Chapter 27

Willa

Harper was in the ICU for a week. All we could do was wait and watch. Dad was with me, Lucas and Chantelle, too. We took turns going in and spending time at her bedside, although she was mostly asleep.

I heard from Sean every day. I didn't answer his phone calls or listen to his messages, and so he resorted to texting me. I didn't want to read them, but I couldn't resist. He felt bad about our last conversation. He was sorry. He hated that he wasn't with me. He apologized repeatedly. I didn't answer. My decision had been made. All I knew was that Sean was in Chicago, finishing up the assignment with some guy named Doug.

It wasn't like I missed him. It'd been so long since Sean had been part of my daily life that he felt like someone I used to know. When I thought about him, I sometimes forgot what he looked like. He had his priorities and I had mine and they were vastly different.

On the eighth day after Harper had been taken to Intensive Care, Dad and I were in a waiting area when John came out of her room with tears glistening in his eyes.

At that moment, I realized. It was over. There was no hope. Harper was lost to us. As hard as it was, I knew I had no choice, I had to accept it. While she'd been barely conscious, I'd still held out hope, riding a roller coaster of optimism that even at this point there was a chance she'd survive.

John knelt down in front of us and took both of my hands in his. It took him a moment to compose himself before he was able to speak.

"Harper's blood counts have drastically dropped."

He didn't need to tell me this wasn't good. "They can go back up, can't they?" My words were full of angst, of hope, desperation.

"Willa," Dad said, his voice soft and gentle. "It's time to let her go."

"No," I sobbed. "Please, no."

"Willa." John's voice cracked as he said my name. "She's ready. All she needs now is for you to give her permission. She loves you, and she doesn't want to disappoint you. It's you who's keeping her hanging on. For her sake as well as your own, let her go."

I frantically shook my head. "I can't . . . I can't . . ." My heart was pounding so hard and fast it felt like it would explode through my chest.

"Willa." It was Dad again. Tears filled his eyes and he wiped his forearm beneath his nose as he sucked in a harsh breath. "Harper needs you. Give her this. Let her rest in peace. She needs you to help her to do that."

"I don't think I can," I said, weeping.

"No, Willa, you can . . . You must. It's time." Dad's voice was gentle yet strong, determined. "You did everything you could. You've carried this weight around ever since we lost your mother. It's time to give it up. I'm here. Lucas and Chantelle are here. We're all with you; you don't need to do this alone any longer."

The tension in my chest was tight, so tight I found it hard to breathe.

John's hands increased the pressure around mine. "She wants to see you, then your dad, then Lucas and Chantelle." His voice trembled when he added, "I don't believe she has much longer."

Unable to remain seated, I stood and started to pace. I pressed my fingertips against my lips, as if they could hold back the sadness and grief that threatened to overwhelm me.

"I'll go in with you," Dad offered. "If you want."

I nodded, and his hand was at the small of my back, guiding me to the door. We stood in front of it for a long moment. "I don't know that I can do this," I whispered, hardly able to find my voice.

"You can," Dad assured me. "You're the strongest woman I know."

Strong? Me? I was falling apart inside, my heart so heavy I could barely function.

Dad cupped my shoulders and I leaned against him, convinced I would have collapsed without his tight hold on me.

"Your sister needs you, Willa. I've never known you to disappoint Harper, and you won't, especially now."

His words gave me courage, more than I thought I had. As if my arm weighed two tons, I lifted it and slid open the glass door that led to the little sister who was so much a part of me. My best friend. My roommate. My lifelong companion. My very heart. We had been through everything together.

When we entered the room, Harper opened her eyes to look at me.

"It's okay, baby girl," Dad said as we approached the bed. "You gave it all you had. I love you so much. You fought the good fight. You're near the finish line now."

She blinked to let him know she'd heard him and did her best to smile.

"When you see her, you tell your mother I have always loved her. It's taken me longer than it should have to learn to live without her. I know she'll forgive me for being weak. Be sure and tell her I'm much better now."

I remembered when we stood at Mom's grave site and Harper mentioned how she'd felt Mom's presence with her when she'd been close to death after she developed leukemia. It left me to wonder if she'd felt our mother at her side this time, and I suspected she did.

Harper's smile widened ever so slightly. "Love you, Dad," she whispered.

"Love you, Harper. So much."

Her gaze shifted to me. Waiting. Wanting.

I felt that pull as if being drawn by a powerful magnet. Harper was waiting, looking for me to release her, to give her permission to surrender. As difficult as it would be for me to say the words, to set her free, I knew I had to do it.

As I struggled to find my voice, my mind flew back to the day we'd left Lucas and Chantelle's engagement party and come to this hospital full of hope and spirit, determined to win this second battle. Determined to defeat this foe, claim victory, and walk away triumphant. In my mind I saw Harper leading the next Relay for Life. She would walk to encourage those facing this fight and show that with modern medicine and faith, they, too, would survive.

Instead, despite her valiant struggle, the hope, prayers, dreams, optimism, and determination, we had lost. My sister's ravaged body barely resembled the woman she had once been. Her fighting spirit was gone, replaced with acceptance.

"You gave it your all," I said, my voice barely above a whisper. "We both did."

"I'm so sorry," Harper whispered, looking to me. "I wished with all my heart to live. You wanted it . . . I did, too."

"Oh Harper, don't be sorry. You tried."

"You're the best sister a girl could ever have."

I smiled though my tears. "Ditto."

"I never got that wedding, did I?" she said sadly. "I would have loved to have been a bride." As an encouragement, I'd talked up all we would do when the time came for Harper to get married. We had it all set, the color theme, her dress, who her bridesmaids would be. She wanted me to be the maid of honor. Those dreams had helped pass the long hours when she'd first arrived at the hospital. Like everything else we saw for the future, it was for naught.

I knew she was thinking of the physician she had come to love: John Neal. In another time, another place, they would have made a perfect couple. How sad it was for Harper to have found love in the last weeks of her life. Cancer had robbed her of that and of the family she might have had.

I bit my lower lip, trying desperately to hold back my sobs. My sister's eyes continued to hold mine. "You're going to be a wonderful mother," she said, her voice trembling. "How I wish I could be there to see it, to be the aunt to your children."

I hadn't given a thought to my own future. Until this moment it had been tied to Harper. Ever since she was born, the two of us had been linked together. She'd encouraged my relationship with Sean, but that relationship was over. I'd never told her and was glad I hadn't.

"You'll always be a part of me," I assured her.

My heart was breaking. I couldn't breathe. This wasn't supposed to be the way it ended. This shouldn't be happening, and yet it was. There was nothing left for me to do but accept this horrible truth and let my sister go.

Even with all the wires and tubes attached to her, I took Harper's hand and pressed it against my tearstained cheek.

Lucas and Chantelle came into the room, almost silently, reverently, as though they didn't know what to expect.

"Hey," Lucas whispered, standing close to our father. Dad's arm went around his son. Chantelle stood at my side.

"Hey," Harper repeated, her voice growing weaker.

"Love you."

"You . . . too." Her eyes went over each one of us. "Love," she whispered.

That was her last word.

Her eyes closed. I could actually feel her slipping away. Part of me wanted to grab her, hold her back, keep her with us. I swayed with the weight of my grief. Chantelle gripped me around the waist and kept me upright.

We stood together as a family, arms around one another, surrounding Harper. Her spirit was gone. Technology was all that was keeping her alive.

Dr. Carroll joined us, and when Harper breathed her last breath, he pronounced her dead, noting the time.

A wailing sound filled the room and I realized it came from me as I doubled over, sobbing with grief and pain and loss so profound it seemed impossible that a single being could hold up under it.

My sister was gone from us. Despite all the medical advancements. All the care. All the love. We lost.

The nurses came and disconnected all the devices and gave us a few minutes to say our goodbyes. Dad and I stood on one side of Harper while Lucas and Chantelle were on the other. No one spoke. None of us could find the words.

For my part, I couldn't stop touching Harper's face, soothing her as I had so often over the last few months.

Dad left the room and returned. "Pastor McDonald will be here shortly."

I nodded. He'd come when we'd lost Mom, too.

The next few hours passed in a blur. We gathered at Lucas and Chantelle's apartment and made funeral arrangements. Pastor McDonald met us there and prayed with us. His words barely registered as grief consumed me. Vaguely, I was aware that once the funeral was over, I would go back to what my life had once been, without Harper. It didn't seem real. Didn't seem possible.

Not until that evening, when I was mentally exhausted and my eyes burned from all the tears I'd shed.

Sean still phoned. Not as often as he had after he'd first left, but I could count on him reaching out at least once a day. When I saw his name come up on caller ID, I thought he should know.

"Willa? Thank God you answered. Babe, we need to talk. I'm sorry. Please forgive me. I'm flying back . . . I should never have left you."

"Stay."

"Stay? What? Why would I do that? Don't you need me?"

I had needed him, but the job was more important. A foretaste of any future we might have had together. "You're too late. Harper died this afternoon."

His shock reverberated across the wireless connection like a sonic boom. "No. Willa, dear Willa, I am so sorry."

"I know . . . We all are." There really wasn't a whole lot

more to say. People generally said the same things in situations like this. They were sorry, as if the death were somehow their fault. Or they were sure the loved one would be at peace now. Or in a better place. In the few hours since Harper had been pronounced dead, I'd already heard them all.

"What happened?"

"Cancer happened."

"I know . . . I mean . . . This is a shock!"

I could tell he was struggling to find words.

"I know she wasn't doing well," he continued, "but I didn't realize . . . you know, that death was imminent."

I had nothing to say.

"I'll be there tomorrow afternoon. Oh babe, I had no idea. I thought . . . I don't know what I thought. I'm so sorry. Will you be in Seattle or Oceanside?"

"Why?" I didn't mean to be obtuse, but why should it matter?

"Why?" he repeated. "So I can be with you."

"You haven't been with me in weeks, why is it important now?"

"Willa, please. I know you're in shock and I hate that I wasn't there for you. But I'll be there soon."

I almost smiled. As far as I was concerned, it was too little, too late. I had nothing left to give.

"Promise you'll talk to me," he urged.

"Promise?" I repeated, as if this was more than I could manage, and at this point, it was.

"Willa, please, tell me what I can do to make this better."

"Make this better?" I asked, as if that was humanly

possible. "My sister is dead, Sean. A bowl of ice cream, a walk on the beach, ten sunny days in a row isn't going to make this better. Nothing this side of heaven could put a dent in this grief. This loss. This pain. I'm empty. Devastated. You aren't going to be able to make this better. No one can."

"Oh Willa . . ."

He seemed to be at a loss for words, which was fine because I wasn't ready to hear anything more he had to say.

"Thank you for calling, but please don't again."

"Willa, don't hang up."

"I'm sorry, Sean," I whispered. "It's over," and I disconnected the call.

Chapter 28

Scan

After my conversation with Willa and hearing the news about her sister, I didn't sleep all night. What I'd said was true. I wasn't clueless. I knew Willa was upset about my leaving so soon after my return from the Philippines. I got the hint when she didn't pick up my calls. At first I rationalized that she was at the hospital with Harper and had turned off her phone. Then my voicemails went unanswered. So did my text messages.

When I'd joined Doug in Chicago, I assumed we'd be able to wrap this all up in a couple of days. I'd been wrong. The last bit was intense. We were putting in long days. I did my best, pressing ahead as fast as I could in my effort to get back to Seattle and be with Willa. We weren't far from completing the comprehensive article with the accompanying photographs. I have to admit that I was proud of how it had come together. Doug knew I needed to leave and said I should go. He would finish up the last bit without me, seeing that I wasn't offering him much at that point.

I was thrilled when I was finally able to connect with Willa.

Learning of Harper's death had left me in shock. I was sick at heart. My stomach clenched with what a selfish, self-absorbed idiot I'd been. I'd gotten caught up in my career the same way I had back when I played baseball. The entire world revolved around me. Everything was about me and my work, my goals.

In my stupidity I might well have lost the one woman I loved. With everything in me, I prayed I wasn't too late and that I could make it up to Willa, that I could help her through this dark tunnel of grief. I refused to believe she meant it when she said we were finished.

As soon as the plane landed, I raced to get home. I collected Bandit first thing, thanking Logan once again for watching the dog. Bandit didn't seem all that eager to go with me. After my long absences, he was probably more comfortable with Logan than with me. It looked like Willa wasn't the only one I was going to have to win over.

On the way from Logan's I stopped off at Willa's apartment and knocked, hoping to see her, talk to her. I knew I wouldn't be able to rest until I could make things right between us.

No answer.

Next I checked in at Bean There and was shocked to see the sign on the door that read: TEMPORARILY CLOSED.

One of her regular customers worked next door at the

candy store. The window displays never failed to attract a crowd, especially when they featured the homemade saltwater taffy.

I walked over and stuck my head in, grateful to see that Allison wasn't busy. "How long has Willa's shop been closed?" I asked, thinking the closure was probably due to Harper's death.

Allison, busy at the counter, paused as if to count the days. "Must be more than a week now."

"That long?" Willa hadn't mentioned anything about needing to close. It left me to wonder what else I'd missed with my selfish ambition. What else hadn't she felt comfortable enough to share?

"Did you hear?" Allison asked, her welcoming smile vanishing. "About Harper Lakey, Willa's sister?"

"I did."

Allison shook her head. "Damn shame, you know. She was young, so full of life. And they were especially close. Willa is going to take her death hard. We're all shaken by it."

"You wouldn't happen to have seen Willa in town, have you?"

Allison shook her head. "Not since I heard the news."

"Do you have any idea where I might find her?"

Again, the shopkeeper had no answer. "If anyone in town would know, it would be Pastor McDonald."

I briefly remembered meeting the man. I'd liked him. He was personable and down-to-earth. I located his address on my phone and drove to the nondenominational church where he preached.

Leaving Bandit in the vehicle, I went to the church and found the doors locked. On my way back to the car, I noticed a parsonage behind the church and decided to check there.

I knocked several times before anyone answered. A middle-aged woman opened the door to me. "Can I help you? Before you ask, we're not interested in buying anything."

"I'm looking for Pastor McDonald," I explained, amused that she thought I resembled a door-to-door salesperson. Sleepless, hours in the air, plus the long drive to the ocean from Seattle—no doubt I looked disheveled.

"Pastor is with the Lakey family."

"Do you know where that might be? I'm a friend of Willa's," I said, hoping that would explain my interest.

She looked me up and down, her eyes narrowing. I must have passed muster, because she said, "Heath mentioned something about them all meeting up at the funeral home."

"Thank you," I said, grateful for the help.

My impulse was to race there, but then I paused, having second thoughts. I had Bandit with me, and I was a mess. This was a private time for Willa and her family to plan Harper's burial. Now wasn't the time or the place for me to go bursting in like some savior and sweep Willa into my arms.

Following our conversation from the night before, I feared Willa never wanted to see me again. As eager as I was to resolve this distance between us, I had to accept that this wasn't the right moment.

Depressed and at a loss for how best to make matters right, I drove home. Bandit walked into the living room, looked around, and sat down on his haunches by the front door. It was as if he wanted to say that if I was leaving again, he was finished with me.

"Okay, point taken."

With a sense of purpose and resolve, I unpacked my bags and started a load of wash. My stomach reminded me that I hadn't eaten all day. The refrigerator was shockingly empty unless I was interested in a mustard-and-ketchup sandwich.

On the bottom of my list of things I wanted to do was go grocery shopping. However, my stomach wasn't the only one I needed to feed. Not thirty minutes after I arrived home, I was in my car again, Bandit curled up and asleep in the backseat.

The following morning, I went in search of Willa a second time. Bandit didn't look pleased when I left the house. Can't say I blamed him. Seemed every time I walked away it was for a good long while. Not something I'd recommend in relationship-building, both with my rescue dog and with my girl.

I connected with Pastor McDonald at the parsonage and met his wife, the woman who'd answered the door.

"You're Willa's young man," he said, remembering our brief meeting.

"Yes. I returned from a business trip in Chicago yesterday. How's Willa holding up?"

He didn't hesitate, his eyes holding mine. "She's taken the death of her sister hard."

"Do you think I should seek her out?" I asked, needing

guidance. "Or would it be best to wait?" I called myself a coward, afraid of what Willa might say or do when she saw me. I was afraid she didn't want me in her life any longer, and I couldn't, I wouldn't, accept that.

"She's at the church now," he said.

That didn't answer my question. "Then I should go to her? Will that help?"

"Can't hurt." He didn't seem to have strong feelings one way or the other, which wasn't encouraging.

"Thank you," I said, and left to walk over to the church.

Stepping into the dim interior of the church, I found Willa sitting in the front pew, staring at the altar. Silently, I slid into the row and sat next to her, leaving a small amount of space between us.

She glanced up when I sat down, paused, and then looked away.

We sat in silence for several minutes. I reached for her hand and gave it a soft squeeze before she dragged it away as though she didn't want or need my touch.

"Is there anything I can do?" I asked.

Willa shook her head.

"What about for your family?"

Again, she declined. "There's nothing anyone can do. Thanks for asking."

Although she didn't say it, I noticed the tension in her seemed to increase the longer I sat by her side. Her back stiffened and she bowed her head as if willing me to leave.

The last thing I wanted to do was walk away. And yet I felt like an intruder, unwanted, a nuisance. I reasoned it was guilt weighing me down. Reluctantly, I stood, wanting her to stop me. She didn't.

"I'm here if you need me."

Willa emitted a soft snicker. "You're a little late for that."

I longed to defend myself. I wasn't a mind reader. If she'd told me, if I'd known how close to death Harper had been, I would have taken the next flight out of Chicago. Screw the project; Willa needed me. Only she wasn't answering my calls, had ignored both my texts and voicemails. Knowing how badly she was hurting, I swallowed down the need to defend myself.

Moving to the end of the pew, I turned back. Willa hadn't budged; she continued to stare straight ahead, as if I'd already left the church. I found it impossible to leave matters as they were.

"I'm sorry I wasn't there when you needed me," I told her.

Silence.

"Can you forgive me?" My heart raced as I waited for her answer.

Then and only then did she turn to look at me, her eyes red and brimming with tears. "Of course."

I should have been relieved, but the indifference in her response had the opposite effect.

"I'm serious, Willa. Words can't express how bad I feel about all this. I should have been with you, should have been the one you could lean on for support to see you through those last days with your sister."

Her face was full of questions when she looked back at me. "I don't know why you would think that, Sean. It's all very sweet of you, but unnecessary."

"Why?" I said, much too loud for being in a church. My voice echoed in the empty space like a bell toll. "You're my girl. Don't you realize how important you are to me? I love you."

It seemed as if my declaration of love went directly over her head. For a long time, all she did was stare at me. "Really?"

"Yes, really," I insisted.

She shrugged, as if my declaration was nothing more than empty words. From all the calls, texts, and voicemails I'd left, she had to know she was constantly in my thoughts. I wanted to remind her that the last time I was home, not all that long ago, she'd slept in my bed. I spent the night with her in my arms. She'd needed me. Sought out my comfort.

This had to be her grief talking. I consoled myself with the hope that within a short amount of time, and with patience, we'd be back on an even keel. As hard as it was to leave matters as they were, it would be best to leave this discussion for another day.

The doors at the back of the church opened and the man I recognized as Harper's friend and physician walked down the center aisle toward us.

Immediately, Willa came to her feet, edged past me, and raced toward him. As I watched, she flew into John's arms, hugging him and weeping on his shoulder. With her face buried against his front, I couldn't make out what she said.

Watching another man hold Willa caused my stomach to tighten. I should be the one comforting her, but Willa didn't want me. It hurt in a physical way I hadn't expected.

Chapter 29

Willa

The morning of Harper's funeral, I rose early and headed for the beach, needing to clear my head. I hoped to find strength and some badly needed peace in the one place I knew I'd find solace.

Sleep had evaded me since my sister's death. I tossed, twisting the sheets about me until exhaustion would finally lay claim to me. Then within an hour, possibly two if I was lucky, I'd wake sobbing, finding it hard to accept the truth that Harper was truly gone.

Everything in our apartment reminded me of my sister. Each item that was hers brought up memories. Her mountain-climbing equipment. The little stuffed mouse she'd purchased for Snowball. Her shampoo tucked in the corner of the shower. She was everywhere I looked.

Eventually I'd need to clear out her bedroom—a task I dreaded. If possible, I'd need to find another roommate, but that was a problem for another day. My rent was paid until the end of the month for both the apartment and Bean There. This month and this month only. My bank account was empty, and I had no way of making the payment for either come December. Today, the one in which we would bury my sister, held enough grief without my dragging my problems of the future into it.

The briny scent coming off the ocean filled the air, and the wind buffeted against me, colder now that it was November. I wrapped my coat more securely around me, hoping to find warmth when everything around me was cold and gray. Gloomy and dark. Miserable.

The overcast sky held the promise of rain later in the day. The burial was scheduled for that morning. The final goodbye. Yet how could I ever really let go of Harper? It would be impossible to release my beautiful sister, even in death.

One of the last things I'd said to her was that she would always be a part of me, and it was true. I would carry her love with me into the future, no matter what it held or where it would take me.

At the appropriate time, Dad, Lucas, Chantelle, John, and I met at the funeral home. The casket was open, and we were given time privately to say our final goodbye before it was closed.

I stood before my sister and looked upon her one last time. Harper's head was covered with her lilac-colored wig. Leukemia had ravaged her body, but it hadn't been able to steal her beauty. She looked nothing like she once had, but it didn't distract from who she was. I touched her face one last time, swallowed my tears, and turned away, bracing myself for whatever this desperately sad day would hold. Of all of us, John lingered at her casket the longest, his grief as deep as our own. His heart broken. He had gone above and beyond in his effort to save her.

The flowers I'd chosen were surrounded with lilac ribbons, bright and cheerful. Harper would have hated to see us grieving; her wish was that we would celebrate her life. Rejoice that her suffering was over and that she was at peace.

The funeral director drove us to the church. I wasn't sure how many from the community would attend and was surprised to see that thirty minutes before the funeral was scheduled to begin, the parking lot was full.

As we exited the car, Dad kept his arm wrapped around me.

"It's going to be okay," he whispered.

This was his way of assuring me he hadn't taken a drink. Although I hadn't mentioned it to Lucas, having our father fall off the wagon was a big concern. Dad had been doing well for two months and seemed better than he had been in years. But this . . . the death of his child was sure to shake that fragile foundation of sobriety. If anything would threaten to cause him to drink again, it would be this day.

I clung to his arm, wanting him to know how proud I was of him. Proud and grateful. "You're doing great." My hope was that he'd remain strong in the aftermath of today and into the future.

We filed into the church as a family and were blessed to find the loving support of our community. Harper was loved, and her death was duly noted by those whose lives she had touched.

I noticed Sean sat in the first row behind the family. As we walked in, he captured my gaze, and while I wanted to look away, I found I couldn't. Emotion clouded his face. Regret. Sympathy. Guilt. I hadn't the strength to deal with his feelings; his actions told me his work would always come first in his life. I needed more than he could give. Realizing and accepting that now was a good thing for us both.

Harper's closest friends, Joelle, Leesa, and Carrie, had insisted on preparing the lunch that would follow the funeral. They were as determined as I'd been to make this as celebratory as possible. They'd cooked and baked, working long into the night to be sure all would be ready. I'd spent a good amount of time with them. Chantelle, too. We'd wept and hugged one another and laughed, remembering Harper and loving her. I'd helped bake dozens of lemon-flavored cupcakes, Harper's favorite, and frosted them with vanilla icing.

Pastor McDonald approached the lectern. He'd been wonderful. He'd prayed with us, but mostly he'd listened. He didn't offer any of the usual platitudes. Instead, he'd sat with us and heard our pain and grief. When I mentioned how angry I was with God, he sympathized and gently said that God understood.

For Harper's funeral he chose the verse from I Corinthians 2:9 to prepare the eulogy.

"No eyes have seen, no ear has heard, no mind has conceived what God has prepared for those who love Him."

It was perfect. He looked out over the packed church and spoke, his words filled with encouragement and comfort. He knew Harper, who had been raised in this same church. She'd attended Sunday school here as a child—we both had. Mom was the one who'd brought us, and Dad joined when he wasn't working and on holidays. Harper had memorized enough Bible verses to be awarded her own Bible. The very one she'd packed with her when she'd entered the hospital all those months ago. Her Bible: Well read, well worn, well loved.

The church had standing room only. While Pastor McDonald eulogized Harper, I could feel Sean's eyes on me. Without a single audible word, I sensed everything he'd wanted to say. How desperately sorry he was to have left me when I'd needed him most. Had he realized . . . had he known, understood how desperate Harper's condition was, he would have found a way to be at my side. He wanted us to go back, start again, and silently begged me to give him a second chance.

For me, at this point in my life, the answer was no. I didn't mean to be cruel. I could forgive him and in fact already had. That didn't change my decision, though. As it was, I was holding on by a thread.

Pastor McDonald looked to me as he spoke. "I know a lot of you feel that your hope, your prayers, your faith, were ignored by God. I'm here to assure you that isn't true. God has answered all our prayers, just not the way we wanted or expected. Remember, Harper is free now: free of cancer, free of pain. She is free. Harper is perfect and whole and in paradise. I can see her now, putting together a yoga class."

A small laugh followed. The thing was, I could envision that scene myself. Harper had never been one to sit still for long. It helped to think of her with her toned body, healthy and happy, free from the cancer that had taken her from us. It was the image I chose to hold in my mind.

At the end of the service, we headed to the community center for the wake, where lunch would be served.

Dad, Lucas, and I stood in the doorway and greeted each person who came through, thanking them for their love and support. Joelle, Leesa, and Carrie took over in the kitchen, along with several ladies from the church. Chantelle and John stayed close by in case we needed anything.

We hugged, wept, and were consoled. No one could ever doubt how deeply Harper had impacted our small town.

Dr. Annie and Keaton were among the last to come through the door. Annie hugged me and expelled a deep breath. "I never thought it'd come to this," she whispered.

"Me, neither." Until the very end, I'd wanted to believe Harper would survive, and I knew she did, too.

"You're a good sister, Willa. She adored you."

Hearing someone I respected as much as Annie say that brought a fresh batch of tears to my eyes. We hugged each other long and hard.

Keaton, always a man of few words, stood awkwardly behind his wife. "Sorry for your loss."

"Thank you," I said, and impulsively hugged him. He was a huge man, and I knew he found my display of affection surprising, yet he returned my embrace and gently patted my back.

Preston followed behind Keaton. I knew the two couples were the best of friends. To my surprise, his wife, Mellie, was with him. She rarely went anywhere when crowds of people were present. For years she'd felt trapped inside her home, afraid to venture out. Only after she'd fallen in love with Preston had she felt comfortable enough to leave the house.

After shaking Dad's and Lucas's hands, Preston hugged me and whispered, "Come see me next week?"

"What for?"

"You need a comfort dog."

I should have suspected he had an ulterior motive. As the head of the animal shelter, he was always looking for good homes.

"My apartment complex doesn't allow pets," I reminded him. I didn't mention that I would likely need to move, unless I found a roommate. Frankly, living with a stranger didn't appeal to me.

When we finished with the reception line, Sean approached with a plate of food. "Eat something," he urged.

The gesture was thoughtful, but I shook my head. "Thank you, but I'm not hungry."

"When was the last time you ate?"

I sincerely wished he'd stop. His gentle care hurt nearly as much as his absence had earlier.

Rather than get involved in a discussion regarding my eating habits, I was grateful to see that many guests were starting to leave. Pastor McDonald spoke with Dad and Lucas, and I saw Dad nod. He glanced my way, letting me know it was time for us to head to the cemetery.

"If you'll excuse me," I said, escaping Sean.

The grave site was prepared, a tent covering the open hole where the casket would be lowered. I knew Dad had expected it would be him who would be laid to rest next to Mom, and not one of his children.

Cars lined the narrow roadway closest to the grave site. As we gathered around, John stood at my side, his arm around my shoulders. I felt his sadness as keenly as my own. How we had hoped for a different outcome. How we had prayed and planned and sought a miracle.

For weeks, I had desperately asked God to heal my sister. My faith was much larger than a mustard seed. I had an avocado-sized faith. And when I was forced to accept that there would be no miracle, my faith was shaken off its foundation. I was angry with God. Angry with the world. Hurting and bitterly disappointed.

Then my thoughts wandered to the eulogy, and my decision to remember Harper as healthy and whole in heaven now, putting together a yoga class.

Pastor McDonald stood at the grave site, read several passages from the Bible, bowed his head, and said a final prayer.

It was finished. Now we were left to carry on.

Without Harper.

Those who'd assembled started to walk back to their cars. The funeral home had provided a vehicle to drive us back into town. I knew Lucas and Chantelle and John needed to return to Seattle.

Dad came to Lucas and me. "Son, I need you to take Chantelle and Willa back home."

"You're not coming with us?" Lucas asked, and seemed as puzzled as I was. He looked to me for an explanation, but I had none.

"Not yet," Dad said. "I'm staying."

I hadn't a clue what Dad was thinking.

"What are you going to do?" Lucas asked, concerned.

Our father placed a hand on each of our shoulders. "I'm not going to let a backhoe bury my daughter. I'm going to do it myself."

"Oh Daddy." I hurled myself into his arms, overcome with love for my father and his tender heart.

"You don't need to do it alone," Lucas said. "I'll join you."

"As will I," John added.

Everyone had left, or so I believed, until I saw Sean walking across the cemetery, with the man I could only assume was the groundskeeper. In his hands were four shovels.

Chapter 30

Willa

Life was supposed to return to some kind of normal now that Harper had been laid to rest. My sister might be *resting,* but those of us who had been left behind had to find a way to return to our lives again. The task felt overwhelming, if not impossible. The one thing that would save me, I decided, was my daily routine. That meant getting my business up and running again. I would need to do that in stages.

My first step was to approach the local bank to see if I qualified for a loan to cover rent until I was back on my feet. This wasn't something I looked forward to doing. I delayed as long as I could. My only assets were a car, which I was still paying off, and my business, which was in danger of folding.

I knew the loan officer, Leon Bent, was sympathetic, but this was business. A few years back he'd briefly dated Harper before she'd introduced him to the woman who eventually became his wife. That was Harper, the matchmaker.

Part of me believed my sister somehow knew she wasn't long for this life. That helped explain why she never allowed any relationship to continue for more than a few weeks. She'd never let herself fall in love. The one exception had been John Neal. She had fallen head over heels for the wonderful doctor and he had fallen hard for her. It hurt to think of all Harper would be missing in life. She would have been a terrific wife and a fabulous mother.

Pushing thoughts of my sister out of my mind, I squared my shoulders and opened the glass door that led into the local bank. Leon was expecting me, and stood when I approached his desk.

"Willa," he said, and extended his hand for me to shake, reminding me this was all business. "What can I do for you?" He gestured for me to take a seat.

I lowered myself into the chair and clasped my hands, which were trembling. Unsure where to start, I struggled to hold back the tears. "As you might have guessed, the last few months have been tough."

"Ellen and I were terribly sorry to hear about Harper."

Glancing down, I swallowed hard and held my breath, fearing if I tried to speak, I'd fall apart emotionally. After several tense seconds, I looked up and managed a weak smile.

"As I was saying, being away from the shop was detrimental to my cash flow." No need to delay the purpose for my visit. "I'm here about a loan, Leon, otherwise I'll be forced to close my doors."

"You're already closed," he reminded me.

"Close permanently," I whispered, nearly choking on the

words and the thought of losing the years of hard work and sacrifice I'd put into Bean There.

Leon asked all the questions I knew he would, then gave me the paperwork to fill out and leave with him. Once I laid it on his desk, he said, "I'll do what I can, Willa, but no promises."

"Thank you." I appreciated his honesty and left with little hope.

Suspecting the bank would refuse a loan, my second and less desirable step was to approach my shop landlord. The property owner lived in Spokane, and I knew Lewis Johnson and his wife depended on the rent money for their retirement. Making that phone call was even more difficult than approaching the bank for a loan had been.

"Willa," Lewis said, answering the phone. "Julie and I are so sorry to hear about your sister." Then, getting right to the point, he asked, "What do you need?"

My mouth was dry. "With everything that's happened, I want you to know I won't have the rent money come December . . . I've gone to the bank and asked for a loan, but—"

"Willa, stop. Your December rent has already been paid, but you should know I wouldn't have hounded you for the money either way. You're a good tenant and I don't intend to lose you."

Stunned, I found myself unable to speak. "Who . . . Who made the payment?" The question squeaked out of the tightness in my throat.

"They asked to remain anonymous."

It could only have been Sean.

"You don't have a thing to worry about. There are a lot of people who want to support you."

"Thank you," I said, stumbling over the words before we disconnected.

While relieved that I had one less worry, I was angry that Sean felt he could step in at the last minute and play hero. Clearly he was looking to absolve his regret and rescue me. If he assumed he could buy his way back into my life, he had another think coming. I wouldn't stand for it. I may not have much, but I wasn't about to forfeit my pride.

Before I could even consider what I intended to say, I leaped into my car and drove out to Sean's place. I slammed the car into park so hard I jerked forward until the seatbelt snapped across my upper body.

I marched up to his front door and pounded against the wood. It didn't take him long to answer. The moment he saw me, he broke into a wide, warm, welcoming smile.

No doubt he'd been expecting me to rush to his side weepy and grateful. Well, that wasn't happening.

"Willa, I'm so glad you're here."

He brought me into the house, and Bandit, who was curled up in front of the fireplace, came to me, his tail wagging with welcome.

"Why would you do that?" I demanded. Then, because I found it impossible to contain my anger, I paced his living area.

"I'm sorry?" He looked confused. He was a good actor.

"Don't play games with me, Sean. I know you were the one who paid my December rent for Bean There."

His eyes narrowed. "I didn't."

"Don't lie to me . . . You're the only one I told, and I immediately regretted it. I regret it even more now."

"Willa, please, listen to me. You can be as angry as you want, but I'm telling you the truth." His gaze dared me to defy him. "The truth is I considered it, but I had no way of knowing who your landlord is or how to get in touch. Besides, I knew you wouldn't want that from me."

He sounded sincere. I blinked, unsure what to believe.

"I want to help. I do. And I would if I didn't believe you'd think I was looking for a way to buy back your favor."

That was exactly what I'd thought.

We stood, staring at each other. "Okay, fine, but if it wasn't you, then who was it?"

Sean's look grew thoughtful. "You may have mentioned it to me in passing, but your family must have known. The shop hasn't been open in nearly a month. It wouldn't take much for someone in town to put two and two together."

Dad knew my circumstances. I remembered him telling me he'd put a bit of money aside. Dad was friends with Lewis Johnson, my landlord. It could only have been my father. Lucas and Chantelle might have contributed, too.

The awareness must have shown in my eyes, because Sean took hold of both of my shoulders and held me at arm's length. "Don't you have any idea of how much you're loved? Bean There is part of the fabric of this community. No one wants you to lose your business, least of all me."

I snickered. "You don't even like coffee."

"True, but I'm crazy about the woman who brews it."

That was the last thing I wanted to hear, especially from him.

As if he could read my mind, Sean added, "Give me another chance, Willa. Let me show you how important you are to me. I've been heartsick knowing how badly I failed you."

Being unnecessarily cruel to Sean or anyone went against my nature. "I appreciate what you're saying; I know you're sincere and I wish things could be different for us, I really do. It would be easy to love you, but I can't let that happen."

"Why? Because I wasn't with you when Harper was sick?"

"No," I said, keeping the emotion out of my voice, although it was difficult. "It isn't only that you were gone when my life was falling apart. It's because I know I will never be able to count on you. You're married to your career.

"You are who you are," I continued, "and I won't ask you to change. Your work is your life, your mistress. You love it and the risks that go along with it. In the short time I've known you, think about all the chances you've taken. Our relationship isn't working for me. I'm sorry, I truly am."

"But—"

"It would be best if we didn't see each other again, Sean. I wish it could be different."

I could see Sean struggling, wanting to argue. He opened his mouth, but when he saw the determined look in my eyes, he closed it again.

Knowing this would likely be the last time I'd see him

outside of Bean There or around town, I leaned forward and kissed his cheek. "Thank you," I said, and moved back one step.

He continued to stare at me as I headed for the front door. I was on my way out when he stopped me.

"Willa," he said with a tenderness I didn't expect, "don't make the mistake of turning away from love. We have our differences, but we can work past them if you'll give me another chance."

I hesitated and then sadly shook my head. After burying my sister, I couldn't face losing someone else I loved. Making an emotional investment in Sean was too much for me.

As if reading my mind, he added, "Loving someone, anyone, including me, will always involve some risk. I love you. I have almost from the first moment we met. It's crazy how long it took me to work up the courage to tell you.

"You shook my world. You still do. One day, and I pray it will be soon, you'll realize that love is worth the cost. Otherwise, I fear you'll end up alone and bitter, thinking about all that you missed out on in life."

"That's my choice," I reminded him.

"It is," he said, walking me to the door. "Choose wisely, my love."

Stepping out into the wind and rain, a chill came over me. Ignoring it, I walked to where I'd left my car, the harsh weather beating down against me.

I connected with Shirley, who I'd spoken to only briefly since I'd moved back into town. I told her I planned to open again on Thursday morning. It would take that long to complete an inventory and purchase what I'd need to get back up and running. I would serve only what I could order in quickly or bake myself. The coffee beans had to be freshly roasted and of the highest quality. No one brewed a better cup of java than Bean There, and I was determined it would stay that way.

As soon as Shirley learned I was opening my doors once again, she stopped by the shop. "Thank the good Lord," she squealed, hugging me hard enough to crack a rib.

I'd been convinced I'd worked her to the point that she wouldn't want to return. "You're willing to come back?"

"You couldn't keep me away," she said, squeezing me again. "If I ever threaten to quit or retire, remind me what it's like at home."

Grinning, I knew she wanted me to ask. "What's so bad about being at home?"

"It's Randy." She tossed her hand into the air. "He expects me to be his personal maid. Cook his breakfast, fix his lunch. Are his clothes washed? I swear, what do I look like? His servant?"

I struggled to hide a smile, knowing Randy well. He had recently retired from work with the city.

"He wants me to bake day and night, and not just for him," she continued. "He promised his poker buddies that I'd provide homemade goodies every week. You'd think I had nothing better to do than see to his every wish."

"I'll be glad to have you back," I said, grateful she was inclined to return.

"I never appreciated the fact that this job saved my marriage."

She released me and I was able to breathe normally again.

"It's good to be back," she said, "but it's even better to have you here with me."

She was right. This was exactly where I needed to be.

"Joelle said she'd be happy to fill in until you could hire a full-time barista," Shirley continued. "I reached out to her after you called. I hope you don't mind."

"Not at all." My one hope was that we'd have enough business to keep the two of us busy.

"Should I let her know we'll be up and running again come Thursday morning?"

"Please."

Standing in the middle of my kitchen, I felt almost alive again. Walking around the room, I ran my hand over the counter and the front of the ovens, getting the feel of it back in my blood, stirring me awake.

Deciding to reopen Bean There felt right. It was where I belonged, where I was most comfortable, where I could forget the pain that threatened to rip me apart.

On Thursday morning, my stomach was a ball of nerves. I'd been up and baking for two hours before Joelle arrived. After she tied the apron around her waist, I asked if she'd unlock the front door and turn on the OPEN sign.

Harper's friend shook her head. "This morning, that's something you need to do yourself."

Surprised that she'd refuse me, I noticed that she trailed along behind me when I unlocked the door. I didn't have a chance to turn on the neon OPEN sign before a line of customers quickly filed into the shop. Most I recognized, and others I didn't.

A very long line of customers.

Stunned, I looked outside and saw the queue stretched all the way down the block. The wonderful people of Oceanside were letting me know how much they'd loved Harper and how much they cared about me and my small coffee shop.

Chapter 31

Sean

I couldn't stop thinking about Willa and her family. I felt at a loss as to how best to help, especially since she'd made it clear she'd rather I stayed out of her life. I knew I needed to be gentle and patient with her. In time, she'd come to understand that I wasn't going away. As far as I was concerned, Willa Lakey was it for me. The yin to my yang, the sun to my moon, the woman I intended to love the rest of my life. All that I needed now was to convince her that we were meant to be together.

I was one of the first people in line the day she reopened her business. I made it my mission to return every day until she got the message. For the first four days, she didn't acknowledge me other than to greet me and wish me a good day. It was the same treatment she gave every customer. As soon as she recognized me, she avoided eye contact, filled my order, and sent me on my way, ignoring any effort I made to engage her in conversation. My frustration mounted, although I didn't allow it to show. I ended every transaction the same way. "See you tomorrow."

On the fifth day, I saw her dad sitting at a table, the very one where Harper once sat. He read the newspaper as he sipped his coffee. This was my chance to seek his advice. Braving it, I took my mocha and approached him.

"Would you mind if I join you?" I asked, pulling out the chair, determined not to take no for an answer.

He looked around and must have noticed that there were several vacant tables. "Sure." He set aside the newspaper and leaned back in his chair to study me. "You're Willa's young man, aren't you?"

"I'd like to think so." I took a sip of my mocha to hide the pleasure his words gave me.

"I appreciated your help there at the grave site. Couldn't have buried Harper alone, as much as I would have been willing to try, my back being what it is and all. You getting those other shovels was a big help."

His appreciation embarrassed me. "I wanted to help . . . It's hard to know what one can do in situations like that."

"You love my girl?" he asked, staring me down.

I appreciated that he was direct. "With all my heart." I held his look, hoping he heard the sincerity in my voice.

His brow folded into a frown, as if he wasn't sure he should believe me. "I haven't seen you around much."

"Willa doesn't want to see me . . . after I failed her. I was away during most of Harper's illness. Willa is finding it hard to forgive me for that; frankly, I don't blame her.

Had I known . . . I've made a mess of this, Mr. Lakey; I need help."

"It's Stan," he said.

"Like I said, I need your advice. Do you have any ideas on how I can win Willa back?" Life without her would be unimaginable. I was determined to make sure that didn't happen.

"Like I said, I haven't seen you around much."

"I've been here every day," I argued. "She greets me like I'm a stranger."

He took a deep swallow of his drink, as if he needed time to think. "Don't suppose you know she walks along the beach every afternoon, usually around four. She seems to find solace there."

"Thank you." My heart throbbed with gratitude. I planned to take full advantage of running into her and had the perfect excuse. Bandit needed exercise. She couldn't fault me if our paths just happened to cross.

Another thought came to mind of how I might be able to help. Willa would need to clear out Harper's bedroom. I could only speculate how difficult that would be. "What's happened to Harper's things? Is there any way I could help with that?"

"It's all been packed up. Willa couldn't do it; she tried and found it too hard. Lucas and I took care of it."

The thought of her dealing with all the memories and mementos caused my gut to clench.

"What's she going to do about the apartment?" I suspected

a two-bedroom place would be too expensive for her to maintain for long, especially since she was having financial difficulties. She'd had enough change in her life, losing her sister and best friend. Uprooting herself would only add to the upheaval.

"Willa and I are talking." His eyes brightened for just a moment.

"Oh?" I hoped he would elaborate.

"There's lots of temptation for me at the casino, if you know what I mean. I let my family down after I lost my wife, turning to the bottle instead of dealing with my grief."

Alcoholic drinks flowed freely at the casino. Being around that wouldn't be easy for him.

"I've been thinking long and hard on what I need to do. Years ago, I worked in the lumber business. Too old for anything that physical these days. A friend of mine mentioned the hardware store was looking for a sales associate. I used to be something of a handyman. Raising a family made it necessary to do a lot of projects around the house myself. I'm hoping they'll be willing to hire me."

I could see the benefit of that for Stan. It would be good for Willa to have him close. She needed him and he needed her.

"If I'm fortunate enough to get the job in town, then I'll move in with Willa."

That would be even better.

He stood and pushed in his chair. "Nice talking to you,

son. Don't you give up on Willa. She'll come around. Just give her some time."

I sincerely hoped he was right.

That afternoon, I was at the beach at the time Stan suggested. The instant I opened the car door, Bandit bounded out, tugging at his leash. Scanning the area, I saw Willa. Her back was to me and a football field away. I released Bandit and watched him race toward her, his feet kicking up sand.

When she saw him, she got down on one knee, wrapped her arms around his neck, and buried her face in his fur. She was still on her knees when I approached, the wind billowing around us.

"Hey," I said, as if it was the most natural thing in the world for us to meet.

She looked up, her eyes puffy and swollen, tears wet on her cheeks. It demanded all I had not to take her in my arms and comfort her.

She broke into sobs and buried her face in her hands. Her pain was so strong, her shoulders shook with the weight of her grief.

"Willa . . ."

"Go," she sobbed.

"I can't."

"Go away," she said again, this time with more conviction.

Kneeling on the other side of Bandit, I reached out to her, placing my hand over hers, and experienced the same shot of warmth and rightness I felt each time we touched. She jerked her arm away.

"Please," she begged. "Leave me alone."

Her words cut me to the quick. I stood, loving her enough to give her what she needed, even though I wanted nothing more than to be the one to comfort her. "Bandit," I ordered, "come."

Although it was hard, I left Willa. Bandit raced back and forth between us as if seeking a way to bring us together. By the end of thirty minutes, he was exhausted and lay down on the sand, panting.

Just as I left the beach, it started to rain. Willa remained, walking in the drizzle as if unaware the heavens were weeping with her.

The following day, I returned at the same time. As soon as I undid his leash, Bandit took off, running to Willa. She greeted him again but didn't look to see where I was. After a few minutes of giving Bandit love and attention, she continued walking. I didn't approach her, although she had to know I was on the beach.

On the third and fourth day she didn't show. I got the message. If I was going to invade this private time she took to grieve, then she planned to not come. My frustration mounted. This wasn't working. If nothing else, I needed to let her know I'd stay away. She wanted that time alone, and I would give her that.

Although I was tempted to stop by the house and tell her,

I waited until the following morning when I went for my mocha. Willa was at the counter. She stiffened when she saw me.

"What can I get you today?" she asked, addressing me as if we were strangers.

"The usual," I said in even tones.

She quickly brewed my mocha and set it on the counter.

I handed her the money, but when she went to take the bill, I held on to the cash. "I won't be going to the beach any longer."

She looked up and I met her gaze. It was the first time since our last conversation at my house that she'd bothered to make eye contact with me.

"Thank you," she whispered.

Seeing my chance, I spoke. "I'd do anything I could to help you, but you need to know something, Willa. I'm here for the long haul. I'm not going away. I love you, and that's not going to change."

Her eyes glistened and she swallowed tightly before she said, "I wish you wouldn't."

"Not happening, love." I started to turn away before I remembered the question I wanted to ask. "Say, did your dad get that job at the hardware store?"

"Yes . . . How did you know about that?"

"He mentioned it the other day."

"Oh." She seemed pleased for him. "He's excited about it."

This was the longest conversation we'd had in weeks. By this time, I was starved for encouragement, some sign that would give me hope. Brief as our conversation was, it buoyed my spirits.

As I left the shop, I saw Stan Lakey climbing out of his car. With my drink in my hand I approached him. "Hey, I hear congratulations are in order. You got the job."

His grin was huge. "I'm grateful." He rubbed his hand down his pants leg. "Have to say I'm not looking forward to the move, though."

"You need help with that?"

He frowned as if he wasn't sure he'd heard me. "Are you volunteering?"

"I wouldn't have asked if I didn't mean it." At his age, packing and hauling boxes wouldn't be easy.

"Willa said she'd stop by after she closed, but I was hoping to get an early start."

"Then I'm your man."

He hesitated, as if he still wasn't sure I was sincere. "You don't need to do this, son."

"Don't need to," I agreed. "Want to."

"For Willa?"

No need hiding my motive. "For Willa and for you. As you said, she hasn't seen much of me lately. This will show her what I've been trying to say with action rather than words."

"Then who am I to stop you," he said with a chuckle.

He gave me the address of the trailer park where he was currently renting and suggested we meet in the next hour. Knowing he'd need boxes, I stopped off and collected a few from various locations.

Stan arrived before I did and opened the door when I knocked. "I didn't tell Willa you were going to be here; she'll find out soon enough when she stops by later."

"Good." That was what I wanted. If she knew, she might stay away, and that would defeat my purpose.

"She's a stubborn one; you need to be patient."

"She's worth whatever time it takes."

Stan nodded. "Glad to know you appreciate her."

He led the way into his small trailer kitchen. "Don't suppose I'll have much need of anything here. Never did much cooking. You'll need to ask Willa what she suggests I do with this stuff."

He winked, knowing I'd welcome any opportunity for conversation with his daughter. "Got it."

The two of us worked together for a couple of hours when I found a half-bottle of bourbon hidden under the sink. "What would you like me to do with this?" I asked, holding it up.

Glancing up, Stan's gaze focused on the bottle. "Where'd you find that?"

I told him.

"Thought I'd done away with all the booze hidden around here. Best thing is to dump it down the sink; I don't have any need for it."

I did as he asked and had just finished when the trailer door opened, and Willa came in. "Dad, is that Sean's car . . ." She paused when she saw me. Her eyes widened when she caught sight of the empty bourbon bottle in my hand.

"Your father asked me to dump this," I said, before she jumped to conclusions.

She stood frozen, looking from her father to me and then

back again. "What's he doing here?" she asked, addressing Stan.

"What does it look like? He's helping me pack up. Doing a good job of it, too, I might add."

"Dad . . . this isn't a good idea."

"Can't say I agree, baby girl."

The last thing I wanted was to cause dissension between Willa and her father. I decided a distraction might help. "Willa, what would you suggest we do with the pots and pans?" I asked. "Your dad seems to think he won't need them living with you."

"Dad." She ignored me and my question.

"He needs an answer," her father said. He carried a box and set it on top of another.

Willa turned and looked pointedly at me. "Sean already has his answer. He knows what I want."

Her words hung in the air like a time bomb.

"It looks like you've got everything squared away here. I'll be waiting at the apartment."

Having said that, she walked out and gently closed the door.

Chapter 32

Willa

I had to credit Sean with being persistent. He was a man of his word. Every morning, right around ten, he showed up at Bean There and ordered a mocha.

As much as possible, I let Lannie, my new hire, wait on him. He never complained, never asked for me personally. He purchased his drink, sat down at one of the few tables until he'd finished, and then he'd leave.

The weather was turning stormy with the approach of winter, so I didn't walk along the beach nearly as often as I had shortly after we lost Harper. Coming to grips with the loss of my sister was never going to be easy, but as the days and weeks passed, I slowly discovered that I could breathe again. As much as I would have preferred to shut myself in a closet and wallow in my grief, life went on. I had responsibilities, commitments. My staff depended on me. I couldn't let down the community that had supported and loved me.

Having Dad live with me had been an unexpected bonus. Now that he wasn't drinking, he was a new man. He enjoyed his job at the Ace Hardware store; it gave him purpose and he liked helping people. I know he grieved for Harper, but he was better at keeping his feelings to himself than I was. He routinely attended his meetings and checked in with his sponsor.

Harper had so often complained about my mothering, but with Dad living with me, I had someone to cook for and look after. It helped me deal with the loss of my sister. We didn't talk about her much, but I felt her presence almost as if she was with me, watching over me.

The holidays came upon us without a welcome. I didn't know how we were going to get through Christmas. Thanksgiving was hard enough. Dad and I gathered at Lucas's house, with Chantelle and me doing the cooking. It was a bleak day for us all.

The one bright spot, although I hated to admit it, was the text I got from Sean.

Spending Thanksgiving with my folks. Back on Monday. Miss you.

I must have read those few lines a dozen times. It angered me that his words meant this much.

On Friday, the day after Thanksgiving, I got another text. Mom and Dad send their love. I do, too.

The temptation to reply had been strong. At first, I was angry, wanting to demand that he stop texting me. I accepted that the only one I'd be hurting, though, was myself. A dozen times the next day I checked my phone, looking for another text. I was furious with myself for caring. I didn't want him in my life. If I gave in, he would only disappoint and hurt me again. I didn't want to love him, didn't want to care. Unfortunately, the message didn't make it to my heart.

The Monday following Thanksgiving, true to his word, Sean showed up as usual at Bean There.

"I thought about you the entire time I was away," he said, after he'd placed his order. "I know how hard it must have been for all of you without Harper."

"It was . . . hard." The empty space at the table felt like an open wound. We'd all tried to ignore the fact that Harper wasn't with us. In retrospect, I believe if we had acknowledged it, and talked about her, it might have helped. Instead we were all more concerned about not heaping sadness on a day meant to be celebrated.

"I wish I could have been with you."

I wished he could have been, too, but I wouldn't say it.

"I thought I should tell you I'm going to be away for a few days."

I stiffened; this was the reminder I needed. "Not my concern," I said, hardening my heart against him.

"Perhaps not. The only reason I mentioned it is so you won't think I'm giving up on us."

"It would be better if you did."

"Not happening, Willa. I love you; I'll wait for however long this takes. I hurt you, and I'll regret that until my dying day. When you're ready to forgive me, I'll be here."

"I already forgave you, Sean. I just don't think it's a good idea for me to become involved with you."

"You're already involved."

"Not any longer," I insisted.

His shoulders sank as he turned away. Part of me wanted to call him back, but I knew it was better to let him go.

For the rest of the day I berated myself over my parting words. I hadn't meant to sound heartless. He was trying so hard to make up to me and I rejected him at every turn. For my own peace of mind, I needed to keep him at arm's length. What I didn't expect was how hard it would be.

For the rest of the week, I was busy preparing for Lucas and Chantelle's wedding reception. From the first time Lucas had introduced us to Chantelle, I'd known she was the right woman for my brother. I'd loved her from the beginning, but never more than when she chose to have their wedding in the hospital so Harper could be part of it.

As promised, I baked the wedding cakes. Two flavors. One Funfetti and one lemon, and I poured all my love into the mix. This was the one thing I could do for them to show how much I loved them and how grateful I was to have them both in my life, now more than ever.

Naturally, Sean was away on another assignment at the time of the reception. That I should even think about him angered me. It was a reminder of what our future would be if I was to welcome him back into my life. There would always be another assignment, another reason to leave. Heaven only knew where he was this time or what risk he would be taking. He didn't tell me, which said everything I needed to know.

It was another dangerous location. Despite his claims of undying love, his camera meant far more to him than I ever would. I was smart to end it when I had.

For Lucas and Chantelle's wedding reception, the hotel ballroom was beautifully decorated with bright red poinsettias and evergreen swags. Small bunches of holly adorned the tables. Chantelle, along with family and friends, had put it all together.

My only participation was to bake the cakes and join the others in the wedding party. I was thankful Chantelle didn't ask me to wear the original bridesmaid dress. That would have brought up too many unwelcome memories, another reminder of Harper's absence.

I arrived well before the time of the event with the cakes. Each had four tiers and looked beautiful, if I did say so myself. I'd worked long and hard on them. Dad helped me cart them into the ballroom.

Chantelle asked me to sit at the head table, but I begged off, explaining that I didn't want Dad to sit alone. There weren't many family members on our side who were able to attend the reception, especially in the winter months, when crossing the mountain pass would be required. Mom's sister had recently undergone a hip replacement and wasn't able to make it. Dad's family all lived on the East Coast, and we didn't have much contact with them.

The tables sat eight. I was about to sit down with Dad when John joined us.

"John," I said, pleased and excited to see him. "You came."

"I got an invitation."

"Yes, of course you did, but I didn't expect you to drive all this way." No wonder my sister had fallen in love with this man.

"I wanted to be here. For Harper, for all of you."

Tears threatened, and I struggled to keep them at bay. "Thank you."

He reached for my hand and gave it a gentle squeeze. "Come on, Willa, this is a happy time. Harper would expect you to kick up your heels and dance with me."

I half laughed and half wept. "I'm a terrible dancer."

"Me, too. Harper made me promise, if she wasn't here for this reception, that I was to dance with you in her place."

Now there was no holding back the tears. "Oh darn," I said, rubbing my fingertips across my cheeks. I was convinced my mascara was running. I rose from the table and excused myself. Making my way across the ballroom, I found the ladies' room, repaired the damage, and started back when I saw him.

"Sean?" Although impeccably dressed, he looked like he hadn't slept in days. "What are you doing here?" I found it impossible to hide my shock.

"Lucas and Chantelle sent me an invitation."

They hadn't told me. Had they asked, I would have persuaded them to take his name off the list.

"I thought you were out of town." I hadn't seen him in more than ten days, not that I was counting.

"I was on assignment. As you can see, I'm back."

I could also see that he had nearly killed himself to make it to the reception. "You're exhausted."

"Yes." He didn't disagree. "No way was I missing this. It's important to you, and that makes it important to me."

My heart melted a little and I had to force myself to keep from showing the impact his words had on me.

"Is there a seat at your table?" he asked.

"Ah . . . It might be better if you sat elsewhere."

"Willa, I've spent the last twenty hours in a cramped oversold airplane, calling in every favor I have to make it to this event. The least you can do is let me sit at your table."

He looked completely wiped out. Turning him away would be cruel, and as much as I should do it, I couldn't. "There's an empty seat at my table. You're welcome to it."

"Thank you."

He followed me to where we were seated. I noticed he paused when he saw that John was positioned next to me. Dad sat on the other side.

"You remember John, don't you?" I said.

"Of course. Good to see you."

The dinner was far better than I expected for hotel food. Of the three options, beef, chicken, or salmon, I chose salmon. Dad opted for the chicken, and both John and Sean asked for the filet.

My brother's two Army friends, Ted and Bill, razzed and teased Lucas something terrible. As the mood lightened, Dad and I couldn't keep from laughing. Chantelle, ever the gracious hostess, spoke of how Lucas and she had met and how grateful she was to be part of our family. Her sister spoke as well. I was grateful no one expected me to give a speech. I'd rather bungee jump than speak in front of a crowd. Had

Harper been alive, she would have had everyone in stitches. We were the opposite in so many ways.

Lucas and Chantelle cut the cakes and they were served. When that was finished, the disc jockey started the music. Chantelle's father led her onto the dance floor for the traditional father-daughter dance before Lucas claimed his bride. Soon other couples took to the floor.

John leaned his head close to mine. "Shall we?"

"You're sure about this?" I whispered back.

"I promised Harper."

"I'd rather wait for a slow dance."

"Okay." As far as I was concerned, the longer we delayed, the better.

Sean stared across the table at John with a narrowed look that spoke of concern and displeasure. He couldn't possibly have known what we were discussing, only that our heads were together. For all intents, it must have looked like we were sharing a private moment, which, in essence, we were.

A couple of songs later, the beat of the music changed to a love song. John stood and extended his hand to me. It was now or never. I took it and rose from my chair.

Sean half rose from his, and then, with gritted teeth, he closed his eyes and sat back down.

John shared a look with me before he led me onto the dance floor. When he turned me into his arms, I was able to look back at the table where Sean sat. His head was bowed as if he found it agonizing to see me in the arms of another man.

"I don't think your man is very happy with me," John murmured.

From Sean's tortured look, I'd say John was right.

The music was slow and sultry. John and I didn't really dance. We shuffled our feet back and forth and swayed to the beat. When the song ended, I breathed easier. "I hope Harper appreciates this," I whispered.

When we returned to the table, Sean was missing. I looked to Dad, who shrugged, offering no explanation.

"Sean left?" John asked my father.

Dad nodded. "Not long after you got to the dance floor."

John frowned apologetically. "I hope he didn't get the wrong impression."

I opened my mouth to say who I danced with was none of Sean's business, but before I could, Dad said, "I don't think it could be avoided." He stretched his arm across the table and locked it around my forearm. His eyes bored into mine.

"Willa, put that poor man out of his misery."

Not until after the party ended did I consider reaching out to Sean. All the way back to the apartment I told myself who I saw or danced with wasn't his concern. If only I hadn't seen how devastated he looked when I left him to dance with John. It was guilt that made me do it. Once I'd changed into my pajamas, I reached for my phone and typed out a text.

I don't want you to have the wrong impression. I'm not involved with John.

No more than a minute later, my phone rang. Caller ID told me it was Sean. I was tempted to let it go to voicemail, but after the fourth ring, I answered.

"Hello."

"Why did you dance with him, then?" he asked, anger echoing with each word.

"Sean, have you been drinking?" He slurred just enough for me to know he'd had at least one or two drinks.

"You answer my question and I'll answer yours."

"Fine, if that's the way you want it. I was Harper's replacement for the evening. There, are you happy?"

"No."

"It's your turn. Answer my question."

"Yes, but I didn't reach for the bottle until I got home. There are some occasions that call for it."

"I told you there's nothing between us. You believe me, don't you?"

"Yes, but I didn't know that when I fell into this bottle."

I'd never known Sean to drink excessively, or at all, for that matter. It troubled me that he would assume there was anything romantic between John and me.

"If you were looking to bring me to my knees or make me jealous, you succeeded beyond your wildest expectations."

"I wasn't. I promise."

"Thank you for that," he said on the tail end of a sigh.

"Sean?"

"Yeah."

"Thank you for making the effort to be with me tonight."

"I'll always do whatever I can to be where you are, Willa. Haven't you figured that out yet?"

I guess I hadn't.

Chapter 33

Willa

The first week of January, I couldn't bear it any longer and made an appointment with Dr. Annie. This shouldn't be happening. Bean There was up and running smoothly. I'd made enough in December to pay rent for January and make a small dent in the loan I'd gotten from the bank. Sitting in the exam room, I hated the thought of taking drugs, but I was desperate.

The door opened and Annie walked in, a chart in her hand. She sat on the stool and rolled it closer to me so we were eye level, and then asked, "What seems to be the problem?" I'd already mentioned the issue to the nurse but guessed Dr. Annie wanted to hear it for herself.

"I'm not sleeping . . . I mean, I do sleep, but never for long." It was torturous. I didn't have trouble falling asleep, but then after an hour or two I'd wake and find it impossible to go back to sleep. This had been going on for weeks, ever since we lost Harper, and I was at my wit's end.

"Have you ever had anything like this happen before?"

"No, never. It all started, as you might have guessed, since we lost my sister . . . and a bit before."

She crossed her legs and spoke to me as she would a friend, which she was. "Tell me about a typical night."

As best I could, I explained what was happening, the long periods of restlessness after only a few hours' rest. "I feel like I'm running on empty. I'm making stupid mistakes at work; I recently ruined a batch of cinnamon rolls. Then I forgot to make a bank deposit and . . . and I'm afraid of what I might do next because I'm exhausted."

"Have you tried taking an afternoon nap?"

"I've tried everything." The frustration was as irritating as my inability to stay asleep for more than a few hours a night. "My eyes burn, but for the life of me I can't go back to sleep." I continued listing the other ideas I'd tried. Reading before I went to bed. Warm milk. Listening to music. Various kinds of white noise: the ocean waves, gentle forest sounds, birds chirping.

Annie listened, nodding now and again.

"I'm desperate," I admitted. "I need something . . . a pill, drug, sleep therapy, something. Anything." If she told me to stand on my head for fifteen minutes before I went to bed, I'd do it.

"When was the last time you had a full night's rest?"

The answer immediately came to me. It was the night I'd

gone to Sean's house when I didn't want to look at Harper's empty bedroom, nor did I want to be alone.

"A while ago . . . a few months." I didn't elaborate with details. My weakness embarrassed me now.

"Was there anything different about that night?"

Avoiding an answer, I shrugged, unwilling to tell her I'd spent the night curled up around Sean. "Can you help me?" I asked.

Annie leaned closer, her look warm and sympathetic. "Insomnia isn't unusual in your circumstance, Willa. You've lost your sister and you're grieving. Our bodies react differently to that kind of stress. There are several drugs I can prescribe that will help you sleep, but I'm not fond of prescribing them. The side effects are worrisome, and in the end I'm afraid you'll become psychologically reliant upon them. And the more you use them, the less effective they become. I suggest we start with melatonin and go from there."

"Melatonin?" Shirley had suggested I give it a try. She said her husband used it and slept like a baby. The local pharmacy carried it, but I brushed off her suggestion, thinking I needed something stronger.

"Can you tell me what it is and why it works?"

"Melatonin is a hormone that regulates the sleep-wake cycle," Annie explained. "It's non-habit-forming and completely natural. Give that a try, and if after a week it doesn't work, come see me and we can discuss other options."

"Okay." I wasn't happy. I was looking for a quick, easy solution, not something I could get over the counter. My problem was serious.

Instead of heading home, I drove out to the cemetery. I hadn't been to see Harper since before Christmas. I'd left a poinsettia at her grave site, weeping until I could barely see, missing my sister to the point I was physically ill.

The marker had been in place a few days before and I wanted to check on it, although Dad and I had given the approval before it was permanently set.

The wind whipped my coat around my legs as I climbed out of my car. I wrapped a knit scarf around my neck, shivering against the cold. January wasn't my favorite month of the year. Since I lived near the ocean, the winter months were often stormy, characterized by strong winds and heavy rain. I missed my walks along the beach. If ever I needed them, it was now.

As I approached Harper's grave, I noticed a bench. It was made of wood and was placed in such a way that it faced Harper's tombstone. I swept aside the leaves with my gloved hands and noticed a small plaque on the armrest. *In loving memory of Harper Lakey.*

My immediate thought was that Dad had done this, creating this bench because he knew I would want to spend time with my sister. Working at the hardware store, he had access to everything he'd need. It was such a thoughtful thing to do; I was surprised he hadn't mentioned it.

Standing by Harper's grave, I looked down at the marker. It had her favorite verse, 1 Corinthians 13:13: "Now of these that remain: faith, hope and love. But the greatest of these is love." Below were the dates of her birth and death. It said little about the vibrant sister who was so close to my heart.

Tears leaked from my eyes. You'd think by now I'd shed all the tears I had inside me, and yet they came without bidding, without warning, leaving me defenseless in my grief.

How long I stood and stared at Harper's grave I didn't know. After a while I sank down onto the bench, grateful it was there. I grabbed a tissue out of my purse to blow my nose. I'd give anything to have my sister back and didn't know how I would ever fill the huge hole her death had brought into my life.

That evening I made one of Dad's favorite meals in appreciation for his thoughtfulness. He deserved something special, and I knew this chicken-and-rice casserole would please him. He came home from work, petted Snowball, washed up, and, seeing that dinner was ready, sat down at the table. His eyes widened when I set the ceramic casserole dish in the middle of the table. This was one I used only on special occasions, because it had belonged to Mom.

"What did I do to deserve this?" he asked. Even before I had a chance to answer, he reached for the serving spoon, piling a large heap of the chicken dish onto his plate.

"I was out to see Harper this afternoon and found the bench you built. It's perfect, Dad. Just perfect."

His gaze shot up and he frowned. "I'd be happy to take the credit, but I didn't build a bench. Wish I'd thought of it, though."

"You didn't? Then John must have had it done." Thoughtful as he was and as much as he loved Harper, his name was the first to pop into my head if Dad wasn't responsible.

Dad took a big bite and then set his fork aside. "Now that

you mention it, Sean was in the hardware store a while back and purchased lumber. I wasn't the one who helped him. He saw me and we exchanged pleasantries. I didn't think to ask him what he intended to make. My guess is it was that bench."

The following morning, just like clockwork, Sean came for his mocha. His eyes immediately sought me out. That, too, was part of his ritual. I pretended not to notice, but he knew. He always knew.

"Morning, Willa," he said when he stepped up to the counter.

"Your usual?" I avoided eye contact.

"Please."

My stomach twisted and I knew I had to say something. Looking up, I asked, "Would you mind if I joined you?"

Surprise filled his eyes, and for a moment he looked speechless. "I'd enjoy that very much."

"Find a table and I'll deliver your mocha."

He paid and then walked to the table in the farthest corner of my small shop, which suited me. I didn't want anyone listening in on our conversation. Once I finished brewing his mocha and poured myself a cup of coffee, I carried our drinks over on a tray along with a slice of coconut cake.

"Cake?" he said when I set the plate down, along with the fork.

"Coconut. I baked it this morning."

"For me?" He reached for it and took a bite. Savoring it, he briefly closed his eyes. "It's even better than I remember."

"You can take the rest of it home if you'd like."

"The entire cake?"

I nodded and then nervously twisted my hands together in my lap. "I . . . I saw the bench."

He grinned a bit sheepishly. "It's my Christmas gift to you and your family. I knew the holidays would be particularly hard. I wanted to do something to let you know I'm thinking of you. Of all of you. I haven't stopped loving you, Willa, and I won't."

I lowered my head, and the knot in my throat made it difficult to swallow.

"I haven't given up on us. I love you and that's not going to change. I'm here for however long it takes to win you back."

I didn't know what to say. He made it hard to resist. I could feel myself weakening and guessed it was all tied up in my lack of a good night's rest.

As though he sensed the protective shield around my heart cracking, he asked, "Would it be all right if we had coffee together once a week? That's all I'm asking. Just once a week?"

By all that was right I should've turned him down, but I found I couldn't. "Only if I'm not busy."

His smile rivaled the summer sun. "Great. How about Wednesday? Didn't you once tell me that was your least busy day of the week?"

That he would remember that small detail told me that he had paid attention. "All right. Wednesday."

I was rewarded with another brilliant smile. My body automatically leaned toward him, as if drawn by a powerful magnetic pull. I fought against it and nearly spilled my coffee, looking to escape him.

By the time Wednesday rolled around, I was agitated and nervous.

"What's gotten into you?" Shirley asked me that morning soon after we opened for business.

"Nothing." I hadn't told her, hadn't told anyone I was taking time out of my morning to sit and talk with Sean.

Hands on her hips, Shirley glared at me. "Are you still not sleeping?"

"No . . . It's worse than ever." The melatonin didn't work any better than the other sleep medication I'd purchased over the counter. Nothing seemed to cure my insomnia. In desperation, I'd made a second appointment with Dr. Annie. I'd given the melatonin a fair shot.

Sean arrived at the same time as usual, collected his order, and returned to the same table where we'd last met. Without a customer in sight, I didn't have an excuse not to join him. Taking my mug with me, I sat down across the table from him.

"Do I look heavier than the last time you saw me?" he asked.

I grinned. "The last time I saw you was only a few days ago," I reminded him.

"I ate the entire cake. It was delicious. I had it for breakfast, lunch, and dinner. Best cake in the universe."

Sean knew exactly what to say to make me smile. "I'm glad you enjoyed it."

"Knowing you baked it for me was the secret ingredient."

Unwilling to let him know how pleased I was at his appreciation, I lowered my head.

"So, how's it going with your dad living with you?" he asked, easing into the conversation.

"Pretty well thus far, although I think we're going to need to find another apartment soon. Snowball is bigger now, and we won't be able to keep her hidden much longer."

"Are you sure you can't talk the landlord into agreeing to let you keep the cat? You're a good tenant and I doubt they want to lose you."

"It will probably be best if we did move," I said, although I hated the idea. "Dad prefers a house. Now that he's working at the hardware store, he's wanting a garage for a work area. That will be good for him. He used to do a bit of woodworking and always enjoyed it."

"If I hear of a house for rent, I'll let you know."

I hadn't made the effort to look, preferring to put it off until necessary. "That would be great."

His gaze held mine. "How are you, Willa?"

"Good," I answered quickly, probably too quickly.

Reaching across the table, he captured my hand. "No, you're not. You're pale and there are shadows under your eyes."

He was smart enough not to mention the weight I'd lost. I heard enough about that from Shirley, who had made it her life goal to fatten me up. So far her efforts hadn't worked. I shrugged, answering without answering.

He continued to look at me, silently demanding an answer.

"I'm having a bit of trouble sleeping," I reluctantly

admitted. "I've been in to see Dr. Annie and have made another appointment. She's not eager to give me a prescription drug, for fear it will become habit-forming." I understood her concerns, but I was at the point that I no longer cared. All I needed, all I wanted, was one night of decent sleep. One good night would change everything.

His hand tightened around mine. "Insomnia is only natural after everything you've been through."

I'd heard that from Annie. That didn't make it any more bearable. "I'm sure it will pass in time."

"If there's anything I can do . . ."

"At this point, I doubt there's much that anyone can." I hated to sound depressed and sad. Lack of sleep left me bone-weary and feeling hopeless.

"I'm serious. If you want to talk in the middle of the night, call. I'll sing you back to sleep."

"Funny."

"I'm serious."

At two in the morning, I stared up at the ceiling, wide awake, fighting back tears of frustration. Was it too much to ask for a good night's sleep? Just one night. I'd prayed, I'd begged God to let me rest, but no matter what I did, my mind refused to stop. Every time I closed my eyes, it was a signal for my mind to start mulling over a dozen senseless thoughts. I'd tried counting sheep, counting backwards from one hundred. My mind would zoom off in a dozen different directions, none of which led to a peaceful night.

Then something Dr. Annie had said came to me. She'd asked, When was the last time I'd slept, really slept? It was the night I'd been with Sean, the night I'd slept in the same bed with him.

Could I go to him? The idea popped unbidden into my head and I immediately shook it off. Still, it persisted. The hope that being in his arms would help me refused to go away. Even if I did go, would he even answer the door?

Then I remembered him saying that if there was anything he could do . . . Well, there was. He probably wouldn't like it; then again, maybe he would. Desperate times called for desperate measures. I was beyond desperate.

While still in my pajamas, I put on my slippers, grabbed my coat and my purse, and snuck out of the house.

All the way to Sean's, I berated myself. This was ludicrous. I would be giving him the wrong impression. I couldn't do it. I couldn't.

Despite all my self-talk, I pulled in to his driveway and sat for all of two minutes before walking up his front steps. I rang his doorbell. I could hear Bandit barking before a sleepy Sean opened the front door.

His concern was immediate. "Willa? What's happened?"

"I can't sleep," I said, fighting back tears. "You said if you could help, you would."

"Of course. Anything."

"Do you mean it?" I pleaded, fighting back exhaustion.

"With all my heart. What do you need me to do?"

"Can I . . . Would you let me sleep with you? Just for tonight. Please."

Chapter 34

Willa

I slowly stirred awake and rolled onto my back. My first thought was that I'd gone the entire night without waking. Then I remembered what I'd done, and where I was. I immediately bolted upright.

I'd gone to Sean, woken him in the middle of the night, and crawled into bed with him. The instant he'd pulled me into his arms, I was out. And I'd slept for . . . I paused to roll my head and look at the clock.

Nine o'clock. I should have been awake hours ago. I should have opened Bean There. With my pulse shooting toward the sky, I tossed aside the blankets and leaped out of bed. I raced around the bedroom, looking for my clothes before I remembered I'd come in my pajamas and didn't bring anything more than my coat and purse with me.

"Willa?" Sean knocked before opening the bedroom door.

"Sean," I cried in a panic. "I need to get to work, I—"

"I phoned Shirley," he said, cutting me off. "She's filling in for you, and so is Joelle. You have the day off."

Because I'd been away from the shop for weeks on end, tending to Harper, I hadn't taken a day off other than Sunday since my return. "But—"

He held up his hand. "It was Shirley's idea."

Sinking down at the end of the mattress, I brushed the sleep-mussed hair from my face as I slowly exhaled the tension from between my shoulder blades. "I slept so well."

Sean sat down next to me and reached for my hand. "I know. Your snoring kept me awake most of the night."

I was horrified and jerked my hand free of his grasp to cover my face. "Please tell me you're joking."

He laughed, letting me know he was teasing.

I playfully elbowed him in the ribs. "That was cruel."

"I'm not kidding when I tell you that you cuddled me all night. I loved having you with me. I had to pinch myself to be sure I wasn't dreaming."

That embarrassed me nearly as much as the earlier taunt. "Did I really?"

"It helped you sleep."

It wasn't like I could deny it. "Thank you," I whispered, unable to find any other words to express my gratitude.

"I'm at your service, Willa."

"I was desperate." He needed to know I would never have come to him if I didn't feel this was my last option.

"I know you had to be to come to me. Never thought I'd be grateful for someone suffering with insomnia."

He was so cute and clever that I found it impossible to

hold back a smile. I loved it when he returned mine with one of his own. Sean had a dimple on one side of his face that I found fascinating. Unable to stop myself, I raised my hand and cupped his cheek.

Sean captured my wrist and brought my hand to his lips, kissing the inside of my palm. "I called your dad and explained that you were with me. He dropped off a set of clothes for you on his way in to work."

"Oh my goodness," I said, and moaned. I could only imagine what my dad must be thinking. "I hope you explained—"

"I told him everything. How you were after my body and—"

"You didn't!"

He arched his brows.

"Sean!"

The way he quirked his mouth told me he was teasing me yet again. "I'll get your clothes and you can dress while I make breakfast."

I noticed he didn't leave me the option, he assumed I'd be joining him. The truth was I doubted I could have turned him down. For weeks I had done my best to push Sean out of my life. He wouldn't let me. He'd been persistent and caring. I was beginning to think that I'd made a hasty decision in ending our relationship. It was time to rethink what I'd done.

After I'd dressed and combed my hair, I joined Sean. He had dished up bacon, fried eggs, and toast. The table was set and waiting for me.

"Orange juice?" he asked as I sat down.

"Please."

He poured us each a glass before sitting down across from me. Because I'd slept, my mind was clear; I felt like a new woman. It was astonishing what a good night's rest could do for a person. The weariness I'd carried on my shoulders slipped away. The day seemed brighter.

"So," he said, once we'd finished eating. He leaned toward me, pressing his stomach against the table. "Willa, I need to know what your being here means for the future."

"The future?" I frowned. I hadn't thought beyond breakfast. "Do you mean you and me? Or my sleeping habits?"

He grinned. "Both. You're welcome in my bed anytime, Willa. I mean that."

I automatically shook my head. "Not a good idea. You'll become like one of those drugs Annie warned me about. I'll become psychologically dependent on you, and that isn't something either one of us wants or needs."

"I wouldn't mind." His eyes were warm and sincere.

"Probably not, but it's not a good idea." Although I had to admit, the longer I thought about it, the more I was tempted. I'd sleep next to a grizzly bear if I could rest the way I had in Sean's arms. But I refused to use him like that.

"Tell you what," he said, leaning forward. "Tonight, if you have a problem, call me. We'll talk."

Not a bad suggestion, and one he'd made earlier. "Do you think you can sweet-talk me into falling asleep?"

"Don't know. But it's worth a try."

"Okay, you're on."

Sean and I spent a relaxing day together. We snuggled up on his sofa and watched movies from the eighties, classics. My favorite was *Ghostbusters,* and Sean was all over *Indiana Jones and the Temple of Doom.* We ate popcorn and ice cream for dinner and then I drove home.

I took a long soak in a hot bath and thought about our time together. I hadn't taken a day off like that since before Harper got sick. I felt lazy, relaxed, and content. The feeling was foreign to me, and I was convinced I would fall straight to sleep and rest the entire night. The dry spell had been broken.

Wrong.

At one-thirty, I was wide awake. Groaning, I tossed and turned for another thirty minutes before in utter frustration I reached for my phone.

Sean answered as if he'd been awaiting my call, his phone already in his hand. "Can't sleep?"

"No. It's so exasperating I could scream."

"Okay, babe, this is what I want you to do. Close your eyes and get comfortable."

"All right." On my back, I nestled into my pillow and closed my eyes.

"Are you comfortable?"

"About as comfortable as I can get."

"Good, now think about me being with you, cuddled up against you. Put the picture in your mind of the two of us spooning. I have my arm around your middle and you're relaxing against me. Can you do that?"

"I think so." It wasn't hard. Must be muscle memory, because I could almost feel my body tucked close to his.

He continued speaking in low tones for several minutes. At some point I must have dropped off, because I woke a few hours later to the sound of my alarm. My phone rested next to my pillow.

It'd worked. Having Sean sweet-talk me had worked. Sleep. Beautiful sleep. I was in heaven. I wanted to dance and sing and leap around the house like a spring lamb. Sean was the key to breaking through my insomnia.

For the next week, Sean talked me to sleep every night. We started texting, too. He'd managed to wiggle his way back into my life. I let him. As much as I didn't want to admit it, I needed him. But even more, I wanted to be with him. I loved the sound of his voice. Nothing soothed me more. The sadness that hung over me like a dark thundercloud shifted and there was light in my life again.

Although neither Dad nor Shirley mentioned it, I knew they were happy to see me back with Sean. We talked every day when he came in for his mocha. I'd gotten him to sample a few other specialty drinks, too. If there was an opportunity, I'd sit with him and we'd work on the crossword puzzle from the newspaper together. Sean was much better at it than I was. I laughed again after what seemed like years. He was quickly becoming my addiction.

Then it happened. The way I knew it eventually would. He didn't tell me in person. Instead, he sent a text.

Babe, I'm leaving on another assignment. I'll be away for a week, maybe longer.

I noticed that he didn't mention where he was headed. I toyed with how best to respond. It wasn't like it was his job to talk me to sleep every night. He was a photographer and travel was a large part of his life. He was passionate about his work. I sent a one-word reply.

Okay.

You mad?

How could I be? If ever I was going to be honest, it was now. I needed to give him that.

No. I'll miss you.

Those three small dots appeared, letting me know he was typing a reply.

Will you stay at my house and sleep in my bed while I'm away?

I didn't need to think twice.

If that's what you want. When do you leave?

Tomorrow morning. Gonna miss you, too.

We spoke again that night. He told me about his assignment in the Caribbean. Can't say I blamed him for escaping to a tropical island. I envied him the opportunity. When I said I was going to miss him, I meant for more than our nighttime conversations. He was the light that brightened my day, the sun my world revolved around. I looked forward to being with him.

The following afternoon, I drove out to Sean's house and spent time with Bandit. My staying at his home was a win-win for us both. He had me to look after his dog and I could sleep in his bed. I didn't know if I'd be able to sleep, but it was well worth the effort. Sean told me he would probably be able to call, but with the time difference, it might be difficult. I'd assured him that he needed to concentrate on his assignment and not worry about me. I meant it. I'd gone weeks without any notable sleep, I could easily go a week.

The first night, I had my doubts. Sure enough, I fell asleep easily, the same as always. About midnight, I stirred awake and groaned.

No, please no.

Grabbing hold of Sean's pillow, I inhaled his scent and let it fill my senses. It was almost like having him with me. Before I knew it, I was back to sleep and woke with my alarm.

Success.

His text was waiting for me the next morning.

Did you sleep?

Sitting up in bed, I answered right away.

Like a baby. You're my muse.

Did you cuddle my pillow?

It was as if he had a video camera in his bedroom and had been watching me.

Yup. It was almost as good as cuddling you.

Don't think so. Be home soon.

Not nearly soon enough to suit me. If Sean was counting down the days, then so was I. Bandit became my constant companion. Dad came to Sean's place for dinner every night.

He'd started looking at houses we could rent and found a small two-bedroom not far from where we were now that he felt would suit us. Although reluctant, I promised I'd go look at it with him. So many changes in such a short amount of time were too much for me.

Sean returned the following week and came directly to the shop before heading home. As soon as I saw him, without even thinking what I was doing, I walked into his arms.

I stated the obvious. "You're back."

"I came straight here. Missed you like crazy."

"Missed you more." I remembered saying almost those same words to him when he returned from Bolivia. And as he had the first time he'd returned from a trip, he drew me into his arms and kissed me. We'd hugged and cuddled since my bout with insomnia, but the kisses we'd shared were more pecks than real kisses.

This kiss was real. So real it made me weak in the knees. It was the kind of kiss that made me curl my toes and lean in more, opening to him like a flower in the sun, reveling in the taste, the feel, the scent of this man I had come to love. It was as though he were starving for the taste of me. The kiss went on for several moments, neither of us willing to bring it to an end.

When we broke apart, Sean leaned his forehead against mine and breathed in heavily. My breathing wasn't any less labored.

"I needed that," he whispered, his hands twined through the hair at the back of my head, as if he needed to keep hold of me, for fear I'd escape him.

"I needed that, too."

He pulled away enough to meet my eyes. "Are we back, Willa? Tell me we're back and that you are willing to be part of my life."

Hugging him, my arms around his waist, I pressed my head against his chest. "We're getting there," I whispered.

"Good. Come home with me."

"Now?"

"Now," he reiterated. "I don't want to be away from you a minute longer than necessary."

"But don't you need to unpack and—"

"Yes, but it can wait. What I need more than anything right now is time with you."

"All right." I found it impossible to refuse him.

To refuse myself.

Chapter 35

Willa

As I had so often in the last few weeks, I sat on the bench Sean had built and spoke to my sister. I knew Harper wasn't really there to hear me; nevertheless, this was where I came to be with her, to share and chat the way we once had.

We'd always been close. Harper was more than my sister—she'd been my best friend, and the hole left in my life wouldn't easily be filled. Time, I knew, was the great healer, and while she was gone, Harper would always remain a large part of who I am. I was learning to live with a new normal, like an amputee navigating life with a lost limb.

"It's Sean again," I whispered. "He's away on another assignment, doing a shoot for an L.L.Bean catalog." I missed him when he was away. In the last month we'd gotten close, even closer than before Harper had gotten sick. It had all started with the bench he'd built and then his help with my insomnia. Now we spent part of every day together, unless he was away on a shoot. Even then we talked and texted, so it hardly seemed that he was gone.

I'd been staying at his home when he was traveling, on the excuse that someone needed to be there for Bandit. What I readily admitted was how much I enjoyed sleeping in Sean's bed. For the most part my insomnia had passed, and I rarely needed to wake Sean in the middle of the night any longer. Although I should confess that I rather enjoyed him sweet-talking me back to sleep. How patient he'd been, caring and concerned, willing to do what he could to help.

He traveled a great deal, but if we were going to be a couple, then it was something I would need to adjust to, and for the most part I had. At least this time he wasn't shooting in a third-world country and I didn't need to worry about him picking up some rare disease. I suppose I should be concerned with him being around all those gorgeous models with their perfect bodies. I wasn't, though. Sean was mine, and I knew it. He'd worked hard to prove he loved me.

"I love him," I told Harper. "I tried hard not to; it was by far the safer bet for me.

"I've been afraid to love him, afraid I'd always be second place behind his camera and career," I told my sister. "Afraid he would take too many chances with his life and health. I wouldn't survive another loss."

I didn't like to think of myself as fragile and looking to protect myself, protect my heart. There was no protection against Sean, though. He was determined to win me over, and eventually I succumbed.

"You knew, didn't you?" I asked, not expecting a reply

but knowing she had one. "The first time you saw him, you knew Sean was the one for me." My sister had known intuitively long before I had.

That wasn't all Harper knew, I suspected. When I'd shared my worries for her with my brother all those months ago, some inner warning, some deep-seated fear, told me Harper was unconsciously aware her time was short. It was all so very clear to me now.

"Dad is doing well," I continued, updating her on our lives. "You'd be proud of the turnaround he's made. He faithfully attends his A A meetings and is making new friends. He loves his job and has already gotten a raise. He's working full-time now. It's good for him. He's happier now than at any other time since Mom died."

Although I hated to move out of the apartment, it had been for the best. There were far too many memories of Harper tied up there, so Dad and I made the big move to the rental house. It was small but adequate. Dad loved the garage and had turned it into a woodworking shop. When I asked him what he was making, his reply was always the same: sawdust.

I enjoyed how he lavished love on Snowball, who was often found in his lap while he watched television. Growing up, we'd never had a cat, as Mom was allergic. It seemed my dad was a real cat person. Snowball didn't have much to do with me these days, and I had the feeling it was because of Bandit, whom she chose to ignore whenever he was around.

I smiled and looked down at my sister's gravestone and the Bible verse we'd had etched there. "But the greatest of these is love." It was love Harper had spoken of in her last words to me. Love. I felt surrounded by it. Besieged by love from Sean, who refused to give me up. From my brother and Chantelle and of course our father. Love was all around and I could feel it, just as Harper had whispered in her final word to us.

My visit complete, I stood up from the bench, running my finger over the metal plate Sean had placed there. *In loving memory of Harper Lakey.*

"You ready, boy?" I asked, as I tugged at Bandit's leash, leading him back to the car.

The sun broke out, rare for a February day, and, wanting to take advantage of it, I headed to the beach. It'd been a while since I'd walked there, and I'd missed the exercise, the feel of the wind on my face, the call of the seagulls, and the rushing sound of the waves as they broke over the sand.

I parked and Bandit jumped out of the car, eager to stretch his legs. I released him from his leash and off he took, bounding over the first sand dune and toward the water with an enthusiasm that had me laughing.

The sound of my laughter carried in the wind and came back to me almost like an echo. After my sister's death, I wondered if I would ever really feel joy again. I could laugh, and that was a start.

I called out to Bandit and he turned at the sound of his name. He raced back to me, his tongue falling out of the side of his mouth in his excitement. I shook my head at his boundless energy. He immediately raced off again, chasing a seagull.

With the sun out, a few others had ventured onto the beach, taking advantage of the afternoon. Feeling the warmth of it, I lifted my face to the sky, letting it spill over me. This was exactly what I needed in the middle of a dreary winter that seemed to go on for far too long.

To think that just a year ago Harper had announced she intended to climb Mount Rainier come summer and had signed up for conditioning classes. A year ago, I hadn't known Sean.

What a difference a few months could make.

"Willa."

Sean's voice came to me and I whirled around to see him walking along the beach, toward me.

I immediately started toward him, my heart leaping with joy. "I didn't think you were due back until tomorrow," I said, holding my hands out to him. He gripped hold of them and brought me close for a hug.

"I wasn't, but the shoot went better than expected." He slipped his arms around my waist and kissed me.

I would never tire of this man's kisses. Oh, the things he did to me made me forget we were in full view of all of Oceanside. I looped my arms around his neck and gave myself over to him, welcoming him home.

Bandit raced to Sean's side and Sean bent down to pet his faithful companion. "Did you miss me?" he asked, glancing up at me.

"I always miss you."

"Good. Missed you, too. Did you sleep?"

"Like a newborn." How could I not? Sleeping in Sean's

bed while he was away, surrounded by his scent, was all that was necessary. Feeling close to him was all the comfort I needed for my weary body to give way to blissful rest.

"I'm thinking you should make sleeping in my bed permanent," he said casually, although the look he sent me was serious.

"You want me to move in with you?"

"I can think of nothing I want more. But there are conditions."

"Conditions?" I asked, wondering at his mood.

"I want you there as my wife."

I leaned my head against his shoulder as we walked arm in arm, the salty scent of the air filling my senses. "Are you afraid I'm going to have a change of heart about us?" I asked. I'd hoped by now he knew how deeply in love with him I was.

He squeezed my hand. "I know what I want, Willa, and it's you at my side for the rest of our lives. You as my partner, the mother of my children. I've had my time in the limelight, entertained a certain amount of fame."

"And beautiful women," I reminded him.

He leaned over and kissed the top of my head. "I have a beautiful woman now."

I looked up at him and smiled. Until Sean, I'd never thought of myself as beautiful. Harper was the one in the family who got all the beauty, but who was I to argue.

"You're the one I want, Willa. You're the one I love. Say you'll marry me."

"Yes," I whispered, tears in my eyes. His eyes held mine

as he removed an engagement ring from his pocket and slipped it on my finger.

Sean turned me into his arms and squeezed me hard. "Thank you. I promise to be the husband you deserve."

The diamond shone in the sunlight and I whispered, "But the greatest of these is love."

He stared down at me quizzically.

"That's the Bible verse on Harper's marker. Life is all about love."

"Yes, it is," he agreed. Bandit bounded back to us, kicking up sand.

We kissed again, sealing our commitment to each other, and then continued down the beach.

Walking together hand in hand toward our future.

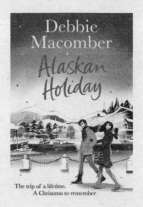

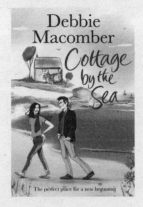